EMERALD CITY

THEY SAY IT'S DARKEST JUST BEFORE DAWN

ALICIA K. LEPPERT

EMERALD CITY

THEY SAY IT'S DARKEST JUST BEFORE DAWN

ALICIA K. LEPPERT

Sweetwater Books
An imprint of Cedar Fort, Inc.
Springville, Utah

DISCLAIMER

In writing *Emerald City*, I tried to stay as true as possible to my beliefs when it came to religious topics. It was necessary, however, to take certain creative liberties for the sake of my story, which is entirely fictional.

ISBN 13: 978-1-59955-864-6

Published by Sweetwater Books, an imprint of Cedar Fort, Inc.
2373 W. 700 S., Springville, UT 84663
Distributed by Cedar Fort, Inc., www.cedarfort.com

Cover design by Brian Halley
Cover design © 2012 by Lyle Mortimer
Edited and typeset by Emily S. Chambers

Printed in the United States of America

10 9 8 7 6 5 4 3 2 1

Printed on acid-free paper

DEDICATION

To Bill and Jen, who both believed I was a writer before I did, and without whom this story would never have made it past the first chapter.

ACKNOWLEDGMENTS

I have so many people to thank for helping make my dream come true:

First and foremost, my beloved cousin Jen, who fell in love with Jude and Olivia before they had names, and who took a *huge* chance on a wannabe writer. Jen, there are no words to describe the gratitude I have for your unfailing belief in me.

My husband Bill, for telling me to *write, write, write*, and for being my perpetual cheerleader.

My amazing kids, Macy and Payson, for giving up their mother days at a time when deadlines had to be met, and only complaining a *little* bit.

My sisters, Amy and Alison, for letting me bounce endless ideas off of them and for dropping everything on a moment's notice to review my first draft.

All my friends and family who brought me meals, took my kids, and helped me in countless other ways to finish and promote my book.

My publicist, Josh, for clueing me in to the unknown world of marketing; my editor, Emily, for fine-tuning my baby; Brian, for designing the most amazing cover *ever*; and all the rest of the good people at Cedar Fort, Inc.

Dr. Peter Later, for giving me much-needed medical info on a topic that is better left un-Googled.

And lastly, but certainly not least, my Heavenly Father, for the incredible blessing that this entire journey has been.

PREFACE

MY WORLD IS A DARK and lonely place. Each day, like the one before it, I drift through, unfeeling, unthinking. Some time ago I discovered that life was semi-livable if I refrained from feeling. I was only ever one thing—numb.

All around me, people go about their lives, talking, laughing . . . living. It used to make me ache—the envy I had for all the happy people. But even that, over time, faded to nothing. Now I don't notice the laughter. I'm oblivious to the smiles, the cheerful banter that surrounds me. It's amazing how alone you can feel in a city of 600,000 people.

Seattle, Washington. The sprawling, industrious city set in a blanket of pine. I have never known a day that wasn't spent inside this concrete jungle. It's my home, and for that I love it. But it's also the setting for the tragedy called my life, and so I loathe it.

I live alone in a cold, empty studio apartment. The tiny square room closely resembles a cell. That's my life: solitary confinement.

Here, in this desolate place that perfectly reflects my soul, my story begins.

CHAPTER ONE

THEY SAY IT'S DARKEST just before dawn. I would soon learn just how true that really was. I lay awake, staring unseeingly out the window that occupied most of the east wall of my apartment. Outside, the city still hummed with activity, despite the hour. In a way, the unceasing background noise was comforting—a constant in my otherwise unstable existence. But it also reminded me just how insignificant I was in this big place . . . how alone.

I never slept. At least, not at night. I couldn't remember the last time I'd had a complete night's sleep. Usually I'd drift in and out of consciousness all night, waking as soon as the nightmares kicked in. It was always at this time, just before the sun rose, that I'd give up on sleep altogether, too terrified to drift off again.

I rolled over onto my back, my eyes moving unconsciously to the ceiling, and listened to the traffic below.

And then, without warning, the floodgates opened and the memories came crashing in, assaulting every cell in my body. The pain, albeit agonizingly familiar, tore through me like a hurricane, and I felt like I was being ripped into pieces. Instinctively, I curled into a ball, wrapping my arms around myself in a desperate attempt at protection. And there, in the blackest night, I traveled to hell and back.

* * * * *

With daybreak came my reprieve. The night took with it the pain and anguish. The day brought numbness—my closest companion. It was no life, to be sure, but it was enough to allow me to get out of bed.

I went through the daily routine: breakfast, shower, and so on. By the time I was done, I didn't remember doing any of it. I left my apartment and began the walk to work.

It was a typical Seattle day: gray, drizzly, the clouds low to the ground. The streets were already busy, the sidewalks crowded. Everyone on their way to somewhere, no one paying any attention to anyone else. I'd heard people—visitors—say before that Seattle is unique in the variety of people that it claims. I didn't know if this was true or not. I had nothing to compare it to, and I didn't see the people who roamed the streets beside me anymore. I looked right through them.

The early morning air was frigid, and I walked quickly to keep from freezing. The warm air in the coffee shop where I worked was welcoming, and the familiar aroma of coffee and bacon enveloped me as I walked through the door.

The waitress behind the cash register, a scowling, silver-haired woman who had worked there for as long as anyone could remember, glanced up at the sound of the bell over the door. I walked past her without saying a word. She didn't expect me to, just returned to whatever it was she was doing. I used to worry about people thinking I was rude. I didn't care anymore.

I tied on my apron, grabbed a coffee pot, and began making the rounds without even thinking about it. I felt like a mouse running through one of those cardboard mazes. I didn't have to think about anything I did. My body just . . . went. The difference was that, unlike the mouse, there was no hunk of cheese waiting for me at the end. No reward of any kind for making it through. In fact, there was no end at all.

The day, as always, seemed to drag on forever. I longed to be back in my bed, burrowed underneath the covers. The end of my shift was near and I was about to have my wish fulfilled. Just one more hour, and then I could leave.

I headed out into the near-empty dining room to a table that was occupied by two guys about my age. I pulled out my order pad and pen as I reached them, pasted a smile on my face and, like a sad little robot, said, "Hi, what can I get for you?"

I saw them peering behind me, obviously looking for something. I turned around to see what it was and saw nothing. Then one of them cleared his throat and said, "Is Bridgett working today?"

Bridgett. Bridg-ett. I repeated the name in my head a couple times before it registered. *Bridgett.* I vaguely recalled another female waitress working this shift. I had no idea if she was Bridgett or not.

"Um . . . I can check." I watched their eager faces as they continued to scan the restaurant.

"Could you?" one of them asked. "We were really hoping she could serve us." I noticed he wasn't looking at me as he spoke. Neither of them was.

I was taken aback momentarily. I had never had anyone

ask for another server to my face before. I was surprised that I cared. But it wasn't just the rejection I felt from their request that stung, it was the fact that they wouldn't even *look* at me. It was weird; I had felt invisible for so long, but no one had ever actually given me cause to feel that way—I was well aware that it was my own doing. But here they were, acting like I wasn't even there.

I turned and headed toward the back in search of Bridgett without responding. I don't think they noticed. When I found someone in the back wearing the same hideous uniform that I was, I glanced at her name tag. Bridgett. I relayed the message, and she gave a giddy little laugh and bounced over to their table. Trying to forget about her and the jerks that snubbed me, I headed over to the front counter to see if there were any other tables I needed to take before I left. As I did so, I heard Bridgett burst into a fit of giggles. Reflexively, I turned and looked and was surprised to see them all staring back at me. None of them bothered to look away and I could feel my face burning with embarrassment. I heard one of them say something about a skeleton and as Bridgett turned away, I distinctly heard her say "freak."

Stunned, I stood frozen like an idiot before turning and heading to the counter. I muttered to whomever was standing behind it that I was going home early. She didn't say anything in response. She didn't even look up.

I don't remember taking off my apron or putting on my coat. I don't remember walking home at all. The next thing I remember was being in bed, buried under the covers where no one could find me, wishing desperately I could cry. But I never did—not even at my mother's funeral only a year earlier. That had been when the numbness had started, when I stopped feeling or expressing anything, good or bad.

But this . . . this I felt. I don't know why, but I let it gnaw away at me, from the inside out.

When had it gotten this bad? Was I really that repulsive to people? Had I truly become a skeletal freak? I tried to remember my image in the mirror that morning, but couldn't recall seeing my reflection at all, although certainly I had to have looked in the mirror at some point. A shocking realization hit me that I had become invisible even to myself. I had succeeded in ignoring all human life for so long, that I had actually taken it so far as to not even see *me* anymore. And in turn, human life had returned the favor.

What had happened to me? How did I get here, becoming this sad, tortured shell of a person? My thoughts began to retrace the path my life had taken over the years before I could stop them and the havoc they would wreak on my soul.

I saw a broken woman standing in a small, green kitchen, looking like she had seen more pain in her lifetime than anyone should ever see. My mom. I saw a man retreat through a doorway, a suitcase in each hand, without so much as a backward glance. My dad. I was five, and I never saw him again.

My chest spasmed, and I found it difficult to breathe. I saw the faceless, nameless people that made up my father's second family, a family that was well under way by the time my mother discovered his secret. They were fuzzy outlines of people and, although I had never seen them, their empty faces seemed to mock me.

At some point I drifted off, never really falling asleep, but going to that place where I was neither conscious nor unconscious. I would remain in this state until a haunting image would shatter my reverie, forcing me awake, terrified and trembling.

The night continued in this way, with periods of trance-like stillness followed by jolting nightmares that left me shaking and covered in sweat. The deluge of rain beating against my window provided morose background music for my chilling visions, which grew progressively worse as the night wore on: An eight-year-old girl, walking down a snow-covered sidewalk to school, a threadbare, holey sweater clinging to her bony frame as children in the background pointed and laughed at her tattered clothing. Me.

My mother standing in a grimy pawn shop, handing her wedding ring to the shady character behind the counter so that we could afford to turn our heat back on.

I knew what was coming then, and I felt my body brace itself in preparation. I tried to fight it—oh, I tried so hard, but I always failed. There was no escaping this image—the one that woke me screaming in the night. I frantically tried to fill my mind with something—*anything*—else, but I was too weak, and the demon was too strong.

My mother staring at me through empty eyes, slumped on the bathroom floor, a butcher knife on the floor beside her lifeless body. Everything was covered in red, scarlet red, everywhere I looked.

Dry, tearless sobs escaped me with each breath. The sobs became moans, and I was gasping for air. I had reached my limit. I couldn't take the excruciating memories anymore. I could no longer handle the physical pain that wracked my body. The piercing sensation in my chest where my heart was breaking apart felt as if a brick wall had fallen on me, and the throb in my head was so intense, I was seeing spots. I had to have some relief.

Stumbling from my bed I made my way to the bathroom and grabbed a bottle of ibuprofen from behind the mirror. I shook three out into my hand and then, three more. I had to be sure it would numb this wretched pain. I swallowed them with some water, then stood shaking at the sink, trying to keep my body upright. As I stood there, my eyes focused on the bottle sitting on the shelf next to the ibuprofen. It was the Valium that some shrink had given me after my mother's death. I had filled the prescription but never taken one. It was fear, I guess, or maybe denial.

But tonight . . . tonight I knew I needed it. I could feel myself breaking apart from the pain and I knew I would never survive the night. This would actually be saving me, allowing me to escape just long enough to let my body heal from the ordeal it had been through. Just the thought of it made me almost smile. Almost.

I carried the bottle and the glass of water to my bed, not trusting my legs to support me another minute. I collapsed onto it and began unscrewing the cap with quivering hands. The bottle dropped out of my hands onto the bed, little white pills spilling out everywhere.

I stared at the pile, cocking my head to the side as I noticed each pill had a heart-shaped hole through the middle of it. *That's ironic*, I thought. *Such a happy little pill for such hopeless people.* I looked closer, and realized it wasn't a heart at all. It was a V. V for vapid. Void.

Vindication.

Feeling like I was moving in slow motion, I reached out to grab one. I watched as my hand, instead of picking up just one, enclosed around the pile, grabbing a handful. I saw the tremor in my hand stop suddenly and felt an odd sense of detachment come over me. It was no longer my arm reaching out—not my hand holding the pills. I was just watching it all happen, a spectator on the sidelines. I watched as another hand grabbed the glass of water, and the hand containing the pills moved toward my mouth.

An inch before it reached my parted lips, though, the hand froze in midair. Somewhere in the back of my consciousness a tiny voice was screaming at me that this was *my* hand, and that I knew exactly what it was trying to do. I considered this for a moment and listened as the voice pleaded with me not to do this. I heard its arguments and knew they made sense. But the detached part of me, the part that was already experiencing the euphoria of not feeling, was far more persuasive. The thought of being rid of the demons not just for one night, but for forever, was much too appealing, and before the tiny voice could fight back, I tossed them all into my mouth, gagging them down with the water.

Falling back onto my bed, I heard the glass drop to the floor and shatter. I didn't move, just gazed at the crack in the ceiling and waited for the darkness to come. I wondered if it would hurt at all, or if I would just fall asleep. I wondered if anyone would miss me, then laughed silently at myself for even wondering. I knew full well that no one would even know I was gone, giving me a small amount of justification that I had done the right thing.

Soon the crack began to get fuzzy, and I could see the room fading around me, closing in like a tunnel. *This is it,* I thought. The only light I could see concentrated into one spot, dead center, and I remembered thinking that all those stories about the bright light turned out to be true. In fact, all the cliché stories had to be true, for, just before the light faded to nothing, I swore I saw an angel, calling my name. And then, even it was gone.

CHAPTER TWO

BEEP. BEEP. BEEP. My alarm. I rolled over to turn it off, but something pulled at my arms, preventing me from moving. Irritated, I pried my eyes open and waited for them to focus. All I saw was white. Fuzzy whiteness, everywhere I looked. I blinked and squinted and tried to make sense of what I was seeing, but the whiteness didn't go away—only sharpened a bit. Scanning my surroundings, I saw another color: silver. Gleaming silver and stark white, all around me. As the sleep fog cleared from my brain, I began to make out machines and instruments that, somewhere in the deep recesses of my mind, were familiar to me. I realized the big machine next to me was the source of the beeping. Not my alarm. Definitely not my alarm, because this wasn't my apartment, wasn't my bed. Wracking my brain, I frantically tried to figure out where I was and why I was here and the last thing I could clearly remember. I came up bone dry. I started to panic, and the beeping got faster. I tried to get up, but again, some unknown restraint kept me down. Looking down, I saw a tangle of tubes and wires attached to various parts of my body, and I began to hyperventilate. Finally, it all registered: I was in a hospital. Why was I in a hospital, hooked up to machines like a lab rat?

Just as I was about to completely lose it, a woman in teal scrubs entered the room and pushed some buttons on one of the machines. Then she turned and smiled at me and said, "Good morning. How are you feeling?"

I opened my mouth to answer her and gagged. She smiled gently and said, "Don't try to talk; it will probably be a little difficult for a while. I'll get you some water." I winced as I tried to swallow. My throat felt like someone had scrubbed it down with sandpaper and acid. I watched as she walked out of the room, which seemed to grow bigger in her absence. The white walls and sterile equipment stared down at me, and I felt as insignificant as an ant. The panic threatened to overcome me again, just as the nurse returned with a large cup of water.

"Here you go," she said, handing it to me. I took a sip and started choking, my throat burning with every cough. She took my cup and dabbed at my mouth with a tissue. "Your throat is going to be pretty sore for a few days. Swallowing will be challenging, and painful. Just try to take it easy. Dr. McNeal will be in soon to check on you." I opened my mouth to ask what had happened to me, but she was already gone.

I waited for the doctor, doing my best to stay calm. I worked on breathing slowly and tried not to think about the terrifying situation I was in, knowing I would get answers as soon as he came. The breathing must have worked, because the next thing I remember was hearing a baritone voice say my name, waking me. I opened my eyes and saw a tall man with a stethoscope around his neck come into focus. He was smiling at me. He had a kind smile.

"Hello, Olivia. I'm Dr. McNeal. It's good to see you awake. You had quite a scare there." He flipped through a clipboard in his hands and glanced at the monitors next to me. "You're one of the lucky ones. If your neighbor hadn't found you when he did, chances are you wouldn't be with us right now."

Neighbor? Lucky ones? What is he talking about?

He must have seen the questioning look on my face, because he started to explain. "You had a very close call. Your neighbor found you in bed, unconscious, with an empty bottle of Valium next to you. He rushed you here, and we pumped your stomach, just in the nick of time."

And with his words it all came back. Every gory detail. The dark room, the shattered glass, the white pills . . .

The blood in my veins turned to ice as I realized it had really happened; it wasn't just another nightmare I'd had. I turned my head away from the doctor, too ashamed to look him in the eyes. What must he think of me? A lump formed in my already swollen throat, and my eyes burned with tears that would never manifest.

Someone entered the room, and I heard Dr. McNeal talk to them, too softly for me to hear. No doubt he was telling the nurse to watch me like a hawk—make sure I didn't try to strangle myself with my IV. Then he cleared his throat and placed a strong but gentle hand on my shoulder.

"You rest now. I'll be back to check on you in a few hours." I listened to his footsteps grow distant as he left the room, but I didn't move, aware that the nurse remained. I didn't want to talk to anyone (not that I could), didn't want to look at anyone. *Just leave me alone.*

It wasn't long before I got my wish, and the nurse slipped out of the room. Immediately I wanted her back.

Nothing was worse than being alone right now. Alone with the realization that the only reason I was alive was because I had failed at trying to kill myself. A cruel twist of fate had robbed me of my last chance at escape, had left me to live a life I didn't want to live. It was as if life itself was laughing at me.

I lay there, humiliation and anger smothering me, wishing for the millionth time that I could just cry. I knew if I could shed even one little tear, it would release some of the pain trapped inside me. Instead, I listened to the beeping machines until they lulled me into a dreamless sleep.

* * * * *

I had no idea how long I'd slept when I woke to yet another nurse beside me, poking and prodding me. She apologized for waking me, although I could tell that she really wasn't sorry at all. After all, she was just doing her job.

"How're you doing?" she asked. She paused and looked at me expectantly, and I realized it wasn't rhetorical. She wanted an answer.

I cleared my throat and rasped out an "okay." It was weird hearing my own voice after not having spoken in . . . how long had it been?

This seemed to satisfy the nurse, who resumed her duties. After bringing me a fresh glass of water, she asked if I needed anything else. I shook my head, and her expression softened. "Dr. Robinson, the hospital psychiatrist, wants to ask you a few questions. She's right outside." My stomach jolted at this news, and the heart monitor betrayed my panic. What would I say? How could I talk about trying to end my life? What if they want to lock me away in some horrific institution? The thought brought with it a wave of nausea and I turned my head away. The nurse left without saying anything else, and, although the room was silent then, I could feel that I was not alone.

A female voice said hello. It was low and raspy and sounded like she'd smoked more than a few packs of cigarettes in her lifetime. I didn't look up, didn't answer. I stared at my new friend, the white wall next to my bed. I was suddenly grateful there were no machines to indicate my level of humiliation.

"Olivia, I'm Dr. Robinson. I just want to talk to you a little bit." I still didn't speak, but this didn't seem to faze her. It occurred to me this wouldn't have been the first time she'd encountered an uncooperative patient.

"I can't force you to speak, but I can't help you if you won't talk to me." She paused, giving me a chance to say something, which I did not take. I wasn't trying to be difficult; when I had something to say, I would say it.

"I want to talk about what happened the other night."

I squeezed my eyes shut, as if this could make her go away. Make it all go away. I found myself longing for invisibility once again.

"Will you tell me about it?"

A direct question. I couldn't ignore her any longer. If I didn't speak, she would only assume the worst and lock me up for sure.

"What do you want to know?" My voice was rough, but it cleared up with each attempt at speaking.

She was silent for a moment, then in a softer voice asked, "Did you try to kill yourself?" The words sliced through me like a red-hot poker. It sounded so wrong—such potent words being said in such a gentle way.

My mind flashed back to my bedroom, to that night.

It was all such a blur. Did I? I know I wanted to sleep, a painless sleep. But did I intend to do more? Utter despair washed over me as I thought of the possibility.

I'm so scared that I did.

"I don't remember."

"What *do* you remember?"

My eyes closed as I tried to remember. It wasn't easy, attempting to dredge up something you'd rather forget forever.

"I remember . . ." I paused, concentrating. It was so hard—every image in my head blurred, every thought a jumble of senseless words. "A headache. Ibuprofen. I couldn't sleep, I just wanted to sleep . . ." I drifted off, unsure how to continue.

"So you took Valium?"

I nodded slowly.

"Did you take the pills just to sleep? Or were you trying to end your life?"

There it was again, the hot poker. I winced, and my brain fought against remembering. I didn't want to remember. Being asked that question made it seem like I had a choice, like there was a possibility I hadn't really intended to kill myself. The idea filled me with hope, and I clung to it with every fiber of my being.

"I—I'm not sure." I really wasn't. Had I tried to end my life, or did I just want to sleep? I couldn't remember, and part of me knew I didn't want to, knew that if I did I would probably remember it happening exactly the way I feared.

Dr. Robinson didn't speak for several minutes.

Then she asked the last thing I expected to hear.

"You have a history of suicide in your family, is that correct?"

My head jerked up, and I stared at her vehemently. "How did you know that?"

She gazed at me with intense eyes and said, "Your chart. Would you like to talk about it?"

"No, I would not," I shot back.

She continued to gaze, unaffected. I think she realized she had reached my limit. This was where it ended with me. I stared at her, daring her to ask me more. She didn't. Smart woman.

She nodded at me, and I could almost see the wheels turning in her head, evaluating my level of crazy. She jotted something on her chart, then started to leave.

"Thank you for talking with me, Olivia. I hope we can continue our conversation another day." *Don't hold your breath,* I thought, staring her down with furious eyes.

She handed me her business card, which I didn't take. She set it on the bedside table. "My extension is on there. If you ever decide you'd like to talk, just call that number and you'll get straight through to me." With that, she turned and left.

My hard exterior crumbled as soon as she was gone, and I dropped back on my pillow, fuming. I lay there thinking venomous thoughts about the psychiatrist for what seemed like forever until, for some inexplicable reason, I suddenly couldn't keep my eyes open any longer.

As my thoughts began to blur together and teeter on the edge of incoherence, I marveled at how drastically sleep had changed for me since being in the hospital. It came so easily, so frequently, without the awful side effect of nightmares. I wondered if the liquid flowing through my IV had anything to do with it—my last clear thought before slipping into nonsensical dreams.

CHAPTER THREE

I WOKE SOME TIME LATER to Dr. McNeal's low voice, speaking to someone just outside my door that I couldn't see. I tried to hear what he was saying but couldn't make it out. After a minute he came over to me, alone.

"Oh, good," he said, smiling that kind smile. "You're awake. It's time we get you out of here. Are you ready to go home?"

"Home?" I repeated, confused. They were letting me go, just like that? I had fully prepared myself for a life spent in a padded room.

"Yes, home." He smiled. "You're doing great. Your vitals have been stable for a while, and Dr. Robinson cleared you this morning: after speaking with your neighbor and getting his story, she is confident that you are not a threat to yourself. After all, accidents happen."

I started to open my mouth to question him but caught myself in time and clamped it shut. My mind was racing, trying to make sense of what he had just said. Had my neighbor lied? Made it sound like an accident? What story could possibly convince a board-certified psychiatrist that downing an entire bottle of Valium was merely an accident? Something was not right here, and it made me uneasy. But it also meant I was out of here, without so much as a follow-up therapy session. I had to play along.

"Let's get you up and dressed, and—" he glanced at the dry erase board next to the door "—Sandra will be in soon to discharge you." I nodded, struggling to digest what he was saying. It didn't add up—something wasn't right, but a voice in the back of my mind told me this was a good thing and warned me to not screw it up.

"Oh, and as soon as you're dressed and ready, there's someone who would like to see you."

This time the surprise could not be hidden on my face, and Dr. McNeal smiled again. "Your knight in shining armor—your neighbor who found you. That is, of course, if you want to meet him."

I hesitated, not quite sure if I did or not. The part of me that was mortified that this person caught me in the act of suicide wanted to scream for him to go away. But the other part, the part that was curious about this mystery neighbor and why he was covering for me, wanted desperately to see who he was and to get some answers. The curious part won. I nodded, and Dr. McNeal left, still smiling.

Sandra came in shortly after and began the process of unhooking me from the myriad of machines I was attached to. When I was finally tube-free, she handed me my clothes and sent me to the bathroom to change.

I was shaky on my feet, and I again wondered how long I had been in that hospital bed.

It was bittersweet, putting on my own clothes. It was one step closer to being home, out of this nightmare. But these were the clothes I was wearing when . . . I stopped myself there, refusing to think about it any more. I had been declared fit to go home, and soon I could forget about the whole ugly thing, pretend like it had never even happened.

When I was dressed, I looked in the bathroom mirror at my appearance. I barely recognized myself. I looked like something out of a horror film. My dishwater blonde hair was thin and stringy, hanging limply around my face. My eyes were sunken with dark circles underneath, making it look like I had two black eyes. My skin was gray and sallow. But the most shocking part was how skinny I was. Every bone in my body seemed to be visible underneath my skin. I truly resembled a skeleton.

I turned away, unable to look any longer. I made my way back into the room and, unwilling to return to the bed, opted instead for an uncomfortable-looking chair. I sat, waiting.

Sandra poked her head in to see that I was dressed, then left again. Seconds later there was a knock on the door, even though it was propped slightly open.

"Come in," I said. I sat up straight and quickly tucked my hair behind my ears in a last-ditch effort to make myself more presentable.

The door slowly opened, and in walked a young man who looked to be about my age. I don't know why this took me by surprise, but it did. For some reason I had been expecting someone older, elderly even. But this guy was definitely in his early twenties. He was tall, at least from where I was sitting, with light-colored hair and shockingly green eyes.

He hovered just inside the door, tentatively.

Of course, I realized with disgust. *He thinks I'm completely crazy. The last time he saw me I had just consumed the contents of my medicine cabinet.*

Trying to appear as sane as possible, I forced a smile and said, "Hello."

"Hi." His voice was soft and deep, almost a hum.

I waited to see if he would say anything else. He didn't. Clearly he was not going to make this easy for me. I shifted in my chair and glanced uncomfortably around the room. What do you say to the person who saved your life? A life you didn't necessarily want saved?

I opened my mouth to say something even though I had nothing in mind, when he suddenly asked, "How are you feeling? Are you . . . all right?"

The concern on his face was so severe it caught me off guard. I cleared my throat and answered, "Yeah, I'm good. Thanks to you."

His eyes shifted suddenly from the floor to mine, and I got the impression he was trying to decide whether or not I was being sarcastic. Did he think I was angry that he had quelled my attempted suicide? My face grew hot in embarrassment, but before I could say anything to clarify, his face relaxed and he said, "I just happened to be in the right place at the right time."

"And where, exactly, was that?" I asked slowly, hoping I didn't sound rude.

"Home. The building next to yours." He shoved his hands into his pockets. "I was walking past my window and saw you through yours. I saw you holding that bottle, and . . ."

His voice drifted off and I quickly looked away, my face burning again. I had never felt so ashamed. I wanted to run out of the room and find a large rock to live under for the rest of my life. Why in the world did I ever think it was a good idea to meet him?

I stared at the floor, willing him to leave, too mortified to say anything else. But he didn't move. After a few moments he said quietly, "I'm glad you're okay."

I glanced up. He was staring right at me, so intensely that normally I would have had to look away, but not this time. This time I stared back, locked in his gaze.

At that moment Sandra reentered the room, almost knocking into my visitor, who still had not moved from his position just inside the door. She smiled at him but did not ask him to leave, and he made no move to do so voluntarily. She went over my discharge instructions and had me sign a release form.

"Okay," she said cheerily. "You're free to go. Do you have a ride home?" It was at this point that I realized I had no way of getting home. The hospital was nowhere near walking distance from my apartment.

"Actually, I was wondering if I could give you a ride home." I looked at the figure by the door, who had been so silent up to this point that I had almost forgotten he was there. I realized I didn't even know his name.

"Oh, perfect," Sandra cooed and led us out into the hall. She either didn't notice or didn't care that I had not yet accepted his offer for a ride. But what other choice did I have? There was no way I could afford a cab, not with the hospital bills that would soon be filling my mailbox. I didn't even have money for bus fare.

We followed Sandra through the labyrinth of halls and outside. I always found it interesting that hospitals will tell you you're well enough to leave, but apparently don't consider you well enough to walk outside unescorted by a medical professional.

Once we were through the automatic doors and out into the damp, foggy air, Sandra said good-bye and headed back into the hospital. I followed . . . whatever-his-name-was to a shiny, white truck. He opened the passenger door for me, and I hesitated, my feet planted a few feet away.

I squinted at his face and said, "I know you saved my life, but I can't just get into a car with a guy whose name I don't even know."

He smiled at this, looking amused, and I watched as dimples formed in his cheeks.

"Jude," he said, stepping forward with his hand stretched out. "My name is Jude."

"Olivia Tate," I said, shaking his hand, which was abnormally soft for a man. He nodded, and I realized he would have already learned my name from the hospital. "Do . . . you . . . have a last name, or should I just call you Jude?"

He chuckled. "West."

Jude West, I thought, trying it out in my head. So that was the name of my rescuer.

"There," he said, smiling. "We're officially introduced. Now you don't need to worry about riding with a stranger." He motioned toward the truck, so I climbed in. I was instantly struck by how good it smelled and how clean it was.

Jude got in the driver's seat and started the engine. He reached over and turned on the heat, and I welcomed the warmth. The March air was chilly, and I had no coat.

We rode in silence for a few blocks, at which point I realized that if I wanted to get answers, I'd better speak up. Chances were I'd never see this guy again. I tried to think of a way to ask him about the story he'd told Dr. Robinson that didn't sound ridiculous or ungrateful, but I couldn't. The only thing that seemed appropriate was to thank him for saving my life. It occurred to me that I hadn't actually done that yet. Even though it may not have been what I wanted at the time, I found myself grateful to him for doing it.

"Um, thank you, for . . . you know." I couldn't say it.

"Really, if you hadn't shown up . . ."

He stared through the windshield, his face expressionless. "I only did what anyone else would have done."

I studied his face, trying to determine if his modesty was put on or if he truly felt what he'd done wasn't a big deal. I couldn't decide.

"Well, anyway, thank you."

He glanced at me briefly and nodded.

The silence that followed felt heavy, as if the thick smog that hovered above the streets outside had seeped into the cab of the truck. I needed to change the subject.

"So, Jude, huh? Were your parents like, Beatles fanatics or something?"

He smiled. "No. I was actually named for the saint."

"Oh." I didn't know what to say to that, so I turned and looked out the window.

A few minutes later we pulled up in front of my building. I hesitated before getting out, feeling like I should say something.

"So . . . thanks again, for . . ." I just couldn't say it, so I changed direction. "For giving me a ride, I really appreciate it."

"Yeah, well, I was headed here anyway." He nodded toward the building next to mine, and I looked, feeling stupid for forgetting.

"Right," I said, the blood rushing to my face. "Our windows face each other." This reminder of what he had witnessed made it suddenly painful to be in his presence, and I needed to leave, fast. I exited quickly, slamming the door behind me a little too hard after muttering one last good-bye. I didn't look back as I hurried to the front doors. I would always be grateful to the guy who saved my life, but I genuinely hoped I would never see him again.

CHAPTER FOUR

JUDE WAITED UNTIL OLIVIA had disappeared through the double doors leading into her apartment before pulling out into traffic again. A few minutes later he pulled off to the side of a busy road in a rare empty parking space. He killed the engine and got out of the truck, then walked over to a homeless man standing on the corner. The man held a cardboard sign that read: "STRANDED, NEED MONEY. ANYTHING HELPS." His face was sun-worn and leathery, most of it covered in a bushy black beard. He was bundled up in a holey stocking cap and faded green army coat.

The man saw Jude approach and quickly looked away. "Hey, kid," he said quietly, glancing around to see if anyone overheard.

"Hey, Hal," Jude responded. He held out the keys to the truck, and Hal quickly snatched them out of his hand and shoved them in the pocket of his coat, eyes still darting around.

"I cleaned it for you. Thanks for letting me borrow

it. And thanks again for the loan. I'll get it back to you, somehow."

Hal shushed Jude and glared at him. "Keep your voice down, will ya? I got a business to run."

"Sorry," he said, lowering his voice. A group of pedestrians were gathering on the corner, waiting for the signal to change to cross the street. Hal waved Jude away and held up his sign. A couple people began digging in their pockets, pulling out loose change and single bills and handing them to Hal. Jude stood off to the side, trying to blend in with the crowd as Hal collected the money and thanked them profusely with a "God bless, God bless."

The signal changed and the cluster of people left. Jude walked back over to Hal, trying not to be obvious. "Hal, I need one more favor."

"What's that?"

"I need to get into an apartment, a certain one. And," he added, "it might already be occupied."

Hal raised an eyebrow but didn't question it, just like he hadn't questioned Jude when he showed up asking to borrow his truck. It was Hal's best quality, in Jude's opinion.

"Where is it?"

"Nearby. Couple of blocks over."

Hal responded, still not looking at Jude. "Got the address?"

Jude reached into his pocket and pulled out a scrap of paper, handing it to Hal. Hal studied it for a moment before quickly shoving it into his pocket. "I'll see what I can do."

"Thanks," Jude replied, trying not to think about what would have to be done for him to move into the apartment if it was already being lived in.

"Well, thanks again." He turned to leave.

"Hey, kid," Hal called out, just loud enough for Jude to hear.

"Yeah?"

The transient reached into his pocket and tossed Jude the keys he'd just returned. "Hang onto it. You need it more than I do." Jude smiled at the irony of that statement, but he knew it was true nonetheless.

"Thanks, Hal."

* * * * *

That night was different. Something had changed since I came home, something inside me. It wasn't as if I was so overcome with gratitude at being given a second chance at life that I was filled with a newfound joy. No, I was still a far cry from joyous. But I had realized something since being home: I wanted to be here. And by "here" I mean on earth, alive. Somehow I still wanted to be living this life that I hated so much, and that was something.

At least one thing remained unchanged: I still couldn't sleep, not without the aid of the magic liquid at the hospital. But instead of my usual nightly ritual of alternating catnaps with hysterics, I forewent the bed altogether.

Instead I sat curled up on my couch, staring out my window. For the first half hour after returning home, I had successfully avoided looking at that window. It was difficult, but it was made easier by the fact that I had a mess to deal with.

Coming home to everything exactly the way it was that night was nothing short of agony. The first thing I saw when I walked through the door was the pile of glass shards covering the floor. My eyes drifted upward to the empty bottle on the bed, the cap lying next to it. I noticed there was not a single pill in sight. Someone had made sure to dispose of those. I wanted to ignore it, hope that somehow it would clean itself up, but there was nowhere I could go in my tiny one-room apartment and not see it. I knew the sooner I got rid of the visual reminders, the better.

But cleaning up had only taken so long, and I found myself standing in the middle of the room, unsure of what to do with myself. At some point I wandered into the kitchen and ate something without tasting it, not because I was hungry but because it was something to do. I saw my answering machine blinking and pushed the playback button, wondering who would have called me. It was my boss.

"Hey, Olivia, it's Bryan. I've been worried about you. How are you doing? I hope everything's okay. Listen, don't worry about work. Take as much time off as you need. Your job will be waiting here for you when you're ready to come back. Take care, Olivia. Bye."

I stared at the machine, wondering how he could possibly know, then decided not to question it, and to appreciate the fact that I could now hole up in my apartment properly. I felt a twinge of something else—surprise maybe, or gratitude. I guess I'd never really realized that Bryan cared at all, or that he was a person outside of the man who sat in his office and gave me a paycheck. It tugged slightly at my heartstrings, but I quickly brushed it away.

I tried not to, but I couldn't help glancing every few minutes at my east wall. I guess maybe I was checking to see if he was watching me. But if I was being honest with myself, I'd have to admit to being curious about him.

Finally, I gave up trying to resist. I sat and stared at the window directly across from mine. It was dark. It had been dark all day. And yet, I continued to stare.

My thoughts inadvertently turned to my rescuer. Jude, named after a saint. Fitting, I thought. Saving someone's life was a very saint-like thing to do. Maybe his parents had a premonition that their son would make it a habit to go around saving damsels in distress.

Without meaning or wanting to, I thought back to that night and tried to picture how it played out, him coming in, finding me, saving me. It occurred to me to wonder how he got into my apartment in the first place. I frowned as I contemplated this, looking over at my door as if it would somehow give me the answer. The door must have been unlocked, I realized. It was the only explanation. I tried to remember if I had locked it that night, but everything about that day was a blur. I thought about how upset I was when I left the restaurant that day. It wasn't hard to see how I could have forgotten a minor thing like locking the door behind me. But then, locking my door had always been somewhat of a reflex, something I did out of years of habit. Growing up in the worst parts of the city with a single mom taught me a thing or two about precaution. Living alone had only increased the need for safety measures, and I couldn't remember a time I had forgotten to lock the door behind me.

This missing puzzle piece led me to think about the other, more perplexing mystery: his fabricated story. Of course, I was only assuming he'd lied for me. I guess there was the possibility that he truly believed it was an accident. But how could that be, unless he was the least intelligent person ever to roam the earth? No, I didn't believe that. It was painfully obvious what I had been trying to do. No one swallows a bottle of pills unless they have a very permanent form of escape on their mind.

But *why*? Why would he lie? What did he have to gain

from it? He didn't know me, so why would he care about protecting me? And what kind of protection was it, really—keeping me from getting the help I so clearly needed? I just didn't get it; it made no sense. And this bothered me to no end.

I was pondering this, gazing out the window once more, when I realized that the spot I had been staring at had changed. The black square I had been accustomed to now had a shape within it. My brain caught up with my eyes and I recognized the shape as a human figure. My breath caught in my throat and I froze, my heart beating wildly out of my chest. It was him. It had to be him; who else would it be? He was staring right at me. Could he see me? I didn't move, didn't breathe for what felt like an eternity. Just when I thought I might pass out, he walked away from the window and disappeared into blackness.

I took a breath but didn't move, trying to calm my heart down. Did he know I'd been watching his window all night? I don't know why this thought terrified me, but it did. I wanted to leave, get off my couch, go somewhere he couldn't see me, but it was a long time before I could bring myself to move. When I did, I went straight to the window and rigged a blanket over it to act as a makeshift curtain. Satisfied that he couldn't see me, I crawled into bed and buried myself under the covers.

* * * * *

I woke up some time later, shaking from head to toe from a macabre dream involving faceless figures wielding butcher knives. When I finally calmed down, I lay there, completely disoriented. I had no idea how long I'd been asleep or what time it was. It was still dark, but I could feel that I'd slept for a long time. I glanced at my alarm clock. 12:43 p.m. This didn't make sense, it was so dark. Then I remembered my "curtain," and the reason I had put it up. A shiver ran up my spine as I recalled his silhouette standing there staring back at me, and I had to shake it off. I jumped out of bed and headed for the shower.

I took my time, letting the hot water rain down on me, as if it could wash away everything that had happened. I stood there unmoving in the near-scalding water for so long that my body started to grow numb to the heat, and I could only feel the sting of each stream of water hitting my back like tiny nails. When I started to feel a change in the temperature and knew I had only minutes before it went cold, I hurriedly washed and got out. I put on my most comfortable jeans and an old sweatshirt. I blow-dried my hair, brushed it out, and put it in a ponytail. Already it looked better than the last time I'd seen it, in the hospital mirror. The rest of my appearance, however, was beyond my control at the moment.

I went into the kitchen to find something for breakfast (lunch?) but nothing sounded the least bit appealing. Once again, I was at a total loss as to what to do with myself.

Before The Incident I had lived like a robot. Worked all day, every day; moving, but not living. Now, I felt like part of me had woken up, like my close call had been a wake-up call and I had this strange new awareness of my surroundings. And they weren't pretty.

I found myself sitting on my couch again, staring at my window, only now it was an ugly green blanket I was staring at. I tried to tell myself I didn't care what was on the other side, but I didn't believe it. I knew better. It took everything in me to not pull a corner back and peek through at his window. I probably would have, if the fear of being seen didn't overpower any curiosity I felt.

Instead I sat and let my mind wander, yet again, to the disturbing questions that seemed to dominate my brain now. Locked door . . . complete stranger lying for me . . .

Over and over again they passed through my mind, each time with the hope that something would make sense, that something would fall into place. But on the contrary, it only became more mystifying.

Finally, I made up my mind. I got up, put on my coat, and grabbed my keys.

I knew where to find him. I had to get answers.

CHAPTER FIVE

IT COULDN'T BE TOO HARD to figure out which apartment was his from inside the building. Fifth floor, like mine, west side, five windows back. The only question was, how many windows did each apartment have?

I could feel the nerves kick in as I made my way down the wet sidewalk. The rain, cascading down, instantly soaked my recently dried hair. My hands started to shake a little as I neared the entrance to his building. Why? What reason did I have to be nervous about tracking down my rescuer and demanding an explanation? *Every reason,* I thought.

My pulse quickened as I pushed through the double doors, and it was then that I realized I had not yet figured out exactly what I was going to say to him. I began working out different possibilities in my head, each one sounding more ridiculous than the next.

"Olivia." My thoughts were stopped short by a quiet voice to my left. I turned toward it and saw *him* approaching.

"What are you doing here?" He seemed surprised, but not annoyed.

"Um . . . actually I was coming to talk to you. I needed to . . ." I trailed off, hearing my words echo off the bare walls of the small area. I was suddenly ultra-aware of the other tenants entering and exiting the building, milling around the mailboxes. I couldn't very well start discussing my suicide attempt right here.

He was watching me, eyebrows raised expectantly, and I couldn't help thinking that I probably looked like a drowned rat. I thought fast. We couldn't talk now. So when? Where? Somewhere public, somewhere safe. But somewhere busy enough that no one would be paying any attention to our conversation. Like a restaurant.

I cleared my throat and started again. "I don't feel like I have really thanked you for . . . what you did. I was wondering if I could take you to dinner . . . as a thank-you."

"Sure."

"O-okay," I stammered, caught off guard by his quick acceptance. "Are you available tonight?" It had to be tonight. Another night of sitting alone in my dark apartment tormenting myself with unanswered questions was too painful to think about.

"Yeah. Should I pick you up?"

I hesitated, thinking how very much like a date this was sounding. I never intended it to be anything resembling a date. But once again, my lack of funds or transportation made accepting his offer necessary.

"That would be great," I replied. "How about . . . six o'clock?"

He nodded. "See you at six."

I gave him an awkward sort of half-smile before turning and walking out of his building.

* * * * *

Jude rode the elevator up to his new apartment. He couldn't tell if it was the quick assent that was making his stomach flip or the run-in he'd just had with Olivia. Nothing could have shocked him more than to see her walk into his building. He felt like he hid it well, kept his cool. But tonight . . . what did she need to talk to him about? He was worried that he already knew the answer.

He got off the elevator and entered his new apartment. He'd lucked out; it had been vacant. A lot of the apartments in the building were, apparently, after the landlord jacked up the rent. Fortunately for Jude, Hal could afford it, no problem.

He stood in the empty room and took in his new home. It was big, not like Olivia's. There were actually walls dividing the bedroom from the living room and kitchen. He thought about the last time he'd been in her place and quickly shoved the memory from his head.

He went to the window and looked across at Olivia's. It was covered now by what had to be a fairly thin blanket, since he could still see her silhouette moving behind it. He could guess why she would feel the need to cover her window now.

His mind subconsciously wandered back to their imminent dinner that night. He sighed, knowing he just had to accept the inevitable. *Maybe,* he thought, *this would be a good thing.* He'd been dreaming up ways to check up on her—make sure she was okay—besides spying on her like a Peeping Tom through her window. He made a face. He hated that that's what it made him. But it was the only way he'd thought of to keep a watchful eye on her.

Now she'd made it easy for him, coming to him and asking him to dinner. Maybe he could simply dodge any questions she might ask, maybe even learn a few things of his own about her.

Maybe it wouldn't be his ruin.

* * * * *

At five-thirty I sat on my couch, watching the clock. I was a wreck. My head was a jumble of negative thoughts, fears, and self-doubt. I had had three miserable hours to get to this point. After trying unsuccessfully to keep myself occupied all afternoon, I finally gave up at five and took another shower. When it came time to get dressed, I stood in front of my closet and stared dejectedly at my pathetic excuse for a wardrobe. Before today I had never needed anything other than some pajamas, some sweats and T-shirts for lounging at home, and the heinous waitress uniform that clothed my body eighty percent of the time.

Thank goodness I owned at least one pair of decent jeans, the ones I'd had on earlier. But going in the old, holey sweatshirt was unthinkable. Somewhere I knew I had a black blouse, the one I'd worn to my mother's funeral with a black skirt. I found it shoved all the way to the side of my closet, untouched for nearly a year. It was a little dusty on the shoulders, but I brushed it off easily. I put it on with my jeans and examined myself in the mirror.

It was definitely a step up from the sweatshirt, but still nothing that would put me on the cover of a magazine any time soon. The blouse that had been form-fitting when I bought it, now hung on me as if it was still on the hanger. I walked away quickly, trying to force the image out of my mind.

I headed into the bathroom, faced with the dilemma of what to do with my hair. There wasn't a plethora of options. Even freshly washed and blown-dry, it hung thin and limp around my face. I ended up putting it back into a ponytail.

After digging out the black flats that had completed my funeral ensemble, I sat on the couch to wait. With nothing to occupy my mind, the full realization of what I was about to do hit me. Hard. I started to panic, to the point of feeling sick.

When was the last time I had sat down and had a conversation with someone for more than a few minutes? What was I thinking? How in the world was I going to *do* this? I didn't know what to say, how to act, and I certainly had no idea how to go about getting the answers I wanted. *Hey, thanks for coming to dinner with me. Now why did you tell the doctors it was an accident when clearly I was trying to kill myself?* My face fell into my hands. This was going to be a nightmare.

I got up to get a drink in an attempt to calm down a bit. As I did, I glanced at the clock. 5:45. The butterflies in my stomach intensified and I worried the water might make its way back up. I was just starting to consider bailing when I heard the knock on my door. Steeling myself, I walked over and opened the door. Jude stood on the other side, looking cool and calm in a polo shirt and jeans. I couldn't help but notice how well he filled out his clothes.

"Ready?" he asked. I nodded a little too vigorously. I put on my coat and grabbed my wallet and keys, locking the door behind me on my way out. I followed him down the stairs and outside. Surprisingly, it wasn't raining, or even foggy, but a bitterly cold wind blew that I felt in my bones.

He led me to the street where his truck was parked. As we neared it, he walked over to the passenger door and opened it, holding it for me. I paused, caught off guard,

I stared at the glove compartment in front of me, thinking of another question or even a comment. Anything but the silence. And then I blurted out the first thing that came into my head. "I like your truck." *I like your truck?* The words echoed in my ears and I heard how idiotic I sounded.

Jude's eyes shifted quickly to me, then back to the road. I thought I saw the corners of his mouth quiver just a tiny bit. "Thanks."

I slumped slightly in my seat, staring out the window. If this was any indication of how this evening was going to go, it was going to be a long, miserable dinner. How was I ever going to get answers?

When we arrived at the pier, I suggested a popular chain restaurant that was well-lit, well-occupied, noisy, and within my price range. After all, I had asked *him* to dinner, which meant I was paying.

But he had something different in mind. He pointed to an obscure-looking seafood place that was almost hidden between the shops on either side. One look at it and my heart sunk. It was sure to be dim, quiet, and outrageously expensive. But what could I do? I wasn't about to humiliate myself anymore than I already had in front of this guy by admitting I couldn't afford it.

He found a parking space a couple of blocks away and I quickly exited the truck before he could have a chance to open my door for me. It wasn't that I didn't appreciate his chivalrousness, I just didn't want to make a fool of myself sitting there waiting for it like I expected it.

We walked through the throngs of people, all gravitating toward restaurants in search of dinner. It felt odd, walking beside this guy like it was nothing. I kept glancing over at him out of the corner of my eye, wondering if people were looking at us and wondering why a guy like him would be walking with a girl like me. Again, I was grateful to live in a place where no one would blink an eye at something even stranger than us.

When we reached the restaurant and made our way inside, I saw that my assumptions were correct. It was exactly as I had pictured it: small, dark, . . . intimate. The dining area was a single room with a dozen or so white-clothed tables lining the walls, each lit by tiny hurricane lamps. Mostly couples occupied the tables. On the walls hung black and white pictures of old fishing boats. A man in a white shirt and black pants led us to a table in the back right corner. I was relieved to see the tables directly around ours were empty . . . we would be able to talk without being overheard.

Our waiter appeared with ice water and menus, and after telling us the special, disappeared into the back. It was strange being on this end of waiting tables. I wasn't used to being the one getting served.

Jude opened his menu, and I followed suit, scared to look. My eyes widened when I saw the numbers staring back at me, and my shoulders fell. Luckily the menu was large, and I was hidden from Jude's view. I wasn't going to get out of here without spending half a paycheck.

The waiter returned to take our order. I got some kind of fish, the cheapest thing on the menu that wasn't an appetizer. Jude ordered salmon, and the waiter left.

My heart started to race a little. I had no more excuses. It was time to start talking. I cleared my throat.

"So, besides wanting to thank you for . . . helping me the other night, I had another reason for asking you to dinner." I was talking to my ice water. I could not seem to look at him as I spoke. His piercing eyes were intimidating. They made me feel like I was standing in a spotlight.

"Oh, yeah?" he asked, and I could hear the curiosity in his voice, mixed with something else I couldn't pinpoint.

"Yeah. I was hoping you could answer some questions for me," I said slowly. "Some things . . . don't add up."

I glanced at him then, just in time to see something pass over his face so quickly that I couldn't even be sure anything had. Before I had a chance to wonder about it, he spoke, totally at ease.

"Like what?"

I hesitated, not wanting to sound ungrateful or accusatory, but not knowing how to accomplish that.

"Well, for starters, I was wondering how you got into my apartment that night."

"Through the door," he answered, without missing a beat. *Thank you, Captain Obvious,* I wanted to say.

"I know," I said instead, "but how? It had to have been locked."

"It wasn't," he said. I couldn't help but notice how his eyes flickered down to the table when he said this. But what could I do? Accuse him of lying? I had no reason, really, to think he was. I myself had considered the possibility that I'd forgotten to lock the door. But still . . . why did I have the nagging feeling that I had locked it?

Considering this, and the possibility that he was lying to me, threw me off for a moment and I almost forgot that I had one more question for him, one that would be harder to ask.

"In the hospital," I began slowly, "I thought for sure they would make me . . ." I struggled to find the right words, so I tried again. "The psychiatrist seemed like she thought I . . . but then my doctor said something about getting your story, and . . . they just let me go, like that. What was . . . 'your story'?" The minute the words were out of my mouth, I regretted saying them. I was instantly positive I did not want to hear his story of what happened that night.

He didn't answer right away, which only fed the sick feeling in my stomach. I was just about to tell him to forget it, when he answered.

"I just told them the truth. That it was an accident." He looked right at me this time, an expression on his face so achingly pure that for a moment I believed him. It was all an accident. For one blissful moment he was telling the truth and I believed him. And then it was gone, and I knew the real truth. The hideously painful, ugly truth. But did he? Did he know my real intentions, or did he truly believe what he was telling me? His face and words were so convincing I had to wonder. For the first time, I considered the possibility that he really didn't know.

Bewilderment caused any potential response to flee from my brain. Trying to process this new development was about all it could handle right now, and luckily I was saved by the waiter bringing our food.

We ate in silence, and I wondered what he was thinking. I couldn't deny feeling frustrated that I had brought him here to get answers, and not only had I not gotten a single one, but I was also more confused now than ever. What a failure this had turned out to be. My only consolation was that the food was worth every dime I would pay for it. I couldn't remember tasting anything so delicious in my life. Actually, it was the first meal I remembered tasting at all in, well, pretty much forever.

The waiter brought the check when we were done, and I braced myself as I reached for it. But Jude's hand shot out and snatched it from the waiter before I'd barely moved my hand. I looked at him and scowled.

"I invited you here. I'm paying." I did not want him to

think for a moment that I thought this was a date, or that he should pay just because he's the guy.

He smiled, the first time all night, and said, "Don't insult me." I had no response to that. He slipped some money into the bill folder discreetly, then got up from the table, so I followed. I realized then that I didn't end up having to pay an arm and a leg for our meal after all, and I relaxed slightly for the first time all evening.

CHAPTER SIX

WE LEFT THE RESTAURANT and walked out into the cold, ocean air. It was almost dark now, the sun a muted red glow on the horizon, covered in a haze of gray. It was mesmerizing. I started in the direction of his truck, but Jude veered off toward the end of the pier, overlooking the sound. He paused and turned toward me, motioning in that direction.

"Do you mind?" he asked.

I shook my head, perplexed.

He walked to the railing and leaned up against it. I did the same.

We stared out at the ocean in silence, the salty air whipping stray hairs from my ponytail around my face and making me shiver painfully under my thin jacket. After several moments, Jude spoke.

"I'm sorry if tonight wasn't what you expected. I'm just not very good at stuff like this. Social stuff."

I looked at him in disbelief.

"You can't possibly be worse than I am." I turned back

to the ocean. "No one can," I added miserably.

"Oh, come on, it can't be that bad. Give yourself some credit."

"I'm not being modest, it's true. I don't do this, ever. I don't socialize. This isn't easy for me, at all."

"Well, you could have fooled me. It seems like it comes pretty naturally for you."

I gave a small, humorless laugh.

"That's nice of you to say, but it couldn't be further from the truth. I'm a bit of a loner, to say the least. I don't talk to people a lot. Well, at all, if I'm being honest."

Jude had turned toward me now, listening intently.

"Why not?" he asked softly. His scrutiny was unnerving, and I suddenly wished I hadn't been so open with him. I had allowed myself to let my guard down, leaving me completely vulnerable. I would not make that mistake again.

I watched the bottom tip of the sun disappear behind Bainbridge Island. Eventually Jude caught on to my silence and turned away from me, focusing his gaze on the sunset as well. We stood like that for a while. Seagulls flew around us noisily, inspecting the pier for stray morsels of food.

When the last sliver of color disappeared off the edge of the world, Jude said, "Ready to go?"

I nodded, shivering. The sun had taken with it every last ounce of heat, and my thin jacket had become completely useless.

Jude saw and exclaimed, "You're freezing! Here." He started to slip off his coat, but I stopped him as soon as I saw what he was doing. My guard was back up, and I didn't feel like accepting any more of his generosity.

He studied my face. "Are you sure? Your lips are kind

of blue." *And my fingers are going numb.* The warm thickness of his jacket was unbelievably tempting, but I had to stand my ground.

"I'm sure. Thanks anyway."

He shrugged, pulling his coat back on. The walk to his truck was miserable, me hunched over against the cold. Once we finally reached it, he beat me to the door again and opened it for me. Desperate to be out of the cold, I didn't waste time with internal arguments. I quickly climbed in and eagerly awaited the heat that would soon be blasting through the vents.

Jude, clearly aware of the brutal cold that had seeped to the center of my bones, immediately turned on the heat full blast, even though it was nowhere near warm enough yet. I didn't care. It was warmer than I was at present, and I longed to stretch out my hands closer to the vents, but I couldn't. One, because they were locked around my stomach like an iron vice, unable to move, and two, because it would betray how cold I really was and I would just look stupid for having refused Jude's coat, which, I realized now, was exactly what I was. Soon, hot air filled the cab and I felt my body start to relax, one joint at a time. The heat felt like a down comforter being wrapped around me, and I devoured it.

Jude drove silently, his face a stone mask. I wondered what he was thinking. I realized I never seemed to be able to figure that out. He was such an enigma, both in how little I knew about him and how jealously he guarded his thoughts. It was as if he refused to let me know anything about him.

The thought was a little upsetting. It wasn't that I had a huge desire to get to know the guy, but I didn't like the idea that he was hiding something from me.

"So . . ." I said. "What do you do when you're not running around saving people?"

"What makes you think I don't do that for a living?"

"What, are you a firefighter? A paramedic?" *How fitting that would be.*

He laughed, and I marveled at the sound. It wasn't something I was used to, laughter.

"No, none of the above. Actually, right now I'm . . . house-sitting, I guess you could say. "

"For your job? You get paid to live in someone's apartment?" *Enough that you can drive this truck and eat at expensive restaurants?* I wanted to ask but didn't.

He shifted in his seat. Or was he squirming? "Something like that."

Why did I get the feeling he was hiding something?

"How long have you been here?" I asked.

"Not long." That would explain why I'd never seen him through my window before. Or maybe I just hadn't been looking.

"What about you?" he asked. "What do you do?"

"I'm a waitress at a coffee shop." I shrugged. "It pays the bills." *Sometimes.*

He nodded.

"So where were you before you came here?" I prodded.

Jude turned and looked out his window. "All over," he said absently. His ambiguity was making me crazy. Every word he said made him more of a question mark. I gave up trying to get information out of him. I could take a hint.

Before long we were pulling into the same spot behind his building. We walked to the front of our buildings together, where I stopped to say good-bye. Jude kept walking toward my apartment. A sick wave of panic shot through me as it all came together in my head—opening my door, paying for dinner, offering me his coat . . . All of these seemingly charming acts were merely a ploy to get something in return.

When Jude realized that I was no longer behind him, he turned and saw me frozen to the sidewalk. Sighing, he said, "Can I please walk you to your door, so I know you made it all the way home safe?"

I debated what to do while he stood watching me. In the end, I played the rescuer card once more, deciding that if he had wanted to hurt me, he would have just let me die that first night. I followed him into my building and up the stairs. Outside my door, he kept a safe distance away, almost as if to prove a point, as he said good-bye.

"Thanks for asking me to dinner tonight. I'm glad we had a chance to talk."

"Thank you, again, for . . . you know. And for dinner, and giving me a ride."

"My pleasure," he said, and smiled. I couldn't help but once again notice the dimples that suddenly appeared. At the top of the stairs he stopped and turned around.

"Good night, Olivia."

"Good night, Jude." I watched as he descended down the staircase and disappeared around the corner.

* * * * *

The emotional strain of the evening hit me like a wrecking ball as soon as I closed the door behind me, and I immediately lost all strength in my limbs. I slid down the door to the hard, cold floor and sat there, slumped, staring at nothing. It had just been so much to handle, the evening of talking, smiling, opening up to another human being. Being normal was as exhausting to me as running a marathon was to a regular person. I didn't feel like I had been fake at all, but holding myself together for that long was completely draining, and I couldn't handle it another second.

When I finally felt like I could, I got up and went to the kitchen. I needed something soothing, but I didn't know what. I searched my nearly bare cupboards before coming across a packet of herbal tea that I didn't remember ever buying. It was exactly what I needed. I filled a teapot with water and set it on the stove to heat, then changed into my most ragged, comfortable sweats and T-shirt. I already felt marginally better.

It suddenly seemed too quiet to me, which was odd, considering it was always that way in my apartment, aside from the outside noise. I went over to my archaic stereo and flipped it on, holding my breath to see if it would still turn on after all this time. Surprisingly, it did, so I dug out my old case of CDs and picked my most melancholy album. I put it in and hit play, and just as the first familiar notes filled the room, so did the whistle of the teapot.

I made my tea and settled into my couch with the steaming cup warming my cold hands. For a while I sat and sipped my tea while listening to the music, which—strangely enough—cheered me. It reminded me of happier times.

I smiled as I thought of the day I got it. I was with Ashley, my best friend in high school. We had gone to the mall that day to shop for prom dresses. I had saved up for months to be able to afford a dress, just in the hopes that someone would ask me to the dance. After scouring every store with formal wear and finally deciding on the perfect dresses, we ate lunch in the food court, then made our way to the music store to check out the new releases. My dress had been on sale, so I had a little bit of money leftover, and

I was dying to buy the new release from one of my favorite bands. As we browsed the selection, we noticed a young sales guy eyeing us.

"Dude," Ashley said to me. "CD guy is staring at us."

"No," I corrected her. "CD guy is staring at *you*."

"Whatever," she said, pretending to be very interested in the albums in front of her. "He's obviously into blondes."

"How can you tell that from looking at him? He is so looking at you, it's not even funny." I was peeking at him from the corner of my eye while trying to appear like I was reading the back of a CD.

"Fine," Ashley said. "When he comes over to ask if we need help—and he will—we'll know who he's after. And I'll bet you the price of this CD—" she held up the one I was wanting, "—that it's you."

"You're on," I said, confident in my prediction.

Two minutes later the guy, an Abercrombie-&-Fitch-model-looking type, came over and asked if he could offer us any assistance, just as Ashley had said he would. I had to hide a smirk as he spoke directly to Ashley, seemingly oblivious of my presence. I snatched the CD out of Ashley's hand and said, "Actually, yes, my friend would like to purchase this." Ashley followed the hunky sales clerk to the checkout counter, smiling and flirting the whole way, not bothered in the least that she had just lost the bet. She gained a three-month relationship instead.

My smile faded as I thought of Ashley now, of what had happened with us. My stomach twisted as I recalled the events that led to the demise of our friendship. As I so often did, I wondered where she was now and what she was doing. And if she ever thought of me.

I had a notion then, and before I could think better of it, I was digging an old photo album out of my closet. As

I took it back to the couch, I knew it was a stupid thing to do, but I knew I was going to do it anyway.

I sat down and, taking a deep breath, flipped open the cover. My heart seemed to break in two as I saw the faces smiling back at me. There was me, with a curly updo and a made-up face that was full and bright and alive, next to a beautiful brunette with long, loose waves and a sparkly tiara. We were both grinning from ear to ear, giddy with excitement as we waited for our prom dates to arrive.

The familiar lump formed in my throat as I turned the page. Me and Ashley in my bedroom, goofing around. Me and Ashley with our prom dates. Me and Ashley in our bikinis, lounging by the side of her pool. Me and Ashley at graduation with . . .

My heart seemed to stop completely. My mom. For a moment I just stared, soaking in every detail of her face. It made my chest hurt so bad I could barely breathe. I touched her image with my finger and ached because I couldn't feel her.

"Mom," I choked out. "Why did you leave me? *Why*? I can't do this anymore. I need you. Why did you leave me all alone?"

I slammed the book shut and threw it across the room. It hit a lamp, knocking it to the floor where it smashed into pieces.

I pulled my knees up to my chest and wrapped my arms around them, burying my head in the space it created, and rocked myself to sleep.

CHAPTER SEVEN

JUDE SAT IN THE DARK on the window seat. He'd been sitting there ever since he'd come home and had scarcely moved. He replayed the evening over and over in his head—the questions she'd asked, his elusive responses. He hated that he couldn't answer her questions, not truthfully, anyway.

He glanced out the window at hers. It was still covered, but he could at least tell that she was awake. Her light was still on, and he could see movement every now and then behind the blanket.

He sighed and shook his head. He thought back to the night that had irrevocably changed everything, and a shudder rolled through his body. Without meaning—or wanting—to, he saw her blank eyes staring past him, at some invisible spot over his head. Her pale white face, the empty bottle and stray pills, the shards of glass covering the floor. He had never felt so terrified. And then . . .

He stood up suddenly, shaking his head to clear the images from it. He started pacing the room, fearful that sitting still would bring them back. What a mess he'd created.

A mess he had no idea how to fix. But he was trying, in the only way he could think of.

He took a deep breath and looked out the window again. He stared across at the green square, turning away only when the glow behind it disappeared into darkness.

* * * * *

I slept well into the next day, after a typical night of terrifying dreams and uncontrollable shaking. The sun was high in the sky when I finally dragged myself out of bed and into the shower, where I leaned against the wall and let the water rain down.

I had begun to wonder if Jude had done the right thing by saving me. Nothing had changed. I was right back where I was. It seemed for a very short time that maybe I had changed since that night, that being saved had given me some appreciation for life. But that was gone now, and all that was left was a shell of a person without the luxury of numbness. I felt everything now and marveled at the fact that, despite what I had once thought impossible, my life had actually gotten worse.

I spent the majority of the day in front of the TV, watching talk show after talk show, absorbing nothing. I had no food in my kitchen to eat, but it didn't matter because I had no appetite whatsoever. When the sun began to set, I started to get anxious, petrified of facing another night.

As my apartment grew darker, the panic worsened, until I felt like I was going to completely lose it. I refused to go to bed, to invite the demons to come terrorize me once more. But I couldn't stay up either, alone here in this empty place another second, with only my miserable memories to keep me company.

I needed to go somewhere; I needed to get out. Never mind that it was getting really late. I needed fresh air, needed to get out of this apartment. I threw on some clothes and my coat and headed for the door. I opened it and screamed—someone was standing there.

"Jude!" I gasped, my heart beating out of my chest. "You scared the crap out of me! What are you doing?"

Jude was standing there looking just as startled as I was.

"I—I'm sorry. I didn't mean to scare you. I was just coming to see if you wanted to go for a walk or something. I couldn't sleep, and your light was on, so I knew you were awake too . . ." He left off there, and I wondered if it was because he was worried that I thought he'd been spying on me or something.

"That's really weird," I said, regaining my composure. "I was actually just heading out for a walk. I couldn't sleep either. Obviously." I eyed him curiously, wondering if he was some kind of mind reader.

He smiled. "Okay then." He gestured toward the hall, so I walked out, locking my door behind me. As I did so, I could feel his eyes on my back and was suddenly incredibly self-conscious of my clothes. I cringed before turning around to face him, when I quickly forced a smile. Trying not to notice his expensive-looking coat and shoes, I led him down the stairs and outside.

The night air, which smelled like rain, bit at my cheeks and made my eyes tear up. I blinked a few times before asking Jude, "Where do you want to go?"

He shrugged. "Let's just walk." We started down the sidewalk. At first I walked my usual swift pace, but quickly realized he was in no hurry, and I slowed down to match his.

We walked in silence, which was nice. The sidewalks were littered with people, even at this hour, although now they were more clustered, standing outside of bars and nightclubs, forcing Jude and me to weave our way around them.

"So, why couldn't you sleep?" Jude suddenly asked, breaking the silence. We'd just maneuvered around a particularly large and raucous group and come to a relatively empty section of sidewalk.

I cleared my throat. "I almost never sleep. At night, anyway."

"Why not?"

I swallowed. How could I answer this?

"I have nightmares a lot."

He thought about that for a moment. "If you have nightmares, then you must be asleep."

I turned and looked at his face to see if he was mocking me, but he just looked contemplative, his brow furrowed over intense green eyes.

"I sleep until the nightmares get so bad they wake me up. After so many times a night, I refuse to sleep anymore." Was I actually telling him this?

"And that's what happened tonight?"

"No. Tonight I didn't even get to the sleep part." I looked at him again, wondering how much more I should say. For some reason, I kept talking. "Tonight, the very thought of going to sleep terrified me."

Jude didn't respond, and I worried I'd made him uncomfortable. But a quick glance at his face told me he was just digesting what I was saying.

"Why tonight?" he finally asked.

I hesitated as the walls I'd built so securely around me shuddered, unsure whether they were ready to come down. Everything in me wanted to tell him, wanted to be able to confide in someone. But the fear was so real, like an animal instinct I couldn't ignore.

"Why couldn't *you* sleep?" I asked after a minute, turning the tables on him. He wasn't the only one who could ask questions.

He smiled, and I knew my evasion hadn't gone unnoticed. "Honestly, I love the night. There's something about it that makes me feel . . . alive. I wouldn't want to miss it by sleeping."

I stared at him. I was not expecting that.

"What is it about nighttime that you love?"

He thought about his answer before he spoke. I noticed he tended to do that.

"I'm not really sure. The dark intrigues me. It has a certain magic to it."

I was astounded by this revelation from him, that he was finally giving me something about himself. I didn't want him to stop. I quickly thought of something to say in response to keep him talking.

"I hate the night," I confided. We walked by two scary-looking men smoking outside of a liquor store. Out of habit I held my breath as we passed, trying not to inhale any of the secondhand smoke. The smell of cigarette smoke reminded me of my father and made my skin crawl.

"I would ask why, but I'm pretty sure I know the reason."

"Yeah, people who suffer from chronic nightmares don't really look forward to the sun going down." I tried to make light of it, even laughing a little at the end. But Jude didn't laugh.

"That must be horrible. I can't imagine."

"Yeah," I agreed, automatically beginning to shy away from the conversation. Not because I didn't want to tell him anymore necessarily, but because I didn't know how. He didn't press it.

As we walked, I kept sneaking sideways glances at Jude out of the corner of my eye. There was something about him, something I couldn't quite pinpoint, that continuously drew my eyes to him. Maybe it was the way he walked so confidently, with his back straight and his head up, and yet still managed to appear so relaxed and comfortable at the same time. Or maybe it was the startling color of his eyes that made me think of sunlight reflecting off tropical waters or a drop of dew on an evergreen sprig. Or maybe it was just good, old, plain curiosity about the kind stranger that had unexpectedly come into my life . . . and saved it.

We turned a corner and headed down a side street. After a couple blocks, we came upon a small park, fenced in with chain link. It was old but looked like it had been kept up fairly well. There was a small merry-go-round, a slide, and a swing set surrounded by dozens of trees.

Jude paused at the entrance. "Does this seem like a good destination?"

"It's closed," I pointed out, wondering exactly what he intended to do at a children's playground anyway.

"Closed, yes." He went to the gate that was chained and padlocked and gave it a shake. "Impenetrable, no."

I raised my eyebrows at him. He wanted to break into the park? I was about to suggest we find somewhere we wouldn't be trespassing, when I had the thought to just go with it. Who cared about something as stupid and insignificant as breaking and entering a tiny little park? What would we be hurting? And obviously, the caretakers couldn't be all that serious about keeping people out, judging by the man-sized gap Jude was able to create between the fence and the gate that the loosely wrapped chain allowed.

He held it open. "After you."

For some reason I had to stifle a laugh as I wiggled

my way through the opening, either from embarrassment at doing something so childish, or excitement from doing something that was technically illegal. Or maybe both. I watched as Jude slipped through the space himself and let the gate swing back into place. I waited to see what Jude planned to do now that we were in here. To my surprise, he headed over to the swing set, where he settled into one of the swings. I timidly followed suit, perching on the swing next to him, praying he didn't actually intend on swinging. Fortunately he sat still, and I relaxed, sinking further into the U-shaped strip of rubber.

"Okay," Jude said, turning to me. "Talk."

CHAPTER EIGHT

"WHAT?" I LOOKED AT him, confused. What did he mean *talk*?

"Tell me about your nightmares," he replied casually, as if he was asking me what I ate for breakfast that morning.

"I . . . I don't . . ." I started to protest, but he cut me off.

"Olivia. I promise nothing bad will happen if you tell me."

And the way he said it left me with no valid reason to object. Of course he was right. Nothing bad would happen if I told him. Nothing except making myself completely vulnerable and subject to possible ridicule and pain.

He must have seen the fear in my eyes, the hesitation, because his face softened and he lightly placed a hand on my arm. "Please?"

My heart fluttered at the physical contact. I was momentarily frozen, locked in his gaze. But then he removed his hand, and I could breathe again.

"Okay," I finally agreed, unable to find any hint of insincerity in the bright jade eyes staring back at me. I knew

I could trust him. "Are you sure you want to hear this?"

"Positive," he replied, shifting his body toward me.

I took a deep breath. "My life hasn't been easy," I said slowly, choosing my words carefully. "When I was five, my mom discovered that my father was not only cheating on her, but that he had been for pretty much their entire marriage and had children with the other woman. He had been living a secret double life, splitting his time between us and them, more with them. My mom wanted to believe that he was working all that time he was gone, but I think on some level she knew. Either way, she came across a box in the back of their closet one day with a family picture inside. His other family, not ours. They had a family picture, like they were a normal, happy family."

I had never said these words out loud. It was bittersweet, sharing these things that had haunted me for so long with someone else.

"My mom confronted him, and my dad, instead of being ashamed and remorseful, blew up. He blamed my mom for driving him to this other woman, for not giving him the life he wanted, so he had to go create it with someone else. He said he was relieved that she knew, that it had been too exhausting keeping it all a secret and now he could just go. She begged him to stay, to leave his other family and come back to us, but he just ignored her and went to pack his things. I stood in the doorway and watched him. He never said a word to me.

"I'll never forget that scene as he left, my mom standing in the kitchen, screaming at him to come back." A hard, painful ache formed in my chest as I spoke. The words tasted like acid on my tongue. "We never saw or heard from him again. I have no idea where he is now."

Jude listened intently with the most curious expression

on his face that I couldn't decipher. A mix between shock and sympathy, pity and anger maybe. He didn't speak, so I went on.

"After that things were pretty rough. My mom sank into a serious depression, and when she finally pulled herself out, she did her best to make a life for us. She got a second job cleaning houses, but so much of her paychecks went to day care and sometimes there wasn't enough money for food. I was hungry a lot, and cold and sad. School was no escape because no one wanted to be friends with the poor, skinny girl dressed in thrift-store clothes that were too small. But my mom and I always had each other. We always knew that." A drop of rain spattered on my arm, followed by another on my cheek. I looked up, knowing it would only be seconds before the skies opened up entirely.

"High school was better. As soon as I was old enough, I got a job and that helped a lot. Pretty soon I could buy food and clothes, and I actually made a friend. We were inseparable. For the first time in my life, I felt like a normal kid, happy even. After our graduation, she went to college at UW, and, since college was never an option for me, I got a job waitressing and got my own apartment. It was hard on my mom when I left, but it was something I needed to do, and I was excited about it.

I stopped then, not knowing if I should continue. The ache in my chest had doubled in intensity and seemed to be cutting off my air. But at this point there was no turning back, no point in even trying.

"Four months after I moved out, I went home—to my mom's—to check on her, like I did a few times every week. I found her in the bathroom . . . dead. She'd taken a knife to her wrists." Jude winced as I choked the words out, each one more painful than the last.

"After that I shut down, basically quit life. I refused to talk to anyone. Ashley—that was my friend's name—tried everything to help me, but when she realized it was in vain, she eventually left too." My voice drifted off as I remembered the last time she walked out my door. I didn't even try to stop her.

"So," I finished, turning to Jude with the most pitiful smile I'm sure anyone has ever worn. "I have a virtual buffet of painful memories for my brain to choose from every night. Hence, the nightmares."

The silence that followed my monologue seemed deafening, muffled only slightly by the rain that was now coming down heavily. My words seemed to hang in the air, on display for anyone to do with what they would, now that I had put them out there. I instantly wished I could take them back, tuck them inside me again where they were safe and secret. I began to feel raw and exposed, and I knew I should never have confided in him. Suddenly I had to get out of there. I stood up abruptly and said in an apologetic tone, "I'm sorry, I have to go," before heading out of the park.

"No! Wait!" Jude called. He caught up with me and moved in front of my path, forcing me to stop. I couldn't look at him, ashamed for telling him all of my horrible secrets, even more ashamed for fleeing like a coward after doing so.

"Please don't," he said softly, a hint of pleading in his voice. "Don't leave because you told me all of that. I promised nothing bad would happen if you told me, and I meant it. Please don't leave."

I stood unmoving, at war with myself. I wanted to believe him, I really did. But in the same way that my body urged me to take my next breath, it screamed at me to run home and crawl into bed.

"What are you so afraid of?" Jude asked so softly, so sweetly it caused me physical pain.

But his question made me laugh bitterly. "What am I *afraid* of? Isn't it pretty clear? I've been abandoned by every person I've ever loved, by all the people who were supposed to be there for me when I needed them most! I—"

Jude cut me off. "I know. You're right, and I'm sorry. It was a stupid question."

I laughed again, but it came out choked-sounding, and I knew I was close to totally losing my cool right there in front of him. I swallowed the lump that had taken up camp in my throat and took a deep, shaky breath.

"You have every reason to not trust people. But I'm asking you to try. Try trusting me."

"Why?" I asked, for the first time stopping to wonder why he had invited me on this walk tonight.

"Why?" he repeated, caught off guard.

"Yes, why? Why do you need me to trust you? Why do you care? Don't get me wrong, I appreciate that you saved my life and all, but you don't owe me anything else."

Jude's reaction to my words was undecipherable. His face, glistening in the downpour, looked . . . hurt? Confused? Ashamed? It was so bizarre; I couldn't figure it out.

And he just stood like that with his face screwed up for so long I was worried I'd offended him deeply. But then he said, "I'm not here out of obligation."

"Then what is it? Why are you here?" I asked, growing bolder with each passing moment. I was finally demanding some answers.

Jude shifted his weight, looking uneasy. I held firm, my eyes locked on his. I was not going to allow him to look away. He would have to answer this one.

"I . . . I just want to make sure you're okay."

Heated frustration filled me suddenly, like a hot air balloon about to take flight. The contrast with my freezing, wet skin made me shiver. "That sounds an awful lot like obligation to me."

"It's not, I promise." He sounded just as frustrated as I was.

I simply stared at him, eyebrows raised, waiting for an answer.

He stared back for a moment before sighing and saying, "If you must know, it's because I'm invested. Not in the obligatory way," he added quickly, "but in a way that has me . . . interested."

I scowled, trying to understand his meaning.

"I can't really explain it myself. I just feel sort of . . . attached to you now. I don't know if it's because of the huge, emotional ordeal we shared, but for some reason I am continually . . . drawn to you."

My pulse quickened and I suddenly felt like that hot air balloon had left the ground. I had no words in response.

We stood there awkwardly, facing each other in the soft glow of the park light, unfazed by the torrent of water falling on us. *Only in Seattle,* I thought. "Jude," I began. "You don't want to be a part of . . . this." I motioned toward myself. "We both know that I'm a colossal mess right now, and I'm the last person you should want to . . . be drawn to. Trust me."

He smiled, an ironic, somewhat teasing smile. "That's what I'm asking you to do." I smiled back, sadly. He didn't know what he was saying. He didn't understand that I was too messed up right now to have any kind of personal relationship, no matter what kind.

"I can't."

"You *can*," he urged. "You just have to allow yourself. I know it will be hard," he continued quickly when I started to object. "I'm not saying it won't be. But how will anyone ever prove to you that they can be trusted if you never give anyone the chance?"

He had a point. I knew he was right, but how? How could I?

I shook my head weakly. I was quickly running out of arguments.

"I'm not proposing marriage here. All I'm asking is for you to let me into your life, even a little. Let me get to know you. Let me prove to you that I can be trusted."

I knew he was close to wearing me down, and he must have sensed it too.

"Please," he said, and that was all it took. Those green eyes bore into mine and I knew before I said it that I would agree. Probably to anything he asked for at that point.

"Okay," I said softly.

"Okay?" he repeated, as if he wasn't sure he heard me right.

"Okay," I said again. "We can get to know each other. Slowly."

His face broke into a smile and all I could see were dimples. "At a glacial pace," he promised, and I couldn't help smiling myself.

We walked home then, quicker this time because of the rainfall, not talking much.

We said good night at my door and a few minutes later, as I lay in bed thinking about how drastically different my night had ended, I fell asleep with a smile on my face for the first time I could remember.

CHAPTER NINE

"Hey, Hal," Jude greeted the haggard man sitting on a park bench. He looked different today, wearing an old flannel shirt, torn jeans, and no stocking cap. His greasy, stringy black hair hung down around his face to the tops of his shoulders, and the beard was gone. Even the cardboard sign was different. This time it read: WHY LIE, I NEED BEER. If Jude didn't know Hal personally, he would never have known it was the same homeless guy.

"Let me guess," Hal replied. "You need another favor."

"Yeah. How'd you know?"

"What else would you be here for?"

Jude nodded. He had a point. "I want to take someone somewhere tonight, somewhere really nice, that's . . . secluded."

Hal raised an eyebrow. Jude rolled his eyes in return. "Knock it off. It's not like that and you know it."

Hal nodded. "Yeah, I know a place. Over in Madison Park. Belongs to a colleague." Jude tried not to smile at hearing Hal refer to someone as a colleague, as if he was some kind of successful businessman. But he kept a straight face and said, "Yeah?"

"Yeah. Real nice place, right on the lake." Hal pulled out a wrinkled scrap of paper and a nubby pencil and wrote down the address, followed by two series of numbers.

He handed the paper to Jude, who took it with mild apprehension. "And this . . . colleague of yours. Will he be there?"

Hal shook his head. "Mac ain't ever there. Always away on business." Jude hated to think what kind of business this Mac was in that got him a lakefront home in Madison Park. If he associated with the likes of Hal, it couldn't be a very honest one.

"And he won't mind two strangers trespassing?"

Hal shook his head again, scanning his surroundings as always. "Nah. Any friend of mine is a friend of Mac's." He pointed to the numbers he'd written just below the address. "That first set of numbers is the code to unlock the front door. The second set is the security code you'll have to punch in once you're inside to disable the alarm."

Jude nodded. "Thanks, I really appreciate it."

Hal waved it off, always uncomfortable with the niceties. "How's the apartment?"

"It's perfect," Jude responded. "I can't believe our luck that it was vacant." He wanted to tell Hal thanks again, but didn't figure the older man would appreciate it very much. By the satisfied look on his face, Jude could see that Hal was pleased he had given Jude what he'd needed. Then the look turned to annoyance. "Go on now, get outta here. You'll scare away potential customers."

Jude fought back a smile at the word "customers."

"You got it."

On the drive back, Jude took a detour and found the

address Hal had written down. As he drove down the long driveway and the house came into view, he whistled under his breath. "Real nice," as Hal had so eloquently described it, was a gross understatement.

He punched in the first code and let himself in, quickly entering the second on the keypad just inside the door. The high-pitched beep that had been blaring in his ears fell silent. He walked through the entire house, familiarizing himself with each room so that it wouldn't be obvious to Olivia that it was as new to him as it was to her.

When he had locked back up and was once again on the freeway heading home, he began to feel a twinge of excitement about taking her there. He scowled, not knowing why. Maybe it was just the act of taking a poor girl who'd never been anywhere or seen anything to what would arguably be the nicest place she'd ever been. A Good Samaritan kind of thing. But deep down he knew that wasn't it. It was something more, and the thought disturbed him greatly. As hard as he tried to dismiss the idea from his head, it refused to leave. He finally gave up resisting and thought of nothing else as he made his way home.

* * * * *

After a week of being home all day and all night, I was going out of my mind. Nothing was worse than this—sitting around with nothing to do, nothing to take my mind off unpleasant memories.

If anything was going to push me over the edge again, it was this.

On morning seven of my sabbatical, I woke up with one thought in my head: get back to work. Besides the aforementioned reason of going stir-crazy, I was in no position to be without a paycheck for another day.

I decided it would be better to go in person rather than over the phone, to show I really was in a state of mental and physical well-being. Well enough to serve coffee, at least.

I got dressed and headed out. The day was fairly nice, for Seattle. Gray, fluffy clouds obscured the sun, but every now and then they would shift just enough to let the sun-rays peek through for a few minutes. I took my jacket off as I walked, enjoying the short periods of warmth.

It wasn't until I was almost there that the awful thought occurred to me that the people I worked with knew some, if not all, of what happened. I wondered with horror how much they knew. They obviously knew something for my boss to call and give me time off. (*How* they would know, I couldn't figure out.) What if they all knew what had happened? Even if only my boss did, that was still enough to make me want to turn around and head back home. But the alternative—like how I had spent the last week—was completely insufferable. Plus, I told myself, if I could face the person who actually witnessed the whole gruesome ordeal, certainly I could handle talking to someone who'd merely heard about it. At least, this is what I told myself. But as I walked through the door of the coffee shop, fear hit me just as strong as the smell of bacon grease.

The woman that was always behind the counter looked up when she heard the bell. *What was her name?* She saw me, apparently decided I wasn't of any interest to her, and looked back down. Relief flowed through me. She obviously didn't know what had happened. Or if she did, she didn't care.

I walked over to the counter. As I got closer I could see the name engraved on her name tag: Rose.

"Hi, Rose," I said. Her head snapped up, her eyes

squinting suspiciously at me. "Is Bryan in?" She didn't say anything, just nodded toward the back.

Bryan was in his office, flipping through receipts, running his hands through his red hair like he always did when he was crunching numbers. When he glanced up and saw me, his eyebrows raised in surprise. "Olivia! I wasn't expecting to see you for awhile."

"Yeah, I wanted to talk to you about that." I spoke carefully, unable to determine what he knew and not wanting to give anything away that he didn't already.

Bryan set his pen down and swiveled in his chair to face me. "Okay."

"I was sort of wondering if maybe you would let me come back. I feel great and I'm going a little stir-crazy. I'd really like to get back to work."

Bryan studied me for a moment before saying, "Actually, we've been a little shorthanded since you've been on leave. If you feel you're really ready, we could definitely use you."

A shimmer of excitement flowed through me.

"Really?" I asked.

"Really. You can start right now, in fact. Go grab a spare uniform in the back."

"Thank you!" I exclaimed, unable to hide my relief. I wanted to hug him for making it so I didn't have to go back to that empty apartment and wallow in self-pity, but I kept my composure. I turned to leave, but Bryan stopped me. "Hey, Olivia."

"Yeah?" I turned back around.

"I'm glad you're okay." And in his eyes I could see that he knew, or at least sensed, what had happened to me. But the fatherly look of concern on his face made any feelings of shame and humiliation vanish. I felt nothing but cared for.

"Thank you," I said genuinely, my insides turning to

girly mush. I slipped out the door, feeling warm and grateful for having the boss that I did.

I never thought I would ever be relieved to be putting on that despicable, faded dress, but I donned it with pride and picked up right where I'd left off. Pouring coffee, taking orders, refilling waters, serving food, pouring more coffee. By the end of the day my feet were aching, but I had a pocket full of tips and I hadn't thought about anything unpleasant all day.

Just as the dinner rush was winding down, I came out of the back with a tray full of desserts for one of my tables and almost dropped it when I saw who was standing inside the door.

Jude smiled when he saw me and gave a little wave with his fingers. I responded with a small, unsure smile of my own. What was he doing here? Had he come here to see me?

I delivered the desserts to the respective table, watching Rose seat Jude out of the corner of my eye. I went over to the booth he was sitting in.

"Hey," I said, the very picture of surprise. "What are you doing here?"

"Well, I heard you guys have the best omelet in Seattle. I had to come check it out."

I knew he had to be joking. No one would ever say that about this place. Which could only mean . . .

"I'm kidding," he said. "I came to see what time you get off work."

My heartbeat picked up. He *had* come here to see me. And unless I was really bad at picking up on stuff, he was about to ask me out. "I was just finishing up."

He smiled. "Perfect. Are you hungry?"

"Sure," I lied. "What did you have in mind?"

"Not here," he said, eyeing the nearby plates of food. "Somewhere else. You'll see."

CHAPTER TEN

FORTY-FIVE MINUTES LATER we were pulling up to an elaborate home on Lake Washington. My mouth fell open when I saw it. I'd never seen anything like it, except in movies.

"What is this place?" I asked in amazement.

"Isn't it incredible? It's a friend of a friend's."

My eyes were huge as we walked up the stone steps leading to the front door. Two giant marble pillars stood ominously on either side of us.

Jude punched some numbers onto a keypad next to the door and let us in. A steady, high-pitched tone greeted us, but it fell silent as soon as Jude entered more numbers into a matching keypad on the wall.

"There," he said. "That's better." I barely heard him. I was completely engrossed in the interior of the house, or at least the vast foyer we were standing in. It looked like something I imagined a celebrity living in, with shiny wood floors covered in expensive-looking rugs, huge framed paintings adorning the walls, and decorative antique vases on every table.

I followed Jude into the next room, too filled with awe to speak. The enormous living room was more of the same, only bigger and full of dark leather couches and chairs. He continued through the house, making his way toward the back. When we entered the kitchen, I drew in a sharp breath.

The entire back wall of the house was windows, huge windows, overlooking the lake. In the dark, I could see the moonlight reflecting off the glassy surface, and beyond the lake, the Seattle skyline seemed to glitter with a million lights. It took my breath away. It was, by far, the most beautiful thing I had ever seen.

When I was finally able to tear my eyes away from the majestic view, I saw that Jude had been watching me. He wore a small, satisfied smile on his face, as if he'd received the reaction he'd been hoping for.

I blushed, embarrassed that he'd been watching me.

"What do you think?" he asked.

"Wow," was all I could say.

He nodded. "I know. It's pretty amazing."

He had wandered into the dining room, next to the kitchen. I followed, still gazing out at the lake.

"Ideally," he said, turning to me, "I would cook you a gourmet meal. But . . ." he paused. "I can't cook. So we're doing the next best thing."

He walked over to the kitchen counter and picked up the phone.

"Do you like Italian?"

* * * * *

While Jude ordered pizza, I walked over to the huge window and stared out, feeling like I was in a dream.

The house, the view, Jude's voice humming in the background . . . it didn't seem real. Stuff like this didn't happen in my world.

I turned around when the room behind me fell silent. Jude motioned toward the living room. "Would you like to see the rest of the house?"

I nodded eagerly.

He led me out of the dining room, through the entire level. Every time I decided a room was my favorite, we'd step into an even more elaborate one that outdid the last. I was gaping at the massive movie screen in the theater room when the doorbell rang.

"Stay here, I'll be right back." Jude disappeared and returned a few minutes later with a pizza box and some blankets in his hands.

"Let's eat," he said. "Follow me." We walked out of the theater and through what looked like a mini arcade, then out a set of glass French doors. I was disappointed to be leaving the house, until we stepped outside and I saw the backyard. I shouldn't have been surprised to see that the outside was just as elegant and extravagant as the inside. Beautiful flower beds and immaculate landscaping surrounded a large swimming pool with a rock waterfall running into it and a hot tub built in beside. We followed a stone path down the sloping hill toward the lake, where a dock jutted out into the water. With each step I became more and more entranced, feeling like I was in a fairy tale. I hardly noticed the chill in the air, or the mosquitoes that I absentmindedly batted away from my face.

Jude dropped the blankets and shook one out onto the dock, motioning for me to sit. I did, unwilling to take my eyes off of the scene in front of me. He opened the pizza box and pulled out a slice, offering it to me on a napkin.

We sat together on the blanket and ate our pizza, enjoying the view and in my case, the company. The pizza was warm and wonderful. When I finished mine, I said to Jude, "This is seriously amazing. I'm so glad you brought me here."

He smiled, grabbing another slice. "I'm glad you like it."

"I love it." I corrected him. "I've never seen anything like it in my life. It's like something out of a movie."

Jude smiled and bit into his pizza. A boat roared by, leaving a wake behind it, lapping against the dock and rocking us.

"My mom and I went boating on this lake once when I was little," I recalled wistfully. "A coworker of hers had a boat and one Saturday he took us out with him. I remember leaning over the side of the boat to dangle my fingers in the water and my mom freaked out and grabbed me and pulled me back in. I remember being so confused as to what the big deal was. I just wanted to touch the water." I laughed, remembering the panicked look on my mom's face, the fuzzy images bringing the old familiar stabs of pain.

Jude was watching me, that increasingly familiar look on his face: pain, sympathy.

"Tell me about her," he said softly.

I hesitated. Talking about my mom would be a little bit like tearing off a piece of my soul and handing it over to Jude. I started to change the subject—something I was becoming pretty good at—but then I remembered what he'd said in the park about nothing bad happening, and I willed myself to talk. "She was beautiful. I always thought so. Even when she was in her work clothes, covered in grime, she was beautiful. She was soft-spoken, which most people mistook for shyness, but she wasn't shy. She would always be the first to talk to someone, to befriend them. She was a hard worker, and proud, but she was always willing to do whatever it took to keep us alive, to make a life for me. She taught me so much. I was always in awe of her strength, her courage. She seemed to me like she could handle anything, like she was superhuman. She was the one person in the world I knew I could trust, the one that would never leave me . . ."

I heard the last few words echo in my head as soon as I spoke them, and the cruel irony of their meaning. Somehow I found the strength to not let it get to me too much in front of Jude. It was a monumental feat.

I forced a smile. "So, I feel like all we do is talk about me. I know virtually nothing about you."

"What do you want to know?" Jude asked warily.

"Well . . . what do you do all day?"

Jude shrugged. "A little of this, a little of that."

I stared at him. "Could you be any more vague?"

He laughed. "What? What do you want me to say? I hang out in an apartment for a living. Not much to tell."

I wanted to press further, to ask how he seemed to have so much money, but chickened out, as always. I thought of another question. "Do you have any siblings?"

"No."

"Okay," I said slowly. "What about your parents? Are you close to them?"

"Both of my parents are dead. They died a long time ago." He didn't sound angry, or even hurt necessarily. Just guarded.

"Oh. I'm sorry." I couldn't believe our situations were so similar and yet all this time we'd only discussed my painful history. How had he never mentioned that?

"Don't be. I'm actually okay with it." And I could tell

that he meant it, as odd as that seemed. I knew better than to ask how they died. It was the question I hated most in the world.

We sat in silence, rocking gently on the dock, side by side. After a while I could feel my eyes drooping. Without even thinking about it, I rested my head on Jude's shoulder. Somehow it felt completely natural and right. For a moment he didn't move. Then he slowly, carefully, lifted his arm and wrapped it around my shoulders. I prayed he wouldn't be able to feel or hear the acceleration of my heartbeat. The last thing I wanted was him knowing how I reacted to his touch.

I savored the heat emanating from his body and breathed in his smell. But more than anything I reveled in the proximity of our bodies, the absence of space between us. It was something I had never experienced before, with the exception of hugs from my mom and Ashley, and even those were distant memories. I had never felt so safe, so warm, so . . . perfectly content.

The rhythm of the waves lapping against the dock combined with Jude's warmth must have lulled me to sleep because the next thing I knew Jude was whispering my name and gently nudging me.

I straightened up, embarrassed, and a blanket fell off my shoulders. He must have wrapped one of them around me after I fell asleep to keep me warm. The cold lake air hit my warm body, and I was instantly shivering. In one swift motion, Jude snatched the blanket off the dock and wrapped it around me again, holding it in place at my collarbone. For one brief moment we sat there, looking at each other, while he kept the blanket on me. I noticed something in his eyes as he stared into mine—something I had never seen before, and it startled me, even scared me a little. It was like I was looking through them, like I could see behind the pupil, the iris—all of it—to what was behind, into his soul. As if I could actually physically see eternity. For that split second, locked in his gaze, I truly believed I could see it: a shimmering emerald eternity. It sparked something inside of me, like a lit fuse somewhere buried deep that was slowly burning through me, warming as it went. No matter how hard I tried, I couldn't look away.

But Jude could. He grabbed my hand softly, bringing it up to hold the blanket where his hand had been and let go. Then he turned away and began cleaning up the dinner mess. I sat, paralyzed, my heart beating wildly, although I couldn't put my finger on why. Absolutely nothing had just happened, and yet something had. I could feel it; I had seen it. But *what* had I seen? I had no idea.

I sat, my heart slowly returning to normal, until Jude had everything gathered in his arms and was ready to go. I followed him in through the house and out to his truck, where we got in and headed home.

As always, Jude walked me to my door.

"Thank you so much for taking me to that house. It really is the most incredible place I've ever been." I tried to convey in my words just how much I loved that he'd wanted to take me there.

He gave a small smile. "My pleasure." He leaned toward me slightly, his face growing serious. "Thank you for coming with me. I had a great time." He looked at me for another moment before saying, "Have a good night."

"You too," I said back, my voice a wisp of sound. I watched as Jude turned on his heel and disappeared down the stairs.

I entered my apartment, closing the door behind me. I stood there for a moment, soaking in the events of the evening, convincing myself they were really real.

Then I turned and walked straight to my window, yanking down the blanket that hung there before crawling into bed.

CHAPTER ELEVEN

OVER THE NEXT FEW weeks I did my best to return to normal, whatever that was. For someone like me, it was a balancing act. I had to resume the routine that I had before The Incident to prove I was okay. But I couldn't become the zombie again, who was so good at the routine that she did it without talking, thinking, or feeling. That was definitely not okay.

I felt like I did a pretty decent job, but every day was a struggle. It took every ounce of energy in me to get out of bed, shower, get dressed, fix my hair, attempt to look human, force myself to eat, brush my teeth, walk to work just to be on my feet all day serving people food, force smiles, force conversations, then walk back home, force myself to eat, maybe take another shower, get into bed, and then will my eyes to stay open despite the fact that my entire body wanted to shut down.

It may have sounded like the same old routine, but the difference this time was that I at least tried to look like I cared, whereas before I didn't care enough to even pretend.

I was fixing my hair, making myself eat a little bit, even wearing makeup in an attempt to look healthier and happier. At work, I wasn't just plastering on smiles to get tips from the customers. I was talking to them, and to my fellow employees, even learning their names.

Was it genuine? No, but I had to get points for trying. And at least this way no one would suspect I was still crazy.

But it was exhausting, mentally and physically. Most days when I got home I went straight to my bed and collapsed in it, wanting to drown in the depths of the sheets and never resurface. The only highlights of my days were seeing Jude. I never knew when it was going to be. He would just suddenly show up at the diner, or my apartment, standing there smiling, flashing those dimples. And then my smile was real, not forced. My conversation was sincere, not put on. I would relax, and all the stress and anxiety would melt away.

For the most part. I still had my reservations, my walls up securely around me. But bit-by-bit, they were coming down. I still held back when we talked, still found myself sharing something, then retreating swiftly into my turtle shell, which he would promptly, gently, ease me out of. Slowly, surely, I could feel myself beginning to trust him, and it scared me to death.

"So why have we never been to your apartment?"

Jude's hand stopped in midair, chow mein dangling from his chopsticks. "Huh?" he asked. We were sitting at my table, eating Chinese takeout one night after work.

"Your apartment. I can see it from here, yet I've never been inside it. Why is that?"

He slowly lowered the noodles back into the cardboard carton. "I don't know. I guess I just thought you were more comfortable here. Besides, it's not really mine. I'm just staying there, remember?"

I thought about that. "I know. But I still want to see it."

"Okay." I couldn't read his face or his voice. But something seemed off. "We'll go sometime. Not now though. It's a mess."

"Okay." I said, trying to hide my suspicion.

We decided on a movie for the evening's entertainment, which is what we'd been doing most nights lately. Jude picked one from my meager DVD collection and got it going. I settled in as I always did, curled up at one end of the couch under a blanket, Jude beside me but with a cushion of space between us. He never tried to move closer or hold my hand, or any of that stuff that guys usually do in a movie-watching situation. I was always relieved and grateful that he didn't push me or expect anything, that he was true to his word about taking it slow and just getting to know me. However, there was always a tiny part of me—the girl part—that hoped.

We watched in silence for a while, and it wasn't long before my eyelids started to droop. I fought to keep them open, but I was completely fatigued. It had been an especially busy day at the coffee shop, requiring me to move at a much quicker pace than normal almost the entire day. My body was definitely feeling it.

As I struggled to maintain consciousness, the line between dream and reality became blurred, and the movie we were watching went from a romantic comedy to a horror film in a confusing, troubling way. Now I was the female lead, walking through a dark, empty house, not knowing what was up ahead but feeling certain it wasn't going to be good. I crept down the hall as eerie, ominous music warned the viewer that something terrifying was about to happen. Up ahead I saw a closed door, a thin line of yellow light glowing at the bottom. Everything in me told me I didn't want to know what was in that room, but it was in the script, so I continued forward. Finally I reached it and turned the doorknob, slowly pushing the door inward. The scene that lay before me was worthy of the most violent, gory horror movie: a dead body; a shiny, stained knife; and blood. Lots of blood. And then my eyes focused on the body, and recognition set in. I realized where I was; I was standing in my mom's bathroom. This was *my* horror film, and that was *my* mother slumped on the floor staring at me through dead eyes. No longer scripted, I opened my mouth and screamed. And screamed, and screamed . . .

Strong arms wrapped tightly around me, pulling me against a strong chest. A soft, deep voice murmured assurances in my ear, the most beautiful sound I had ever heard. I reached for it, pulling myself closer to the source of the comfort, curling against the strong chest, burrowing deeper. The arms formed a vice-like grip around me, a protective cocoon of safety where nothing bad could happen. Slowly the blood, the dead eyes, the bathroom all faded away, and I was on my couch in Jude's arms.

He held me, slowly rocking back and forth, his voice a gentle hum whispering words of consolation as I tried to stop shaking.

It seemed like forever before I calmed down, despite the peace Jude's presence gave me. Even when I didn't have so much as a tremor in my body, he held me, not relaxing his hold on me even a fraction. I must have fallen back asleep at some point because some time later something woke me. I had no idea how long I'd been out. My head ached slightly, and my throat was raw from screaming.

The atmosphere in the room had changed since I was

last awake. It was darker, almost pitch black, like the dead of night. Silent except for the rain now pounding outside on my window loudly, which I realized was the source of my wakening. My apartment had grown colder, but I wasn't cold. Why wasn't I cold?

I shifted and instantly felt the body beside me. Panicked and confused, I froze as comprehension flooded my head and I remembered who was here with me, wrapped around me on my couch, and why. He was sleeping—I could feel his slow, shallow breaths rise and fall beneath my head. From where I lay on his chest, I could see that our legs had become entwined. I could feel his arms still around me, tightly. I slowly lifted my head and turned to look at Jude's face. In the near-total darkness, his features took on an ethereal look that took my breath away. Both angelic and demonic at the same time. The very picture of serenity. Peace and contentment radiated from his face as he slept but was contrasted sharply with dramatic angles of his brows, cheeks, and chin, which were thrown into dark shapes and shadows by the thin streams of light coming through the window.

I stared, unable to look away. It was so powerful, so . . . otherworldly. It opened my eyes to something I had never seen before, caused me to look at him in a way I never had. Now I was sure that there was something more to him, something I knew, with an absolute certainty, that he was keeping from me. All the secrets, all the missing pieces . . . I knew it now. There was more to this guy than he wanted me—or anyone for that matter—to believe. I could feel that it was something big. I had no idea what, but I was intrigued, and I determined once and for all to flush out what it was.

I felt like I was on full alert now, my heart racing and

my mind sharp. Looking at Jude's face like that affected me in a wholly other way, one that was both disconcerting and thrilling. It stirred something inside me, something I hadn't felt in years. It made me want to reach out and touch his porcelain skin and prominent cheekbones, his dark, full eyebrows. I suddenly longed to touch the tiny, almost undetectable indents where his dimples appeared when he grinned, and the one in the center of his chin that I had somehow never noticed before. I wanted to stroke his smooth-looking forehead, softly slide a finger down the plane of his nose. And his lips . . . I wanted to know if they felt as soft and full as they looked . . .

Jude's eyes fluttered open then, boring right into mine. I instantly went motionless, holding my breath. For one eternal moment we stared at each other in the dark, and I was convinced I would never breathe again. But then Jude's eyes fell closed, and his breathing told me he'd fallen back asleep. I lay frozen for several minutes before slowly laying my head back down on his chest. It seemed like hours passed before I fell back asleep. When I woke up in the morning, he was gone.

* * * * *

Pike Place was crowded with early morning shoppers. The ocean air was cool and damp and left a fine layer of mist over everything. Jude carved a path through the throngs of people, his shoulders squared. He must have looked like some kind of menace, drifting aimlessly alone through such a busy, energetic place with his hands shoved in his pockets, a scowl on his face. He passed the endless rows of fresh cut flowers, stepped around a couple of tourists debating a purchase, and barely noticed the fishmongers yelling and tossing whole salmon to each other. He moved with the crowd, lost in his thoughts.

He needed someone to talk to, really talk to, but there was no one. Hal was less than the optimum choice, and the only other person he knew was Olivia. He certainly couldn't talk to her. He'd had no idea what he was getting into when he saved her. No idea that weeks later they would be spending almost all their time together. He had never imagined on that fateful night, when he ran to her bedside and stood over her, yelling her name, that he would become so invested, so irreversibly involved with her. He had no idea what to do about it.

And now . . . now it was even more complicated. Up until now he had convinced himself it was just him, that he was the only one feeling anything, that he was the only one at risk of getting hurt. But last night changed all of that. He saw it on her face. He saw it in her eyes, the way she was looking at him. It nearly stopped his heart to see her looking at him that way, but whether from being thrilled or terrified he didn't know. He only knew that this complicated everything.

He closed his eyes for a moment, reliving the night before, a smile unwittingly spreading across his face. He could still feel her in his arms.

He opened his eyes, his smile gone. *No.* He shook his head, trying to clear it and come back to reality. It couldn't be like that. Ever. He had to bury it deep down where no one would know, and no one would get hurt. Where *she* wouldn't get hurt.

It was true that he was the one who had pushed to be in her life, but not for that reason. Not then, anyway. Then, she was just the girl he had saved, someone he had an obligation to (yes, he had lied to her when he told her the contrary), that he had to make sure was okay. But then . . . it changed somehow. He couldn't even pinpoint exactly why or when, it just did. The way she smiled when she talked about her mom (it had become his personal quest to get her to smile), the way she always had to have a blanket to wrap up in when they watched movies because she was always so cold. The heart-wrenching sadness in her eyes when she told him her story in the park, which made him feel like his soul was being ripped apart.

This had never happened before, not to him. It was wonderful, and warm, and happy. It made him feel completely alive. But it was complex and confusing, and . . . impossible. It could never go anywhere, could never turn into anything.

That thought weighed him down, and he walked through the crowd a smaller man, defeated. He passed booths of jewelry, artwork, handmade journals, and clothes. The myriad of trinkets blurred together. He mindlessly scanned row after row of little glass figurines, animals carved out of wood—all things he would never buy in a million years. A waste of money. Then suddenly his eyes fell on a particular item, causing them to come into focus. He made his way over to it and bent down, examining it closer. His breathing picked up as he saw what looked like it had been placed there specifically for him. He carefully picked it up and cradled it in his palm, where it fit perfectly. Without pause, he pulled out his wallet and paid the vendor behind the table. Shoving it in his pocket, he continued on his way, heading nowhere.

CHAPTER TWELVE

I COULDN'T DECIDE IF I was more relieved or disappointed that Jude was gone when I woke up, so I settled on being both. As I went about getting ready for work, however, the disappointment won out, and I was plagued with paranoia about his absence. My heart sunk at the memory of him witnessing my nightmares, and I no longer questioned why he had left. I was sure that I knew.

Instead of leaving for work, I found myself sitting on my bed, staring at my window. I couldn't go near my couch, couldn't even look at it. In the daylight, Jude's window was only a gray square, revealing nothing of what lay beyond. What would he be doing right now? The idea that he would rather be there, alone, than here with me was almost more than I could bear.

I felt myself slipping back into that place, being pulled under by old, familiar demons determined to have me for their own and it scared me to death. I never wanted to go back there. I couldn't. I refused to.

My eyes fell on the bulletin board in my kitchen above

the phone. I slid off the bed and walked over to it, pulling off the little white card pinned up next to a bus schedule. I took a deep breath and dialed the number on the front.

"Hi, Dr. Robinson? This is Olivia Tate."

* * * * *

The chairs were oversized and comfortable, and I noticed with relief that there was no couch in the room. Stupid, stereotypical movies. I gazed at the cluster of framed diplomas and licenses in an effort to reassure myself that I had made the right choice, that this stranger could possibly help me. Dr. Robinson sat in front of her desk, but she had rolled her chair away from it, facing me. I took a deep breath and waited. Even though I was the one who had initiated this meeting, I knew I would not be able to speak until she prompted me. Fortunately, that's exactly what therapists are trained to do.

"I have to say, I was surprised to hear from you," she began in her smoky voice, leaning back in her chair and crossing her legs. "I'm glad you decided to come in." She smiled, a genuine one as far as I could tell. But the jury was still out on her. No verdict yet on whether or not she could be trusted, or if she was in fact qualified to dig into my head, my soul, my past, and pull out whatever she considered to be of importance. I would let her in at my pace, layer by layer, as I deemed her worthy. But if she thought for one moment she could slice right into me, tear me open, and leave my insides raw and exposed, well, then she was in for a rude awakening.

"So, Olivia, how have you been since you left the hospital?"

Such an innocent question to open with, and yet it unleashed a torrent of conflicting emotions. So much had happened since I'd seen her last, but really only one thing had: Jude.

Dr. Robinson waited patiently as I sorted through this in my head, wondering what to say and where to begin.

"Well," I began cautiously, "it's been a roller coaster ride. The first few days back were . . . rough. I couldn't sleep, didn't know what to do with myself." I was giving her the bare minimum. Who knew what she would do with this information once she had it? I clamped my mouth shut in defiance, regretting what I'd already shared.

"That's to be expected. Anyone who went through what you did would be expected to react in a similar manner. If they didn't, well, that's when we would worry. That would mean they were holding it all inside, pretending nothing happened, and not dealing with their feelings. And with something this extreme, keeping it in and not admitting what you feel could lead you right back to where you'd been."

Now she had me, hook, line, and sinker. I had to talk now. We both knew I had been through something extreme, and therefore had to talk about it if I ever wanted to get better. There was no way I could pull off the silent treatment now. I sighed inwardly. This chick knew what she was doing.

"So," she led, "things were bad for at least a few days after returning home. How are they now?"

"Better," I answered without having to think about it. "Not better as in, fixed, but better as in, improved."

The doctor raised her eyebrows. "Really? That's encouraging. How so?"

Well, I no longer want to pop Valium like they're Skittles. "I got my job back. I couldn't handle being at home all day, every day."

"Great! So you're already returning to your regular daily schedule. That's wonderful!"

I ignored her enthusiasm and went on. "I've been eating regularly too, and . . ." I hesitated. "I made a friend."

"Oh? Tell me about . . . her? Him?"

"Him." In a matter of seconds, I debated how much to tell her. It didn't take long for me to decide not to disclose the fact that it was my rescuer, the very person with whom she'd discussed my level of sanity.

"Uh . . . he's a neighbor of mine, lives sort of by me. We hang out, eat dinner, watch movies, stuff like that." I shrugged as if to say it was no big deal, very casual. Which it was, technically. But why did I see it as anything but?

She was nodding. She wanted more.

"He's a really sweet guy, always making sure I get home safe, opening car doors for me, and paying for dinner."

"Wow," Dr. Robinson gushed. "This guy sounds like a keeper. So is it strictly friendship, or do you think it could be more?"

Was that within her rights to ask me?

"I—I don't know. For now it's strictly friendship, but . . " I drifted off, not knowing how to answer that even for myself.

"Are you attracted to him?"

I stared at her, totally caught off guard. What kind of therapy *was* this? My face felt hot and I'm sure it was visible on my cheeks. I stared at my lap and stuttered something completely unintelligible.

"Olivia, it's a simple question," she said, smiling. "Do you find him attractive?"

I raised my head slowly and looked at her. "Yes," I said quietly. "I find him very attractive."

Dr. Robinson nodded and jotted down something on

the clipboard she'd been holding in her lap. She must have known I would not be keen on this line of questioning going any further, because her next question had nothing to do with Jude at all.

"Can we talk a little about the night of the incident?" My body automatically went into lockdown mode. My insides recoiled, wanting to get as far away from this conversation as possible. I opened my mouth to tell her I wouldn't but closed it again when I remembered why I had come here in the first place. I knew I had to do this.

"Sure," I said through clenched teeth.

"Tell me about that day, leading up to it. Did anything out of the ordinary happen to upset you?"

I remembered back to the jerks in the coffee shop that were staring at me, calling me names.

"Yeah, something happened." I relayed the story to her, again making it seem like it was no big deal, because in telling it, it did seem like a really ridiculous thing to push someone completely over the edge.

She listened with a sympathetic look on her face, and once again I was struck with the thought that she meant it.

"And then what happened? You went home, and . . . ?"

"Basically fell apart. And then I had my typical nightmares, which led to hysterics, although I wasn't crying. I never cry." Dr. Robinson's right eyebrow raised so subtly I almost didn't catch it, and she made a note on her paper. "My head felt like it was going to explode, so I went to get some painkillers." I stopped there, knowing what I would be admitting to if I said more.

"And that's when you saw the Valium?"

My shoulders and head dropped in a heavy sigh, and I could only look at the carpet as I nodded almost imperceptibly.

"And so you decided to take them and end your life?" She was talking so softly now it was barely above a whisper. If it weren't for the complete silence in the room, I would never have heard her. Shame and regret burned my cheeks. I was done deluding myself into thinking maybe it was an accident, that maybe I hadn't meant to kill myself. I had no interest in pretending anymore. I absolutely knew what I was doing when I downed those pills, and saying—or thinking—otherwise wasn't going to help anyone.

I nodded, still unable to look at her.

She said nothing, either out of respect for me and the humiliation I was obviously feeling or from the shock of hearing me admit the truth, that I actually had tried to kill myself. No one spoke for several moments, the only sound in the room a faint ticking from a clock on the wall.

Finally, she asked, "Have you had any suicidal thoughts since that night?"

"No!" I answered defensively, then felt embarrassed when I realized she wasn't accusing me, merely asking a valid question, one she needed to ask as a therapist. But then I had to think about it. "There might have been a time or two when I thought maybe it would have been better if I'd succeeded, that maybe Ju—my neighbor shouldn't have saved me, because I wasn't any better off. But nothing even close to doing anything about it."

Did she believe me? I prayed that she did. Because it was true. It was all true. I wasn't holding anything back now, except for the parts about Jude, but that wouldn't hinder my recovery in any way.

She was writing on her tablet again, and when she looked up, she looked as if she was studying my face, trying to decide. I guess I passed, because she started in on some psychobabble about the human mind recovering from traumatic experiences. I shut her out, nodding and mm-hmming in all the right places, just praying for it to be over.

Finally she set down her pen and said, "Well, I think that's enough for today. We made a lot of progress and I like what I'm hearing so far. I want to see you back here next week, same time." It was not a suggestion, she made that clear by her tone of voice. She tore a slip of paper from a smaller pad and handed it to me. "I want you to start taking these, once a day." I glanced at it. Scribbled gibberish that may as well have been written in Swahili for as much as I understood it. I looked up at her for help. "It's a prescription for an antidepressant that I believe you would benefit from. It will help with the nightmares, and with any feelings of . . . depression you are having." I got the distinct feeling that she was really going to say "suicide," then thought better of it.

I shoved the paper into my pocket and gathered my purse and jacket. She walked me to her door and opened it. "You have my card with my number on it. I wrote my cell on there too. Feel free to call any time." I thanked her and left. I felt strange, but in a good way. Had I actually just had a therapy session? A—dare I say—*successful* one? There was the matter of the drug she wanted me to start taking, which deflated me a tiny bit. I pulled the little paper out of my pocket and stared at it dubiously. I just didn't know about this. Pills and I had an ugly history, and I was less than convinced that anything that small could help the epic amount of problems I had. But I knew I would do it, that I would take them. Because suddenly, there was nothing in the world more important to me than getting better.

* * * * *

"Hal, I need to tell you something."

"What's up?"

"It's about this person I've been hanging out with, the one I took to Mac's. Hal . . . it's *her.*" Jude only had to look at Hal's face to know he knew exactly who "her" was. "But," he took a deep breath, "there's more."

CHAPTER THIRTEEN

I WALKED OUT OF THE building feeling lighter on my feet. On the bus ride home, I allowed myself to feel good about the steps I had made toward progress today. It was a foreign feeling, and it actually felt wrong at first. But the facts were undeniable. I was making the first moves at crawling my way out of the black hole that I'd been in for so many months. I still had a long way to go before I was out of it completely, but for the first time ever, I believed it could happen.

The bus let me off a block from my apartment. I strolled down the crowded sidewalk, unhurried, with my jacket slung over my arm. The days had grown noticeably warmer, the sun breaking through the clouds more regularly. It heated the top of my head and my shoulders as I walked past a young street performer in Rasta garb. He was playing various buckets and cans as drums, and he had obvious talent. I paused to listen for a moment, captivated by the steady rhythm of the sticks hitting the canisters. I pulled out my wallet and found a dime and a quarter—leftover bus fare. It made a chinking noise as it hit the pile of change filling an upside-down beret. The drummer nodded to me in thanks, and, after listening for another few seconds, I continued toward home.

I walked through a cluster of seagulls that were scuttling around on the sidewalk looking for morsels of dropped food. They didn't scatter or fly away as I passed, too intent on finding a meal. No one paid them any attention; they were part of the landscape, as permanent a fixture in this city as the concrete giants towering over my head.

I reached my building a few minutes later and trudged up the five flights of stairs to my floor. As I rounded the corner at the top of the fifth, I was startled to see someone sitting on the floor outside my door. His head was down with his elbows propped on his knees and hands clasped together against his forehead. I recognized the huddled figure immediately.

At the sound of my footsteps, Jude looked up. His face was drawn. It took me a second to understand why, and then I remembered the last time I had seen him . . . the night before . . . his disappearance this morning.

"Hi," I said, because I didn't know what else to say.

"Hey."

No one said anything else. There was only an awkward silence that seemed to echo in the empty hall and down the stairwell. Finally I couldn't take it anymore and asked him if he wanted to come in. He clearly had something to say, and I didn't want to hear it out in the hallway.

He accepted and pushed himself up off the floor. Inside, we sat on the couch, and I turned to face him but couldn't seem to make eye contact. I had this sickening feeling that something was coming, something I didn't think I wanted to hear at all. Something I didn't want to imagine trying to deal with.

"I owe you an apology," Jude said. Now I looked at his eyes, trying to find there the thing that would either confirm my fears or reassure me. As always, when I needed answers, his face gave me nothing.

"For what?" I asked, because I was supposed to, and he was expecting me to, but I didn't really want to know. Not at all.

"I think I crossed a line last night that I shouldn't have, and I'm sorry."

I frowned as I tried to figure out what exactly he meant. Was he sorry he'd comforted me? That he'd witnessed my meltdown? That we'd shared such an intimate, personal experience? Either reason would kill me just a little.

He watched me, then quickly explained, "I shouldn't have stayed. I shouldn't have fallen asleep. I should have been more careful, more responsible. I'm . . . sorry that I slept here and put you in that position. Our agreement was that we would be friends and I wouldn't ever do anything to make you feel uncomfortable or to not be able to trust me and I feel like I failed you. I'm so, so sorry." He looked like he was about to cry. I was shocked into silence. I had no idea what to make of it.

When I didn't speak, Jude asked, "Can you ever forgive me? Or have I ruined things completely?"

I opened my mouth to answer, then closed it again, having no idea what I was going to say. He was sorry because he thought he'd let me down? He was worried he had ruined things between us? He wasn't breaking it to me that last night was a mistake because it was more personal than he wanted to be with me?

"Is that why you were gone this morning?"

Jude nodded. "I thought it would be easier for you. I worried that it was the wrong move, that somehow you would take it as a sort of abandonment, but after weighing it back and forth, I decided it would be worse for me to be here when you woke up." A panicked look crossed his face. "Did I choose wrong?"

I shook my head, still trying to get caught up to speed, to wrap my head around the direction this conversation had taken. "No. I mean . . . I did sort of assume the worst when you were gone, but now that I know . . . it's fine."

Jude didn't look convinced. He scooted closer to me, grabbing my hand. My stomach did a little flip.

"Last night was . . . wonderful. Not the part where you were in pain, obviously," he quickly corrected, "but the part where you let me . . . be there for you while you were in pain. I've never felt so . . ." He trailed off, and I knew I would die wondering what the end of that sentence was. "I am so grateful that you let me, that I could be there to comfort you, all night. But not if it's not what you wanted, if you had any regrets this morning. All I want is for you to feel safe and secure."

I closed my eyes, savoring every word he had said, reveling in the warmth of his hands. I willed time to stop, to never have to move on from that moment. Because in that moment I felt joy. Pure, utter joy. And I felt like I could conquer the world.

I opened my eyes to see his boring into mine, looking scared and unsure. I smiled and said shakily, "Last night *was* wonderful. Every single second of it. Please don't think for a moment I would change one part of it, with the exception of this morning, when you were gone. But"— he opened his mouth, I was certain to apologize again—"now that I know why, I'm glad that you were."

My words hung in the air, and we sat looking at each other. I was ultra-aware of the fact that we were still holding hands. Jude looked like he was considering something, like there was something he wanted to do or say but wasn't sure how.

"So . . .," he said, studying my face. "Are we . . . good?"

I smiled. "Yeah. We're good."

Jude's shoulders relaxed, and he smiled in relief. "Okay, good. So, do you wanna get something to eat?"

"Yeah, that sounds great."

* * * * *

The next week continued on in the same fashion: Work, and Jude. Jude, and work. He'd started taking me to and from work every day now, and I had begun to watch the clock obsessively toward the end of every shift, in anticipation of seeing him. And when he appeared in the doorway every night just before nine, looking like a movie star and smiling that dimpled smile for *me*, I felt like the luckiest, happiest girl in the world. And then I would have to remind myself that we were just friends, that *I* had been the one to make it very clear that it would never be more. Stupid, stupid girl that I was.

Thursday was my day off, and we spent most of it walking through the shops along the pier. We were sitting on a bench eating ice cream cones, watching a tour boat slowly fill with people, when Jude said, "So, tomorrow night. Can I take you to my favorite restaurant in all of Seattle? Maybe even Washington State?"

"Wow," I remarked, catching a drip of ice cream with my tongue before it hit my fingers. "Those are some pretty serious accolades. I might have to let you."

"You won't regret it." He paused. "You'll probably want to wear something. . . that's not jeans."

"Okay," I replied, feeling uneasy. He was taking me somewhere with a *dress code*?

When the sun started to set, we headed home. By the time we had walked the few blocks to where we'd parked the truck, it had grown almost completely dark and had begun to rain. Hard. We were almost to his truck, which was parked in a now-empty parking lot on an abandoned street, and I started to run the last several feet to avoid getting drenched. I only made it a few steps before Jude grabbed my hand, pulling me to a stop. I turned, surprised. We were standing under a lone lit streetlamp, the fat raindrops looking like diamonds cascading down in the light. Jude drew me in closer, and I swallowed hard as he wrapped his right arm around my waist, pulling me against him. My heart began to pound out of control, and I was terrified he would feel it. He wove the fingers of his other hand between mine. All I could do was stare at his face, unable to move or speak. The rain had flattened his hair against his head, steady streams of rainwater running down his face, soaking his eyebrows and eyelashes and making trails around his nose and over his lips. Never had his lips looked so desirable. Never had his face looked so dream-like.

He looked me square in the eyes and asked, "Have you ever danced in the rain?"

I couldn't find my voice, merely shaking my head as he raised my right hand to his chest and began moving us in slow, methodical circles, never taking his eyes from mine. The traffic in the background and the sound of the raindrops overlapping as they hit the ground provided the music, and the shimmering sidewalk gave us our dance floor. We turned to the beat of the rain, lost in a world that was completely our own. It was like a fairy tale, like we'd transcended time and space to some magical place in some fantasy world. Because all around us I swear the light and the water came alive, dancing along with us. I was lost in our world, where time stood still and space didn't exist to create any distance between us. If this moment never ended, I would die the happiest person on earth.

And then Jude stopped turning us in circles, and my spirits fell as I waited for him to let me go. But he didn't. He held me in the same position, as if we were dancing, but we weren't moving. He stared deep into my eyes, and I suddenly realized what was about to happen. My heart stopped altogether, and I watched as Jude's face moved closer to mine. I closed my eyes, waiting for that blissful moment when I felt his lips on mine, my entire body screaming for it, but it never came. Instead I felt his forehead touch mine. I dared to open my eyes and saw that his were closed, clenched tight even. His whole face looked like he was in pain, and I didn't understand. Had I been wrong? Had I misread the signs? Had he not been about to kiss me? My heart began beating again, each one an ominous thud in my chest. I wasn't sure what I felt more of: foolishness or disappointment.

He pulled away after a minute, opening his eyes and smiling sadly. "You're soaked," he said, apologetically, taking my hand and leading me to the truck. "Let's get out of this rain."

As we got into the truck, I couldn't help but thinking that standing in the rain under that streetlamp, in Jude's arms, was the only place I wanted to be.

* * * * *

"I have to tell her, Hal. I'm gonna do it. Tonight."

Jude was standing under an overpass where Hal had set up camp to get out of the rain. He was covered in newspapers, and Jude noticed the beard was back.

"You're out of your mind, kid." He was shaking his head at Jude like the young man was the biggest idiot he'd ever laid eyes on. "Are you *trying* to push this girl back over the edge? You may as well hand her the pills and pour her the glass of water. Hell, shove 'em down her throat—make it easier for her."

Jude cringed at the image, feeling desperation and rage build up inside of him. "You know that's not what I want, Hal!" His voice rose with each word. "You know that's the opposite of what I want. But I can't . . . keep . . . *lying* . . . to her!" He spat out the last few words, feeling like he was losing his mind.

Hal glanced around to see if anyone had heard. There were a few other derelicts lying around, most of them sleeping, and the few that weren't didn't seem to hear anything over the roar of traffic whizzing by.

Hal sighed. "Why don't you sit down so I can talk some sense into you."

"I don't need sense talked into me." He wasn't yelling anymore, but his voice was shaking, along with the rest of his body. "I know what I have to do. There is no other choice. If I don't tell her, she'll find out eventually and it will destroy her, far worse than if I tell her."

Hal leaned forward, his eyes narrowed. "And how do you suppose she's gonna take it? How do you think she'll handle being told your little secret? You already screwed yourself over when you saved her. Why would you risk the only chance you got at redemption by doing the one thing that would guarantee you can never go back? That's quite the life you'd so easily give up, especially for someone like you."

Jude looked at Hal, his eyes burning with madness. When he spoke, his voice broke. "Because I don't know what else to do. Because . . ." He paused, knowing that what he was about to say wouldn't go over well with Hal. "Because I would rather take that chance, even if it means"—he swallowed—"the worst, than to continue letting Olivia believe I'm someone I'm not."

Hal's eyes widened, and he slowly leaned back, folding his arms over multiple copies of the *Seattle Times*. He sat pensively for several moments before saying, "You're falling for this girl." It wasn't a question.

Jude didn't respond. He stared at his feet.

Hal slowly began shaking his head, muttering something under his breath that Jude couldn't make out. He was sure he didn't want to hear it anyway.

"Boy, you're more of a fool than I thought. Do you have any idea what you're getting yourself into here?"

"Of course I do," growled Jude. "Why do you think we're here, having this conversation? If I was oblivious to the consequences, I would have told her a long time ago."

"This can't happen. It's impossible. It's not right."

"I KNOW!" Jude shouted. "I know all of this, Hal! You think I don't know this? You think I wanted this to happen? You think I didn't try everything in my power to fight against it? I did, as hard as I could, and it happened anyway. I'm scared out of my mind, Hal. I don't know what to do. I don't know what's right and what's wrong anymore. All I know is that I have to do whatever won't destroy Olivia."

"And what's that?" Hal asked quietly.

"Nothing," Jude choked out the word. "There's no way out of this that won't destroy her. *I've* done this. *I'm* the reason this is happening, and I can't undo it. It's either tell her or don't tell her. One way she hears it from me and maybe I can lessen the blow. The other way, she finds out eventually anyway, and I can't control when or how that will be."

Hal was silent for a long time, thinking through Jude's predicament.

"So. You tell her." The old man said it with resignation, unable to deny it was the lesser of two evils.

"I tell her."

CHAPTER FOURTEEN

After I showered, I dressed in the only skirt I owned—the black pencil skirt I'd worn to my mother's funeral. I paired it with the only thing that went with it—the black blouse I'd worn to the funeral as well, the same one I'd worn with jeans the first time I'd gone to dinner with Jude. Knowing what kind of place we were going to, I decided to step it up a bit. I outlined my eyes in black eyeliner, followed by mascara and some charcoal eye shadow. Suddenly my eyes looked twice as big. I didn't want to look like I should be standing on a street corner, so I went light on the blush and lipstick. Then it was time for hair. Blowing it dry, I couldn't get over how much it had filled out recently. It actually had substance, body even. I could finally move beyond straight-and-stringy, or ponytail. I dug a forgotten curling iron out of the back of a drawer and spent the next half hour curling big, loose waves all over my head, like I'd noticed girls wearing lately. When I was finished, I stepped back to get a good look at the finished product. I inhaled sharply at the girl in the mirror, who was more woman than girl. It wasn't me. It couldn't possibly be me. This person looked healthy, content. She filled out her clothes and had thick, shiny hair and a fuller face. She didn't have dark circles under her eyes or sunken cheeks. Her skin was a blend of peaches and pinks instead of a sickly gray. This woman was . . . *pretty*, I had to admit. I smiled, allowing myself to appreciate what I was seeing, to celebrate the loss of the wan creature that had stared back at me for so long. "Good-bye, skeletal freak," I muttered as I walked away.

Jude was going to be here any minute, but I just needed one more thing to complete my look. Dragging a chair over to my closet, I climbed up and stood on my tiptoes, reaching to the far back corner of the shelf. After several attempts, my fingers finally brushed against the item I was seeking. Straining, I got my hand around it and pulled it down. My heart did a funny little dance as I gazed at the intricately carved wooden box. I gently traced my finger around the floral design, each deep cut that formed the roses and leaves that covered the surface. I had admired this small chest that sat on my mother's dresser my entire childhood, never knowing what was inside, at first because I was too small to reach it and then too scared of getting caught peeking. I don't know why, but somehow I always knew it was private, that whatever was inside was sacred to her. Then, once I was big enough to reach it, I had moved on to more interesting things (interesting, at least, to a teenager), the mystery and appeal was lost. Last year, when I inherited the little rosewood box along with all my mother's other possessions, I shoved it to the back of the closet, still ignorant of its contents. It hadn't moved from that spot since. Until now.

I carried the small chest to the couch and, taking a deep, unsteady breath, gently unhooked the little gold clasp and lifted the lid. Immediately my chest constricted and something akin to a sob escaped me as the achingly familiar smell seeped out and permeated the air I was breathing. A smell that made me think of baking cookies in a tiny, green kitchen, and of huddling together in bed on cold winter nights. It made every square inch of me ache. I fingered the contents inside, taking each item out and holding it, inspecting it, smelling it, one at a time. My mother's treasures, her most cherished possessions.

There were two hospital bands, an adult-sized one and a teeny tiny one, from when I was born. A ticket stub from when my aunt took us to the Woodland Park Zoo, worn and soft around the edges, the ink so faded I could hardly read it. I smiled as I recalled traipsing through the rain that day, determined to see each animal despite the downpour.

A deep sadness overcame me, as I pulled out a yellowed marriage certificate and a small, faded wedding photo—a sadness that wasn't my own. I saw these items for what they were: a woman's inability to let go of a man who had crushed her heart. It was something I had never considered—what my dad leaving had meant for my mom, instead of just me. It hadn't just meant the loss of financial stability and a father to her child. It had meant lost love. Deep in thought, I gazed at the picture another moment before setting it to the side and reaching into the box again.

There were some things I didn't know the significance of, like a brittle rose whose petals had fallen off and crumbled into a powdery layer that covered the bottom of the box, and a shot glass that said "Viva Las Vegas." And curled around each item like an ivory snake was the object that I was certain would be in there: my grandmother's pearls.

I gingerly lifted them out of the box, admiring the way they hazily reflected the light as they turned in my hand. I had always loved this necklace, and had often begged my mother to let me wear it when I was young. She never would, always saying they were too valuable to risk getting broken. I never knew what kind of value she was referring to: sentimental or monetary. Or both.

A loud knock shattered my reverie and I jumped. Jude! I quickly (but carefully) replaced the contents of the box—all but the necklace—and latched the lid.

I went to the door, took a deep breath to steady myself, and swung it open. Standing on the other side was a male model that looked suspiciously like Jude. My mouth opened slightly as I appraised the utter perfection standing in front of me. His dark blond locks had been perfectly coifed, looking like he had placed each individual wave in its proper position on his head. He wore an olive dress shirt that made his eyes the greenest I had ever seen them, with a solid black tie, black slacks, and black leather shoes. He was . . . striking. And he was staring at me.

"Wow," he breathed. "You look . . . *amazing*." I ducked my head in embarrassment and felt my cheeks burn. "You look pretty good yourself," I mumbled softly.

Jude stood frozen for an unnatural amount of time, before suddenly thrusting a gorgeous bouquet of mixed flowers at me. "These are for you."

"Thanks." I took them, giving the obligatory sniff, and said, "They're beautiful. Let me go put them in some water before we go."

I went to the kitchen, wondering if I even owned a vase. I had never been given flowers before, other than corsages for the formal high school dances. I searched through my highest cupboards, hoping against hope that a vase would magically appear. No such luck. Improvising, I grabbed a tall glass and filled it with water, then wedged the cluster of stems into it. It was top-heavy, and started to fall when I let go, so I propped it up against the wall in a corner. It stayed, at least for now.

Turning around I saw Jude standing next to the end table where I had set my mother's box and the necklace beside it. He had the pearls in his hands, and when he saw me looking, held them up. I didn't say anything. He walked over to me, his face inscrutable.

"Turn around," he said softly. I conceded, already tingling with apprehension. I felt his hands gently move my hair to the side, his breath on my neck as he leaned in to fasten the clasp. I stood rigid as his fingers brushed the back of my neck so subtly it could have been a slight breeze that drifted by. I shivered involuntarily; every pore in my skin rose conspicuously. Then I felt my hair fall back into place and Jude's hands were on my shoulders, turning me around.

We were face to face, no more than a few inches apart. My bones turned to jelly as the realization came again that he might kiss me. I reminded myself that the last time I'd thought he was going to kiss me I'd been wrong, but I began to shake anyway. Not enough that I thought he noticed, but enough that I knew I couldn't talk or the tremor in my voice would give me away. So I stood there waiting, willing myself to stay upright, to keep my heart from stopping altogether.

Then I noticed Jude's face contort slightly, the same face he'd had the day before in the rain. His eyes were fixed on mine in such a way that made me think of a starving man begging for food, knowing there's none to be had. Again, I didn't understand and it hurt me, but before I could delve too deeply into its meaning, he spoke. "We should go. We have reservations." His voice had a faint edge to it, but he held out his hand and smiled, his eyes betraying the conflict behind them, whatever it was.

I tried to hide my unease as we drove to the restaurant, tried, yet again, to suppress the ball of nerves in the pit of my stomach that was always accompanied with a string of questions that would never be answered. *I'm becoming a pro at this,* I thought bitterly. I deserved some kind of medal for all the times I'd bitten my tongue when something didn't fit, didn't make sense. For all the questions he'd dodged, and all the times I'd let him.

But deep down there was something far more disturbing than evasive responses and tormented looks, something that I wasn't even allowing myself to think about. Because Jude's mysteriousness, as frustrating and agonizing as it could be, was something that I could handle. The idea that maybe he just didn't feel about me the way I felt about him, however, was not.

We pulled up to a small but very posh restaurant that emitted a bluish light through its few front windows. A man in black and white came up to Jude's truck before we'd even come to a complete stop in front of the building, and I looked questioningly at Jude. He didn't notice though; he had put the gearshift in park and was starting to get out. That was when I realized that the guy was a valet, something I had only ever seen in movies. I exited the truck as Jude spoke to the man and gave him his keys. I think he gave him some money as well, but he was always so subtle about those things. Then his truck was gone, and he held out his arm to me in that old-fashioned way that invites the lady to link hers with the gentleman's. I might have laughed at the cheesiness if it didn't fit the setting so perfectly.

"Wow," was all I could say.

"You haven't even seen the inside yet."

I had a distressing thought as we approached the entrance. "We don't have to eat snails, do we?" This looked like the kind of place that would serve snails.

Jude looked at me solemnly and said, "Only first-timers." I looked at him in horror. His face broke into a smile, and he started laughing. I punched him in the arm. "I believed you!"

We made our way through the doors and immediately I felt like I'd stepped into a different world. What had looked so small from the outside was actually a fairly large dining room, with linen covered tables, eclectic art pieces, and geometric-shaped light fixtures hanging above each table that were the source of the blue glow. A band played on a low stage set off to one side, and along the wall opposite them was a bar stocked with what seemed like every bottle of liquor known to man, and then some. Just off from where we stood was the waiting area, a small, enclosed space that was sectioned off by black leather couches, which were barely visible under all the bodies that occupied them. Jude went and spoke to the maître d', who, after confirming our reservation on his list, grabbed two menus from the front podium and led us through the maze of tables to an empty one next to the bar. As I surveyed the other patrons of the restaurant, I was incredibly relieved and grateful that Jude had made sure I'd dressed for the occasion. Even though most of the other women there were wearing cocktail dresses, at least I didn't stand out like a sore thumb in my black skirt and top.

Our waiter appeared shortly, and we listened as he went into extensive detail about the night's specials, then asked us if he could get us anything from the bar. Jude looked at me, and I shook my head, asking for ice water. He did the same.

When the waiter left, Jude asked, "You don't drink?"

"Nah. My dad drank a lot before he left. I guess it turned me off from it. I did a little bit in high school, but it never did much for me, except make me sick. Besides," I said, smiling slyly, "I'm only twenty, remember?"

"Right."

"What about you?"

"What about me?"

"You don't drink?"

Jude shook his head. "Nope. Never have."

I stared at him incredulously. "You *never* have? How is that possible?"

He shrugged but didn't say anything else, not that this surprised me in any way. I picked up my menu and started scanning the entrees. Then I saw the prices. I whistled under my breath. I had assumed this place would be spendy but no way had I expected it to be that much. But I didn't worry. Jude had chosen this place, and I knew he would pay because he always did. He never let me spend a dime when we did anything together.

When the waiter came back, I ordered a chicken dish and Jude ordered steak. The man left and returned shortly with a loaf of bread on a little cutting board. Jude sliced off two pieces, handing one to me, and I began munching on it hungrily. I couldn't remember when I had last eaten that day, or if I had at all.

"So what do you think?" Jude asked.

"The restaurant? I think it's amazing. I feel like I should be wearing a tiara or something, but other than that, it's pretty cool."

Jude laughed. "I'll admit, it's a little . . . upscale. The people who come here can be snooty, but it's totally worth it for the food."

I raised my eyebrows. "You've talked this food up quite a bit. I'm not so sure anything can live up to the level of excellence you're making it out to be."

"This food can. You'll see."

I nodded, looking skeptical. "All right, if you say so," I teased him.

We ate the bread in silence for a while, and then without really thinking about it first, I said, "So I went and talked to that doctor. The one from the hospital. The . . . psychiatrist." It was hard getting the last word out. "About a week ago." I glanced down at the table.

Jude didn't say anything for a moment, but I could see out of the corner of my eye that he'd stopped eating.

I glanced up.

"Oh yeah?" he said in a carefully neutral tone. "How did it go?"

"Fine. Well, better than fine, actually. It went *well.* I never thought in a million years that it would, but it did. I go back tomorrow."

"Really? That's great!" Now he smiled, and I couldn't help but smile too.

"She put me on some medication too," I said, thinking I should feel embarrassed about this but didn't. "I think it might be helping."

Jude grabbed my hand and squeezed it. "Olivia, that is so great." He paused and stared at me. "I think that's really brave of you, to go and do that on your own."

My face got hot and my throat tightened. He thought I was brave? How can that be? No one had ever called me brave before. I was the weakest of them all.

"Thanks." I replied, playing with my napkin.

"*Olivia?*" My head jerked up at the sound of a female voice saying my name. A familiar brunette was walking toward our table. Recognition set in as I looked at the face that was almost as familiar to me as my own. Stunned, I barely managed to open my mouth and speak as she reached us.

"Ashley!"

CHAPTER FIFTEEN

"How are you?" Ashley asked, her eyes shifting back and forth between Jude and me. I just stared. She looked the same . . . but different. Her hair was shorter, and a little lighter than the last time I'd seen her. Her face was still the same face, the one I'd carefully applied makeup to before prom, the one next to mine in an endless amount of pictures. But it was different to me now. It had something foreign about it that put a dull ache in my stomach.

"F-fine," I sputtered, feeling my face flush.

Moments of charged silence surrounded our table, until a girl I hadn't noticed before stepped around Ashley and stood beside her. Ashley looked at her, then shook her head quickly as if to clear it and said, "Sorry. Olivia, I don't think you know my cousin, Marilyn."

Marilyn stepped forward and held out her hand. "Nice to meet you," she said, giving a friendly smile. I shook her hand and mumbled something in agreement. I'd seemed to have lost the ability to form coherent sentences, or even thoughts. My eyes floated between Ashley, Marilyn, and

Jude while my brain worked on processing the situation.

"So . . . how have you been?" Ashley posed the question carefully, timidly, as if unsure if she should ask.

"I . . ." I shrugged awkwardly. The words I needed to answer were gone. They had literally escaped my brain for a simpler place to dwell.

More awkward silence. Marilyn cleared her throat uncomfortably. And still I stared, mute.

Suddenly Jude thrust out his hand to Ashley. "I'm Jude," he said, smiling in a natural way that put everyone at ease, in the way that only his smile could.

Ashley shook his hand. "Nice to meet you, Jude." He continued introducing himself to Marilyn, while I looked on in a daze.

"You're Olivia's friend from high school, right? She's told me a lot about you. It sounds like you guys had some pretty good times." I looked at Jude, and I saw him glance at me, so subtly I doubt the other girls saw.

Ashley laughed. "Yeah, we have our fair share of crazy memories." Jude laughed too, so I joined in, although it came out louder than I intended.

"Were you guys headed to a show?" Jude nodded at a printout in Marilyn's hand with the words "Paramount Theater" across the top.

Ashley glanced at the paper. "Yeah, we're going to see *Wicked*. Marilyn's in town for the week and really wanted to see it."

Marilyn was nodding enthusiastically. "I can't wait."

"Actually," Ashley added, glancing at her watch, "we'd better go. Seating begins soon." She looked at me. "It was good seeing you, Olivia. You look well."

Despite the ache in my heart at her words, I managed a small smile. "Thanks. You too."

"It was nice to meet you both," said Jude. "Enjoy the show. I hear it's a good one."

"We will." They said good-bye and headed toward the front of the restaurant. When they were out of sight I looked at Jude, then down at my lap. My face and hands and scalp were burning and I just wanted to go somewhere and hide. I felt sad, hurt, and confused at seeing her. And humiliated and small at the way I had crashed and burned when I did. All I wanted was to be home in bed in the safety of my dark apartment. The lights in this place were too bright. I felt too exposed.

Just then the waiter showed up with our food. Jude looked at me, then at the waiter, and asked him quietly if we could please get it to go. I'd never felt such gratitude in all my life. The waiter nodded and whisked the tray away.

"Ready to get out of here?" Jude's voice was like a soft symphony in my ears. I nodded. I suddenly felt like we couldn't get out of there fast enough.

When the waiter returned with our food in bags, Jude paid the bill, then escorted me out of the building. As soon as the valet had brought Jude's truck around, he helped me in and began driving home. In the dark cab, I stared out the window at the blur of lights streaming by.

When we reached our apartments and he'd parked in his usual spot in the back, he came around and opened my door for me as always, offering his hand to help me down. He kept my hand as we walked toward my building, and I could feel myself relaxing by degrees from his touch alone.

We got to my apartment and I let us inside. Jude followed me wordlessly. I didn't turn on any lights on my way to the couch, just dropped down onto it and stared out my window toward Jude's darkened one. I felt him sit down beside me.

"I wasn't ready for that," I said into the dimness. My voice was quiet and emotionless. "I don't think I handled it all that well." I laughed humorlessly. Jude didn't laugh, didn't speak.

"I don't know what I thought would happen when or if I ever saw her again, but it wasn't that. I knew that it would be awkward, that it would be hard, but I wasn't prepared for the onslaught of pain that hit me like a freight train. Like it had all just happened yesterday."

Jude sat, listening. If I hadn't felt him sit down beside me minutes earlier I would have thought I was alone.

"Every time I think I'm making progress, getting better, handling life, something happens to prove to me I'm not."

Jude spoke. "That's not true." He said it forcefully, almost harshly.

"It is true!" I countered. "Maybe I'm fine when I'm with you, and maybe I took a step by going to therapy, but those things are nothing compared to the way I still fall apart when I'm alone. You don't know."

"I do know," he said softly.

"What do you mean you know?" My eyes narrowed at the silhouette beside me.

"I mean," he said, sounding tired, "that you don't fool me as much as you think you do. I know you still struggle." He paused. "I know you."

Inwardly I melted a little to hear him say that, but I was already shaking my head. Not in argument, but in frustration, confusion, anger. "I just . . . I just want . . ."

"What?" Jude interjected, pulling me around to face him. Even in the dark I could see his eyes pleading with me for an answer. "What do you want?"

But before I could even think of one to give him, his lips were on mine, so suddenly I barely knew what was happening. A jolt of electricity shot through me and with it every ounce of tension, anxiety, and distress that had just been wracking my body was gone. I could feel him in every pore of my skin, every cell in my body. He was flowing through my veins. His lips moved delicately against mine, and I melted into him, sure that this was what heaven must feel like. His mouth was even softer than his hands, and the sweetest thing I'd ever tasted. I wrapped my arms around him, pulling him closer, *needing* him to be closer. He did the same, and for a few precious moments there was only Jude and me, and the world was revolving around us. But then, just as instantly as it had started, it stopped. Jude pulled away from me and dropped his arms.

I opened my eyes, disappointment crashing through me like a wrecking ball. *No, not yet.* It was over too soon. Jude was staring vehemently back at me, and I noticed then that I was shaking. I prayed he couldn't tell. He reached up and touched my cheek, so tenderly I wanted to cry. I closed my eyes and savored the touch, my heart beating wildly in my chest. When I opened them again, Jude was looking at me with that tortured look I had seen way too many times on his face. My forehead creased in concern, and I searched his face for clues as to what was going through his mind.

"I have something for you," he murmured, straightening up. He reached into his pocket and pulled out a small brown paper bag that had been folded and tied with twine. He set it in my hand. "I saw this a few days ago and wanted to give it to you."

My curiosity was piqued as I carefully untied the string and opened the bag. I reached in and pulled out something small and hard. I couldn't make out what it was in the lightless room. Jude reached over and turned on a lamp, which instantly cast a glow on the tiny trinket in my hand. I could see now that it was a figurine, carved out of a solid piece of white stone, possibly marble. It was a faceless figure lying with its head buried in its hands as if defeated. On its back was a set of small, ivory wings. An angel. The saddest angel I had ever seen.

"Thank you," I breathed, turning it carefully over in my hands, admiring it. "It's beautiful." There was something about the sorrowful look on the angel's face that was heartbreaking. Why would an angel be so sad?

"It reminded me of you . . . the night I first saw you."

My eyes fluttered to Jude's. We hadn't spoken of that night in a long time, at least, not to each other. It had become a sort of unspoken agreement between us.

"You were lying there, so small and broken . . ." He trailed off and I followed his eyes over to my bed. I knew he was back there, mentally standing at the tragic scene. "I'd never seen anything so helpless, so . . . heart-wrenching."

I sat, entranced. I'd never heard him tell it from his perspective. In fact, I'd never actually stopped to wonder about what it must have been like for him, finding me like that. How selfish of me to not realize how much it must have affected him.

He touched the miniature seraphim in my hand. "So broken, and yet since then I've come to see," he paused, ". . . an angel."

Surely at that moment the world stopped spinning. At least mine did. I reached for him, but he stood up then. "I gotta go." He smiled and began walking through my apartment. I jumped up, startled by the abrupt conclusion of our night—we still hadn't eaten—and caught up to him at the door.

"Jude," I said, a little desperately. But then I stopped, not sure what to say. *Please don't go? Stay with me? Kiss me some more?* I could think of nothing that didn't sound needy and clingy, so instead I said, "Thank you for dinner, and for the gift. I absolutely love it."

He grinned and opened the door. But before he walked through it, he turned and leaned forward, kissing my forehead. His lips lingered on my skin, and I didn't move for fear he would stop. When he did pull away, he whispered, "Good night, Olivia." I was trembling and could only manage a nod before he closed the door behind him.

I walked in a daze to my bed, grinning from ear to ear. I almost laughed out loud, I felt so deliriously happy. I wanted to sing and dance around my apartment and open my window and shout to the world how happy I was, but something in the back of my mind was gnawing at me, like an itch I couldn't scratch. Something I couldn't pinpoint but was troubling nonetheless.

I sank onto my bed, hugging my gift. I replayed our kiss over and over in my head. It was so emblazoned in my memory, it was as if I was still experiencing it. I could still taste his lips; my forehead still tingled where they'd been.

I fell asleep that night in a whirlwind of thought and emotion, the tiny angel clutched in my hand.

* * * * *

Jude didn't go home. His stomach was roiling and he felt like he was going to be sick. He walked through the lamp-lit streets, shoulders hunched, head down. He was breaking apart, one agonizing piece at a time.

What had he done? He had made an epic mistake, that much was certain. He had gone to dinner tonight resolved to tell her the truth about who he was, no matter how hard it was going to be. But then Ashley showed up, and everything changed. He had watched Olivia revert back to the person she was when he was first getting to know her. It had killed him seeing her like that again after how far she'd come, to see the insecure, unstable girl he'd met instead of the amazing, strong, beautiful one he knew now. One chance meeting and his resolve had crumbled in a matter of seconds. His natural instinct to protect her overpowered everything else and all that mattered to him after that was helping her come back from the dark place she was revisiting.

And then . . .

He grit his teeth as he thought about his moment of weakness, the stupidest thing he could have possibly done. Unbelievably, he had not only failed to tell Olivia the truth to try and fix this catastrophic situation he'd created, but he'd done the one thing that could make it even worse.

What have I done?

He pushed through a crowd of people on a street corner, ignoring the angry protests spewed at him as he crossed the street without waiting for the signal to walk. A car zoomed past, narrowly missing him as he reached the opposite curb. He barely noticed the driver's rude hand gesture as the car sped away.

He had to do something, had to think of *something.* He couldn't let Olivia become any more attached to this person she thought he was. He couldn't continue to be with her, day after day, pretending and fighting against what were quickly becoming the most potent feelings he had ever experienced.

He found himself on an empty side street, and he was relieved to be alone. He slid down the wall of a brick building to the sidewalk below, running his hands through his hair. What was the answer here? How could he fix this? Even the one idea he'd had up till now—coming clean with Olivia—seemed like too little too late. He shuddered at the thought. He couldn't even think about how it would ruin her. Any progress she had made in the previous month would most definitely be set into reverse, and not just for an evening, like seeing Ashley did. It would be . . . *permanent.* The word filled his mind like poison, spreading throughout his body and making it difficult to breathe. The thought that he could do that—undo everything that she had worked for and accomplished with one simple sentence—sickened him. It wouldn't even take a whole sentence. Just three small words.

No, he couldn't do it. There had to be another way. Some way of fixing this without killing Olivia. Because that's what telling her the truth would do. It would kill her. Maybe not physically, but in a way that, for her, was far worse.

Jude wrapped his arms around his torso and let the darkness swallow him whole.

CHAPTER SIXTEEN

"Tell me about your week. How's it going with the medicine? Any side effects?"

Dr. Robinson leaned back in her desk chair, a pad of paper in her lap, a pen in her hand.

I shook my head. "Not really. I've maybe been a little bit more tired, but it's hard to tell when I'm always so tired as it is." Then, before she could question why I was always so tired, I threw in, "Because I'm on my feet, working all day."

She nodded, scribbling on her pad. "What about your appetite? Any changes there?"

I thought about it. "I have been eating more. Wanting to eat at all is new for me." Was that from the drug, though? It seemed like I had been even before I started to take it. I didn't know, so I didn't say.

She scribbled some more. "That's good. You're looking much healthier."

"Thank you?" I said it like a question, feeling like I should say it but unsure if it was meant as a compliment or merely a clinical observation.

"You're welcome," she replied, smiling. "Have you noticed a difference in the way you feel? Do you feel like the medicine is helping at all?"

"That's hard to say. I feel like I'm doing better, but I can't say for sure that it's from the medicine."

Dr. Robinson nodded, making a note on her pad. "Do you think there are other factors involved, or just that with time things are getting easier?"

I cleared my throat. "There might be . . . other factors involved." The corners of my mouth twitched as I fought back a smile.

"Such as . . . ?"

"Well, things seem to be progressing with . . . the guy. My neighbor, the one I mentioned before."

"Oh?"

"Yeah. I think maybe it's going somewhere. I mean, I'm no expert at relationships or guys in any way, but I don't think I'm misreading things or seeing things that aren't there. We're together all the time, he takes me on dates to the nicest places, and he's always so concerned about me and how I feel. He's a complete gentleman, always making sure I know that he knows where the boundaries are between us. He gives me gifts and tells me things that make me think that maybe . . . possibly, I don't know . . . he feels *that way* about me. And . . . he kissed me." A rush of heat hit my face as I spoke the words.

"And do you feel that way about him?"

"Yes," I answered without missing a beat. Dr. Robinson chuckled softly. "You seem pretty sure about that." My face burned hotter, but she quickly said, "That's good. It's good that you're sure of your feelings, and that you're allowing yourself this kind of happiness. The change in your demeanor is . . ." she paused, shaking her head. ". . . remarkable."

I smiled, feeling happiness at my newfound happiness. I was a regular greeting card.

Then her expression turned to concern. "Just be careful. It's easy to get caught up in feelings of love and romance, especially when it follows a period of severe depression. It can act as a drug, masking the pain that is still present underneath the euphoria. Just make sure this is real, something that you believe you would respond to the same way in any given situation."

I nodded as if what she was saying was something I'd already considered, but inside I was reeling. Of course this was real. I wasn't some stupid schoolgirl so low and insecure that I'd fall all over the first guy that smiled at me.

Was I?

It was an unsettling thought, one that I quickly dismissed.

Dr. Robinson was watching me closely. "So, anything else happen this week?"

I started to shake my head when I suddenly remembered running into Ashley the other night at the restaurant.

"I saw an old friend." I picked at a fiber on the stuffed chair I was sitting in, my mood completely deflated now.

"And? How did that go?"

"Disastrous."

"How so?"

"I froze like a deer in the headlights. Couldn't think of one lousy thing to say. I was so overcome with this crazy mix of feelings: hurt, betrayal, shock, embarrassment, nostalgia, joy at seeing my best friend again. Well, what used to be my best friend. The good feelings were worse. I was ticked off at myself for feeling them."

"What happened between you and your friend?" She

was speaking in her "I'm concerned and want to ask these questions delicately" voice.

I sighed. After spilling it all out to Jude not too long ago, I wasn't keen on reliving it again just yet.

"Let's just say that when I reached my low, she couldn't handle it anymore, so she left. She was all I had, and she left me. With no one." *Story of my life,* I thought bitterly.

Dr. Robinson didn't say anything, just nodded slightly.

An awkward silence filled the small office, and I yanked harder on the fiber. Wasn't the hour up yet?

Finally, she asked, "What was her reaction to seeing you?"

I shrugged. How could I have known what she was thinking when she saw me? "I don't know. She seemed normal. Which made it even worse. Like I was the only one having a hard time with it. But she was with her cousin, so maybe that helped her keep her cool."

"And you were alone?"

"No," I said, realizing the problem with my logic. "Jude was with me."

"Who's Jude?"

I faltered, realizing I'd never mentioned his name before. For one panicked second I wondered if Dr. Robinson would make the connection between "my" Jude and the Jude she'd met in the hospital. Somehow I guessed she'd have some strong opinions about me falling for the person who saved me from my attempted suicide, and not positive ones. But her face showed no signs of registering, so I relaxed.

"Jude is the guy I've been telling you about."

"Ah," she nodded knowingly. I waited for her to punch a hole through my strength-in-numbers theory but she didn't, and I was grateful.

"And what was he doing during this reunion?"

I thought back. "He was quiet at first, but then he came to my rescue, actually." Huh. I'd never thought of that before. That's twice now he'd saved me.

"How's that?"

"He jumped in when it was apparent I'd gone catatonic and started talking to Ashley and her cousin. He was a pro, making small talk, asking about their plans for the evening. Made all the painful awkwardness go away."

"He sounds like quite the guy."

"He is," I agreed, realizing how true her statement actually was. "He really is."

"So how did it end, the conversation between the four of you?"

"All right, I guess. She told me I looked well and I managed to say thank you, so that was a plus. Then they left." I shrugged, trying to convince Dr. Robinson (and probably myself) that it was no big deal, a pattern I'd noticed in these therapy sessions.

She did her silent nod thing again, and I was beginning to wonder if this was her signature trademark. I found it a little infuriating. What was she thinking when she did that?

When it was clear I had nothing more to say, Dr. Robinson set her pad of paper on her desk and said, "I'm happy with what I'm seeing, Olivia. You're really progressing."

I smiled and tried to let her words give me a reason to mean it, but the wave of bliss I'd been riding at the beginning of the session was gone, only a weak ripple in its wake. I left the office with Dr. Robinson's words echoing in my head like a blazing red warning light flashing over and over. *Make sure this is real . . .*

* * * * *

I couldn't get her words out of my mind as I worked my shift that afternoon. It was beginning to eat at me, devour my insides. Why was I letting it get to me so badly? But I knew the answer. Fear. Fear that she was right. That all of this, whatever it was with Jude, was not real. That it was nothing more than a lonely, tortured girl falling for her handsome rescuer. I tried to imagine what things would be like if we'd met under normal circumstances. If it had been a year ago, when my life was vastly different, when I'd had friends and family and a normal, healthy self-esteem, would Jude have pursued me the same way? Would I have fallen for someone so secretive, trusted someone so obviously hiding things from me? Would we have met at all?

I finally had to push aside all thoughts about it. I was too distracted and I'd already messed up three tables' orders. I was going to lose out on some serious tips if I didn't pull it together. Instead I focused on seeing Jude at the end of my shift. He always came to pick me up after work now. We'd never discussed it or made plans to do it, he just always showed up. On the way home each time, we'd decide what we wanted to do that evening. It varied between several different things, but always included food, since lately I was so hungry after work.

I had to close that night, which meant I had to wait longer than usual to see him. It also meant two extra hours for the nervous anticipation to build. I hadn't seen Jude since we'd kissed and I wondered if things would be different between us. Would it be awkward, or would he kiss me hello and it would just become something we did all the time, like a regular couple? The butterflies in my stomach danced at the thought, and I had to take a deep breath to calm my nerves. By the time the other closing waitress and I finished cleaning the dining room, I was a jittery mess. Jude hadn't shown up yet, so I headed to the back to change. Bridgett was still back there, already changed into what looked like a tube top that she'd stretched down to make a dress. She was applying thick black eyeliner in front of a grungy mirror when she saw me enter. She'd hung around after her shift, flirting with a table of guys who didn't feel the need to leave when we turned the "open" sign off and started cleaning up. They'd all just barely left, but not before making plans with Bridgett to meet up at some bar.

"Hey!" she said, glancing at me out of the corner of her eye. "So tell me about this guy." Her voice was animated, and she drew out each word in a sort of drawl. "He's super hot."

My jaw tightened hearing her talk about Jude like that, but I forced a smile and said, "He's a friend."

"Honey, a friend doesn't show up at your work every single day looking like a centerfold." She grabbed a tube of red lipstick and made an "O" with her lips as she smeared it on. "Trust me, I know."

I'm sure you do, I thought. "Maybe not," I shrugged as I moved past her toward the bathroom. I slipped in and closed the door before she could say anything else. I quickly changed into a new pair of jeans and a red shirt I'd recently bought and then sat on the toilet lid for another five minutes until I heard Bridgett leave. When I thought it was safe, I grabbed my stuff and walked out of the bathroom. I walked over to the now-unoccupied mirror and was checking my appearance when I heard a voice behind me say, "Bridgett's an idiot."

I spun around to see the waitress I'd closed with. She was sitting in a folding chair counting her tips. She was tall and kind of quiet, and had only worked here for a few weeks. Since neither of us seemed to be big talkers, we hadn't spoke much while we'd cleaned together that night.

"Oh, hey," I said, giving a small, nervous laugh. "I didn't know you were still here."

She smiled. "Sorry. I move pretty quietly. Don't like to draw a lot of attention to myself, you know?"

I nodded. *Boy, did I ever.*

"Olivia, right?"

"Yeah, and you're . . . Jen?" I was relieved that I'd remembered. She'd already taken her name tag off.

She nodded. "We've worked together a few times, but I don't think we've actually met." She got up off the chair and came over to me, holding out her hand. I shook it. "Nice to officially meet you." She smiled and returned to her seat. "Anyway, just ignore Bridgett. I went to high school with her, and she's always been that way." Jen made a face. "An idiot."

I couldn't help but smile. "Yeah, that pretty much sums her up."

Jen grinned then. "She might be popular with the boys, but she can't solve an equation to save her life."

I laughed, thoroughly enjoying the image of Bridgett straining to do a math problem. I knew it was evil of me, but it felt good to have something to laugh about with someone else, almost like having a . . . friend.

"Anyway, I gotta go," Jen said. "Do you work tomorrow night?"

I didn't have to think about it. I worked every evening shift, with the exception of my one day off a week. Jen must not have figured that out yet; she seemed to jump between days and evenings.

"Yeah. You?"

"Yeah," Jen replied, grabbing her jacket off a hook. "See ya tomorrow." She smiled as she walked to the back door.

"See ya," I echoed, watching as she disappeared outside. I turned back around to the mirror, feeling good. Who knew I'd been working with someone so nice for almost a month?

Satisfied with the state of my hair, I hurried out to the front of the restaurant, anxious to see Jude. But when I walked out front to the dining room and skimmed over the few remaining customers, my spirits fell.

Jude wasn't there.

CHAPTER SEVENTEEN

I STOOD STUPIDLY IN THE entrance to the dining room, scanning the perimeter once more, then a third time, hoping that maybe I'd missed him but knowing I hadn't. I frowned, wondering why he wasn't there. He had come to pick me up every single day for the last three weeks, without fail. A sense of foreboding hovered over me like a rain cloud ready to burst. Something wasn't right.

I debated whether I should wait for him a little longer or not. I glanced at the clock on the wall behind the cash register. He was half an hour late. I had to resign myself to the fact that he probably wasn't coming. Heavy-hearted, I headed for the front door, readying myself for the walk home.

"Olivia."

I spun around when I heard the male voice calling from behind me. Bryan had come out of his office where he'd been working on revising the schedule all evening and was walking through the dining room toward me. "Can I talk to you for a minute?"

Human instinct had me recoiling slightly from that question, but he didn't look upset at all, and his voice was calm and friendly. He probably wanted me to start working some day shifts too. Or maybe things were slow and he needed to cut back my hours. I frowned inwardly at that thought.

Bryan came over and motioned toward the closest booth. "Care to sit?" I nodded, sliding onto the padded bench. Bryan did the same across from me.

"What's up?" I asked, timidly.

Bryan linked his fingers loosely together. "I just wanted to talk to you, see how things are going. We haven't spoke much since you came back. You usually jet out of here as soon as you're done; I thought I'd take advantage of this rare opportunity." He smiled, but I had a hard time smiling back, since the "rare opportunity" he was referring to was Jude not showing up.

I shifted in my seat, still unsure of where this was leading. Was he here to tell me I wasn't cutting it at work? That I'd come back too soon? Paranoia engulfed me, even as I told myself that couldn't be possible. I had worked harder the last few weeks than ever before.

"So . . . how are things?" Bryan repeated, when I didn't answer.

"Um . . . good. Great, actually." I shrugged one shoulder, not sure what else I should say.

"Really?" Bryan asked, scrutinizing my face. Did he think I was lying?

"Really," I repeated, emphasizing the word in hopes of convincing him.

"Okay, I just wanted to make sure. You seem better, that's for certain. But I know that how things look on the outside don't always reflect what's really going on on the inside. Thought I'd ask, just to be safe."

I nodded. I still had no idea where this was going, but everything Bryan had said so far seemed like genuine concern. If he really was just checking up on me to make sure I was okay, well, then, that was really sweet. Something totally foreign to me, but sweet nonetheless.

"So tell me about this guy. Jude, is it?"

I nodded, and my skin flushed as it always did when someone mentioned him.

"How'd you meet him?"

Aaaaaaaaand . . . freeze. Everything in me locked up; every muscle, every joint, every breath. I couldn't move, couldn't think. *How would I answer this?* I couldn't very well say "he saved my life when I tried to kill myself," and in the moments of panic that followed Bryan's question I could not for the life of me think of a single lie.

I creased my forehead, hoping to look like I was trying to remember the exact details of our first meeting, but really I was just stalling. *How did we meet? How did we meet?*

"Uh . . . well . . ." *Just tell what you can!* my inner voice yelled at me. "Well, he's my neighbor, and he helped me out during . . . that whole thing." I still had no idea what Bryan did or didn't know about what *had* happened to me, so I wasn't about to risk talking about it by assuming he did. "He was there for me when no one else was." I said a silent prayer that he wouldn't ask me what had happened to me. My prayer was answered.

Bryan nodded, looking like I'd just confirmed something he'd been thinking. "He seems like a pretty decent guy, from what I've seen. Is he? As decent as he seems?" His question caught me off guard. This was a little more personal than Bryan had ever been with me, but after his message on my answering machine the night of The Incident, and of course the line of questioning now, I knew that he was just looking out for me, in a fatherly way. It made me feel safe, secure. Cared about.

I smiled, hoping I would be able to convey the truth to what I was saying. "He is. He really, really is. I've seriously never known anyone like him. I've definitely never known anyone who's treated me the way he treats me. What you've seen of him—holding doors, pulling out chairs, paying for every meal—that's him. That's really who he is. There's no pretense, no show that he's putting on when people are around. He doesn't have a fake bone in his body."

I stopped, suddenly embarrassed at how quickly my answer had turned into gushing. I just wanted Bryan to know what an amazing person Jude truly was.

Bryan smiled. "Good. That's what I was hoping to hear. I suspected as much, due to the complete change in your demeanor since you came back. You're like a different person, you know that?"

My eyebrows lifted in surprise. I knew I was happier, obviously, and more sociable, but other than that I felt like the same person I was. Sort of. Not really. *Not at all,* I realized. He was right. I was a totally different person than the one that'd worked there a month earlier.

"I shake my head in disbelief sometimes when I see you now, laughing and talking with the other waitresses. Even your appearance," he said, and I felt my cheeks burning in embarrassment. For some reason, I had never been comfortable with anyone pointing out anything about me physically, even if it was a compliment or a simple observation, like I knew Bryan's would be. "I hope you don't take this the wrong way, but, before . . . you looked kind of sickly. I actually worried you had some life-threatening illness. And now . . . well, you know what you look like," he said, picking up on the fact that my cheeks were now the color of a boiling lobster. "Anyway, my point is, the difference is undeniable, and it's nice to see you happy and healthy."

"Thank you, Bryan," I said, wondering if this was what it felt like to have a father who cared about you and looked after you. "That means a lot. Really. You're a great boss. The *best* boss. I feel lucky to have you."

Bryan patted my hand. "Well, I do what I can." We both laughed.

As we scooted out of the booth, Bryan asked. "So, where is your boy tonight?" The question brought me down from the clouds, crashing back to reality. For some reason, I couldn't tell Bryan the truth: that I didn't know. Not after I had just got done telling him how wonderful and trustworthy Jude was, how well he treated me. So I lied. "Oh, he wasn't feeling well today. I'm just going to walk home."

"Nonsense," Bryan said. "I'm headed home now too. Let me give you a ride."

"You sure?" I asked, thinking how very nice a ride would be right now.

"Positive."

Bryan and I talked a little more on the drive to my apartment. It was dark and rainy, always a scary combination with Seattle drivers. But Bryan managed to stay relatively calm, weaving in and out of traffic in his little Ford Focus. I asked him about his wife and kids; he grinned with pride and pointed to a picture tucked up under the passenger visor. I flipped it up so I could see. It was the whole family—all seven of them—at the Aquarium. I commented on how happy they all looked, and he proceeded to tell me the latest hilarious things his four-year-old had said.

I was still laughing when we reached my building,

where I hopped out and thanked Bryan for the ride. As he drove away, I glanced up at Jude's window to see if his light was on. It wasn't. I trudged up the stairs to my apartment, hoping against hope that maybe he was inside waiting for me. Again, I chided myself for being so ridiculous. He would have had no way of getting inside with the door locked. Although he had somehow managed it once before . . .

I walked into a dark, empty apartment and sighed. I couldn't help it. I was freaking out a little. Was it the kiss? Had he regretted it? Had I scared him off with my obvious desperation when he went to leave right after? Panic welled up inside me, and my conversation with Dr. Robinson resonated once more in my head.

Maybe she was right. Maybe this was more to me than it was to him. Maybe it was a stupid schoolgirl crush, and I'd fallen so hard for him simply because he was there, and he was nice, and handsome, and caring, and wonderful . . .

No, I didn't believe it. I couldn't believe it. I hadn't been seeking out a boyfriend. The last thing I'd had on my mind when I met Jude was a relationship. Wasn't I the one who convinced Jude that I wasn't ready to get close to anyone? Yes, I had been smart. I had taken precaution against exactly what Dr. Robinson was talking about. And yet still, somehow, I'd managed to fall. Hard.

I went to the kitchen and made myself a sandwich, willing myself to think of something else, anything else. I flipped on the TV, found an old sitcom, and sat down to eat. I tried—really tried—to pay attention to the clichéd family playing out less-than-realistic situations on-screen, but my thoughts inevitably returned to Jude, and three bites into my sandwich, I couldn't stand to eat or watch anymore.

I shut the TV off and moved to the couch, curling up in

the corner and pulling a blanket over myself. I noticed the little stone angel that Jude had given me lying on the coffee table. I picked it up and thought about when Jude gave it to me, pictured his face in the soft light of the lamp, creating a halolike glow around his body. He had looked especially striking at that moment, almost taking my breath away.

I turned the figurine over and over in my hands, rubbing its smooth surface with my thumb. I noted again the sorrowful expression on its face and thought how remarkably familiar it seemed. It was the look I'd seen on Jude so many times . . .

My mind began to wander, in the way that minds do when time passes by with nothing around to distract or entertain. My thoughts bounced around between random, silly things that had no significance of any kind, and bigger, more important things, some good, some not-so-good. I thought of my mom, trying hard to focus on our life together instead of the tragic way we were torn apart. It cut at my soul, and I only managed to think of a few happy memories before quickly moving onto something else. I thought of my dad, and for maybe the nine hundredth time in my life wondered where he was, and if he was happy with his other family. I thought of Ashley, of the countless times we'd laughed together and did stupid things that only we found hilarious. I recalled running into her at the restaurant with Jude, felt again the humiliation at my pathetic reaction. But then I thought of the way we'd said good-bye, how she'd smiled and paid me a genuine compliment, and a small portion—a very small portion—of the humiliation faded away. I thought about work, and about the surprising conversations with Jen and Bryan. It made me smile. And, of course, I thought about Jude. A lot. Of meeting him at the hospital, our first "date" on the pier, our talk in the park, the house on the lake, when he held me all night long, when he kissed me after running into Ashley . . .

I thought about everything, the whole time turning the little figurine in my hands. I couldn't believe how much had happened between us in just a few short weeks, especially considering the way it all began. That night . . . that night that was burned into my brain like acid. Of course I thought about that night. The harder I tried not to think about it, the more I did. I thought about the sequence of events as they unfolded, remembering odd little details that I hadn't thought of since it happened. Things like how the boy that called me a skeleton at the restaurant had his eyebrow pierced, and how I'd taken the phone off the hook when I got home in the very slim chance that someone decided to call. How I'd nearly choked trying to swallow six ibuprofen at once and how haunting my face had looked in the mirror in the bathroom, like something straight out of a horror movie. I remembered lying on my back after swallowing the Valium and watching the crack in the ceiling grow fuzzy and the light condense around me into one bright spot above my head, like tunnel vision. I laughed now, remembering how I'd thought it was the famous light that everyone says appears when you die, and that there was an angel there, ready to escort me into heaven.

I realized with a start that it was Jude, already there, trying to save me. I had never made that connection before, never thought about what happened at the end in so much detail. He was the figure standing over me; it was his voice I heard calling my name . . .

I froze suddenly, the angel dropping from my hands mid-revolution. He had *called my name.* How was Jude calling my name when we'd never met, never spoken before? My blood turned to ice as I went over it in my head, trying to make absolutely sure I remembered correctly, that it wasn't the drugs, wasn't the loss of consciousness playing with my head, that I had actually heard him say my name, yell it even. But there was no uncertainty in my mind. I had heard it.

My heart racing, I raised my eyes to the door, wondering once more how he had got into my apartment. And suddenly I remembered. Another forgotten detail, this one much more significant. An answer to the question that had plagued me since that night. I *had* locked my door. I remembered it vividly now: Rushing home from work, distraught, not able to get into my apartment fast enough. Dropping my things on the floor and heading straight for my bed where I instantly crumbled into a pile on my bed. Then, having the thought to take my phone off the hook in case Bryan decided to call and see why I'd bailed early, and then, just in case he decided to stop by on his way home from work to check on me, I walked over and locked my door, which I *had* forgotten to lock in my distress.

All the blood drained from my face, and I could hardly breathe. I stood up, the blanket dropping to the floor. I felt like the walls were closing in around me. I had to get out before they crushed me. I ran from my apartment, slamming the door behind me, and went down the stairs, outside. I didn't know where I was going or what I was doing, but the fresh air did nothing to help me breathe, and soon I was standing in the lobby of Jude's building. I walked over to the wall with the inset mailboxes, not planning or meaning to. My feet just took me there, having taken on a mind of their own.

I scanned the metal rectangles, seeing names that didn't make any sense to my jumbled brain. Finally, my eyes fell on what I now realized I'd been looking for: *West, J. 515A.*

Bingo. I moved robotically to the elevator, a loud buzz filling my head, replacing all sound. I stumbled out when it came to a stop on the floor that I'd told it to and made my way down the hall until I came to the door that said 515A.

There I stopped, still not having any kind of a plan. What if he wasn't home? What if he was?

I lifted my hand to knock, but ended up pounding on his door. There was no answer. I pounded again. Nothing. He wasn't there.

Now what? I dropped my hand, taking long, deep breaths. I looked around—for what I don't know—then back at his door. I knew it had to be locked, but I grabbed the handle anyway and turned. I was startled to feel it unlatch. I pushed the door open. It was pitch black. I fumbled around until I found a light switch, and flipped it on. A faint cry escaped my lips, taking with it all the air in my lungs.

I was standing in an empty apartment.

CHAPTER EIGHTEEN

I BARELY MADE IT TO the window before collapsing onto the built-in window seat below it. I was gasping for air, feeling dangerously close to passing out. I leaned my head against the cool glass, then slowly turned and looked out through it. There was my window, straight across, just as it should have been, just as Jude had said.

I swallowed hard, trying to keep the stomach bile down that was threatening to make an appearance. He was gone. He had left, without saying good-bye. Without looking back. Just like my dad. And my mom. And Ashley. A wave of cold sweat washed over me, and I felt like I was trying to breathe under water. I was drowning. It had happened again. It would always happen. Everyone I would ever love would always end up leaving me. I was unlovable. I wasn't worth sticking around for, to anyone.

The darkness in the room was seeping into me, pulling me under. That place that I'd escaped weeks earlier, and held at bay ever since, was reaching its black arms into my soul and sucking me into its abyss. I had fought so hard for so long to stay away, to never go back. But I was so tired of fighting. I had nothing left to fight for. I should just give up . . .

And that was when a second thought came to me, one that stopped me cold. Another possibility, I realized. One that hadn't occurred to me until just now, one that I wasn't sure was any better than the first.

Maybe Jude had never lived here at all. Maybe that's why he'd never wanted to bring me here. Maybe it was just another lie.

I had to get out of there. I retraced my steps out the door, down the hall, into the elevator. I'm sure I must have freaked out several of the tenants who passed by, my skin white as a ghost, my eyes bugged out as if I'd just seen one. Once I got back down to ground level, I hurried outside before emptying the contents of my stomach into a large potted plant. Then I stood, gripping the back of a bench, shaking like a leaf. I was scared to let go, certain I would collapse onto the concrete below. But I couldn't stay here, out in the open where everyone could see. It felt like all eyes were on me, everyone staring at the crazy girl who'd just thrown up in a plant. It was enough to get me to let go of the bench, and I walked in a daze through the dark night back to my building, back up the stairs, back into my apartment. I stood just inside my door, wondering how to wake up from this nightmare. Maybe my nightmares had gotten so out of control that they'd combined into one super-nightmare, the mother of all nightmares. I was ready to wake up.

I slowly walked over to my couch where the blanket was still puddled on the floor. The stone angel was peeking out from under it, and I bent over and picked it up. It looked completely different to me now, although nothing about it had changed. I was disgusted by it, furious, devastated.

Scared. I was spiraling downward; the world was imploding and sucking me inside to its fiery, molten core. Nothing made sense. All I could think about were secrets, lies. Lies and secrets. *Who was he? Why was he doing this to me?* My eyes burned with rage as I raised my arm to throw it as hard as I could against the wood floor, to shatter it into as many pieces as possible. But I couldn't bring myself to do it. I set it down on the coffee table and crawled onto the couch, curling onto my side. I wondered bitterly why my life always circled back to this. It was as if someone had decided long ago that I could only ever experience happiness for so many weeks or months at a time, and then I would have to fall back into the pits of hell. It was just so unfair.

Underneath it all, my heart was breaking. It was what I felt the most. Not the fury I felt at being deceived and abandoned, or the debilitating fear that maybe this person meant to harm me in some way, but the pain in my heart as it was ripped to shreds. At losing this person who had saved me in so many ways, the only person in this world I had left to love.

My stomach twisted at the word. *Love.* Because I did love him. I knew that now, like I knew the earth was round and water was wet. I loved him. More than anything or anyone I had ever loved in my life. He had brought me happiness at a time when I was certain I would never smile again. He was the sunshine in my world of perpetual rain. He was everything good in my life. He was the reason I *had* a life, the only reason I still existed at all. And now . . . I didn't know what he was. I didn't know anything anymore. I didn't know good from bad, joy from misery, up from down. Because it was all a lie. Everything was. He had lied about my door being unlocked. How could he have possibly gotten in through a *locked door*? And how could he possibly have known my name, when we had never met, never spoken? And if my guess was correct—that he'd lied about being my neighbor—how, *how* had he known to come save me that night?

It was so perplexing that for a moment I forgot about my anguish. Somewhere there was an answer to all of this—an explanation. I could feel it in my bones now, an overwhelming feeling that I was missing something—a *big* something—the missing puzzle piece that would complete the whole picture and reveal what I was searching for. *But what?* I began running through it in my mind, the things that didn't add up. Getting into my apartment somehow when the door was locked. Knowing my name when we'd never met, and somehow knowing I needed help that night. Lying about living in the apartment across the way, lying to Dr. Robinson (I was sure of that now) about it all being an accident. Never answering my questions, never giving me any information about his family, or where he came from, or why he didn't seem to have any friends or anyone he even knew in the entire city. The fact that he had no real job, yet he always seemed to have plenty of money.

Each unexplained mystery swirled around in my head until they all wound together into one giant cyclone of confusion. I began to see flashing images, a mental slide show of Jude. I saw his eyes like sparkling jewels as they bore into mine on the dock, and again when he woke up in the middle of the night and caught me staring at him. Both times I had felt . . . *something*, something that I could never explain. I saw the light glowing behind him as he gave me the gift, and the tortured look that so often plagued his beautiful face. Around and around they all went, the images and the questions, until I thought for sure I was losing my mind: sparkling eyes, locked door, calling my name, lies, secrets, halo of light, dodging my questions, knowing I needed help, no family, empty apartment . . .

Somewhere through the whirlwind, I realized my eyes had focused on the white marble angel.

And the cyclone came to a crashing halt.

I sat up slowly, staring at the small figurine, my eyes growing wider with each passing second. *No,* I thought, shaking my head. *No, it can't be. It's completely ludicrous. Don't be stupid.*

But it would explain everything. And as impossible as it was, I knew that it had to be. The missing piece. The thing that connected all the other pieces, made it all come together into one big picture.

He knew my name because he already knew everything about me.

He knew I needed help that night because he saw the whole thing happen.

Only it wasn't from the window next door like he'd claimed, it was from right here. In my apartment.

He hadn't needed to get through a locked door to save me.

He was already in here.

Shaking violently, I reached forward and picked up the angel. There was one lie that I'd missed. One glaring falsehood I'd overlooked. I wasn't the angel, as Jude had told me when he gave it to me.

He was.

CHAPTER NINETEEN

I UNDERSTOOD NOW WHAT IT was like to suffer from Post-Traumatic Stress Disorder. My body was in shock, my mind had shut down. I didn't move after my revelation, just sat staring at the angel, not believing it could be possible. If I was right, my entire world had just been turned upside down. Everything I'd ever known to be true was in question. Was the earth actually flat? Would gravity suddenly cease to exist one day? Was there a God after all?

I had never really been religious. It was something that my mom had never addressed. I got the impression that any belief she ever had in God followed my dad out the door. It didn't take long for me to adopt the same ideals.

But now . . . if there was a chance that angels might actually exist, wouldn't that mean there was a chance that other celestial beings, like God, must exist? It wouldn't make sense for there to be angels with no God. Wasn't that their whole purpose, to serve God?

That is, assuming there really were angels, and I wasn't convinced yet. It was all too much. It was making my head hurt. I moved from the couch to my bed, wanting to go to sleep to make the whole complicated thing go away. But sleep wouldn't be coming any time soon, and I knew it. I lay awake the entire night, trying to sort it out in my head. I went over everything again and again, convinced there had to be another explanation. I was so determined to find one I even embraced theories that were equally alarming, if not more so. Such as a stalker, or a psycho killer. But neither of these would explain why he saved my life, or how he got into my apartment, which was virtually impenetrable. Plus, I knew without question that Jude could never be either of those things, or anything close to it. The only thing he could be was something my brain couldn't comprehend, something that couldn't logically be explained. Something otherworldly. And yet, even knowing that, I still couldn't accept it.

By the time dawn broke, I was more than ready to escape the exhausting task of trying to solve an unsolvable problem. Although my eyes burned from lack of sleep and my head was foggy, I relished the chance to get out of the house for several hours, to be distracted by mindless physical exertion. I had to sit around for an excruciating amount of time before work, but finally it was close enough that I started to get ready. I showered and dressed in record time, and speed-walked the entire way to work, the whole time trying not to be reminded of the fact that I was having to walk to work once again and the reason why. So of course it was all I could think about. Where *was* he? Why would he just up and disappear like that? He didn't know I was on to his secret; he didn't know anything had changed at all. So why would he leave? And where did he go? It made my stomach twist to think about, so I was relieved when I reached the coffee shop.

In the back I tied on my apron, then went to the server area and poured myself a Coke to kill time, since I'd arrived early. As I stood there drinking, waiting to clock in, Jen came back with an empty tray and began loading it with glasses.

"Hey," she said brightly when she saw me.

"Hi," I responded, pasting on a smile. I watched as she dumped ice into each glass and began filling them with varying soft drinks. "Need any help?"

"No, I got it. Thanks, though." Jen smiled and disappeared into the dining room. A minute later she reemerged with a tray full of dirty dishes. She took them back to the kitchen, then came back to where I was standing.

"How has your shift been so far?" I was proud of myself for initiating the conversation. It definitely wasn't an easy thing to do.

"Typical," she answered, shrugging. "Except for the part when I spilled water all over an old woman. That wasn't typical, thank goodness." She laughed, grabbing two coffee mugs. As she reached forward, something shiny caught my eye. A silver chain swung away from her neck, a delicate cross hanging from it.

She saw me looking and reflexively grabbed the necklace. "It was my grandma's. I never take it off."

Embarrassed that she caught me looking, and that she felt she needed to explain it, I tried to think of something to say. "It's pretty."

Jen smiled. "Thanks." She fingered it, craning her neck to see the charm. "I always admired it on my grandma. She left it to me when she passed away a few months ago."

I nodded, knowing I should say something along the lines of condolences, but I had only one thing on my mind just then, something that had taken up camp in my head the night before and quickly grown into an obsession.

"Uh, can I ask you something?" I wasn't sure how to say what I wanted to say without looking like a complete nut job.

"Of course." Jen filled the mugs with coffee and set them carefully on the tray.

"Do you . . ." I swallowed, "believe in angels?"

She glanced at me somewhat quizzically, but not so much that I regretted asking.

"Yeah," she answered. "I do." Then, "Why, don't you?"

I stared back at her feeling slightly lost. "I . . . I don't know. I've never really believed in any of that . . . stuff."

Jen nodded. "I guess, for me, it makes more sense for them to be real than not to be."

"Why's that?"

She thought for a minute. "I'm not sure. In my mind, it's more believable that there's some greater power up there who created everything, than to think there was a big explosion and *bam*, here we were. Or that after we die, that's it, there's nothing more, just an empty void. I just can't believe that. And so it's logical to me that if there's God, and there's heaven, then there must be angels." With that, she turned and carried the tray of coffee out of the room. When she returned a minute later, she came over to me and said, in a softer voice, "But . . . more than the logistics of it all, I *feel* that it's real."

Something in her words struck me deep, and a strange feeling came over me that was both alien and familiar at the same time. I'd never felt it exactly like this before, though. The closest thing I could compare it to was what I felt when I looked deep into Jude's eyes for the first time, on the dock.

I struggled to regain composure, and, in a quivering voice, asked, "Do you believe there are angels here, on earth?"

"Sure," she nodded. "I think they're all around us, watching us, protecting us." She shrugged. "Maybe I'm wrong, but it's what I believe." Then she left once more, and I pulled myself back to reality long enough to see it was a minute past the time I was supposed to clock in.

I darted over to the time clock and punched my card, then quickly got to work, my head an infinite amount of miles away from earth.

* * * * *

As soon as my shift was over, I began the walk home. I let my feet carry me along the streets of Seattle, the city I thought I knew inside-out but that now looked and felt completely foreign to me. When I reached home I just kept going, right past my apartment. I had to keep moving or I'd think too much about what I didn't want to think about. Working had been the perfect cure, forcing me to think of taking orders and cleaning tables and counting tips, instead of things much too deep for my fragile brain.

Now that I was done with work, I'd managed to continue to keep these thoughts at bay, and I would do whatever it took to keep them there.

So I kept walking.

I walked around in a daze for I don't know how long, wandering the darkening streets, unaware of any danger it may have put me in, not caring if it did anyway. The night was colder than nights had been of late, but I didn't feel it. My body must have been chilled, but the message never made it to my brain.

I couldn't wrap my head around it, couldn't reconcile the world I had always known with one where angels could be present, in plain sight, walking around, and talking just like everybody else. Eating, sleeping, making people fall in love with them . . .

Now everything was different in this world. Everything looked different, felt different to me. I took nothing at face value. Everything I saw had me wondering what it really was, what I just wasn't seeing. Everyone around me was a potential mythical creature or celestial being.

And yet it was just so absurd. Believing that it was possible, that there was even a chance it could be, that Jude could be . . .

I could hardly finish the thought.

At some point during the night I wound up at a bus stop. I sat on the bench for a while until a bus pulled up in front of me. I stared at it, wondering why it had stopped for me and opened its doors. I didn't need to go anywhere. But since it was there, I got on anyway. I dug out some tip money and dropped it into the box. Hoping it was enough to allow me to curl up on a seat and ride out the night in solitude, I made my way to the very back. Luckily, not many people needed public transportation at this hour, and I had the entire back of the bus to myself. I huddled in the corner, pulling my feet up under me.

As the bus began moving, I leaned my head against the cool glass of the window. I stared out into the night and numbly watched the buildings and car lights flash by. It put me into a trance, and it felt wonderful to concentrate on such simple things. Inanimate objects that could never cause me pain. At least, not the kind I couldn't heal from.

I rode for hours, always moving, going nowhere. I gazed at the scenery through half-lidded eyes, my breath fogging up the window. I wiped it away absently and watched the condensation trickle down in erratic paths with dull fascination.

I had almost fallen asleep when the bus stopped in a familiar-looking neighborhood. I glanced up and saw two teenagers get off, and I suddenly had the urge to get off as well.

I got up and made my way down the narrow aisle and the three small steps. The bus drove off, and I was alone on a dark, quiet street. I recognized where I was now.

I wrapped my arms around myself, the cold registering now after the warmth of the bus. I strolled briskly through streets and around homes that tugged at my memory. It had been years, but I knew exactly where I was and where I needed to go.

CHAPTER TWENTY

A FEW BLOCKS LATER I was standing in front of an old, dilapidated house that had once been white, but was now the same color as the dirt that used to be a lawn. It was abandoned, and had been for some time, based on the state of it. Wondering if it had been turned into a meth house at some point throughout the years, I wandered up the familiar concrete walkway that was now broken up and almost completely overgrown with weeds. I reached a tattered screen door that was hanging by one hinge. I gingerly pulled it open, a shrill creak piercing the silent night.

The wooden door behind it took a few tries to get open. It was stuck from disuse for who knew how long. Inside was pitch black, and it smelled of old, stale air and other much more unpleasant things. I should have been scared to go in but it didn't occur to me to be. I left the door ajar, allowing a small amount of light from the street lamps to come in. It was enough that I could see where I was, not that I needed light to tell me which room I was in. I was young when my mom and I were forced to move into a cheaper apartment, but I would never forget this room as the last place I saw my dad.

It was filthy now, full of dead leaves and covered in dirt. The walls had holes in them and the carpet looked like someone had parked their car on it and changed their oil without bothering to use a drip pan. It was hard to see in the lightless gloom, but it only made it that much easier to see it as I remembered it, with the blue flower-print couch and my grandma's old hutch over in the corner.

I sat down on an overturned crate in the dark room and remembered what it felt like to be a family. All together, my mom, my dad, and me. It hadn't been that way in fifteen years, but I could still remember what it was like, how . . . *normal* I felt back then. Things were so simple, so uncomplicated, just my five-year-old self, playing with dolls in my shoebox-sized bedroom. My biggest worry at the time was what was for dinner that night, my only problem a broken shoelace.

Of course, that wasn't true, but I didn't know it at the time. I had a father who was lying to me and my mom, hiding his secret life, about to shatter ours. I guess the old saying is true: ignorance really is bliss.

Just like with Jude.

Nothing had changed except the knowledge I now had. He had always been . . . whatever he was, but not knowing . . . it had been blissful. Admittedly, it had been frustrating, all the secrets and mysteriousness, but I had been happy. So very happy.

Now . . . everything was different. Now I knew, and I couldn't handle it. I couldn't handle knowing what he was, and I especially couldn't handle knowing we could never be. Because as impossible as it was to believe that he was an . . . *angel* . . . I knew now that I believed it all along, from the second the idea occurred to me. It just made sense—it was the only thing that explained it all. And it meant we could never be together.

And with that thought, the last thing I ever expected to happen, happened.

I began to cry. Real, honest to goodness tears that didn't stop at my tear ducts. They filled my eyes, then spilled over onto my cheeks and continued to come in a torrent of saline. And I was wrong. All this time I thought that if I could just cry I would feel better, and I was so wrong. It doubled the pain, made it that much harder to breathe. I'd never known hysterics before this. I was sobbing, crying harder than I'd ever cried in my lifetime. I wanted to lie down on the filthy floor and curl up in a ball and cry myself to sleep, because it would be the only way to escape this agony.

I cried thinking of all the time I'd had with Jude. I cried thinking of all the time we would never have. I cried at the injustice of finally finding someone to love, someone I was certain would never hurt or leave me, only to learn I could never be with him. I cried over my broken heart, over lost love, over the sick joke that fate had played on me. But that was my life. It had always been my life. It was only fitting that the best thing that had ever happened to me would end up this way.

But why did I care? What did it matter now? He wasn't who I thought he was, and we could never be together. Did I want to be with him, anyway? With someone who hid his true identity from me and told me lies, knowing what a fragile, vulnerable state I was in? Someone who let me love him, knowing all along he would abandon me like every other person in my life?

Yes. I did. Because that someone was Jude, and somehow my shattered heart still loved him more than I wanted to admit.

This made me cry harder. My sobs echoed through the empty house, making it sound haunted. I was certain this would be the death of me, this unbearable anguish. When my body finally had no more tears left to give, I sat mute, staring into the void, at the spot where our family picture used to hang.

I laughed derisively. *Family.* We weren't worthy of the word. A father who abandoned us, a mother who didn't love me enough to stay alive. Once again I saw the scene of my mother's death, felt the familiar stabbing pain as I relived the nightmare.

"You coward!" I suddenly screamed. It echoed through the empty room. "You weak, pathetic excuse for a mother! Things got hard so you *quit*!" I spat the word venomously. "You just *quit*, like the coward that you are! Now you're not here, when I need you most! When I need a mother!"

I listened to the heavy silence that responded, as if mocking me, reminding me that I was screaming to no one, that I was alone. All alone. And then, shattering the noiseless air, one word filled my head with a deafening roar: *hypocrite.*

I flinched. Had that been *my* thought? I looked around to see if someone else was there, but I knew no one was. It was my own voice accusing myself. And I was right. I *was* a hypocrite. I was the biggest hypocrite that had ever walked the face of the earth. How could I possibly sit there and judge my mother for doing the exact same thing I had tried to do? When things got too hard—had seemed hopeless—I had given up too. The only difference was that my attempt to escape failed. If Jude hadn't been there to save me, I'd have ended up just like my mom. I'd had a guardian angel there, watching over me, protecting me. And if I hadn't? I would have had the same fate as her. What right did I have to hate her for her choice? She obviously felt she had no other way out, just like I had felt only a few weeks ago. She had been just as abandoned as I had been when my father left and had worked herself to the bone trying to make a life for us every day that followed. She'd had the hardest life of anyone I'd ever known. And when I moved out and left her all alone . . . it must have destroyed her.

The thought struck me like a bolt of lightning. How had I never realized this? Because I had been so consumed with making a better life for myself. I had been so anxious to get out of there, to distance myself from the impoverished existence I'd endured for so long. But my mom couldn't leave. She had no escape, no prospects for a brighter future. All she had was a husband and a daughter who'd left her behind, and years of hardship that had wreaked havoc on her body and soul.

I wasn't making excuses for her decision to end her life, just like I didn't make excuses for mine. But at least now I had somewhat of an understanding *why*. She hadn't left me because she didn't love me enough to stay. She hadn't seen it as leaving me at all. She merely saw it as the only way to escape the endless pain. And unlike me, there was no one there to stop her.

Why was that? I suddenly wondered. *Why had no one been there to stop her? If an angel prevented me from ending my life, why hadn't one prevented her from ending hers?*

The thought wedged itself into my mind, refusing to let me think of anything else.

Why me? Why had Jude saved me? Not only did he save my life, but he stuck around afterward to make sure I was okay. And why had I seen him, when no one to my knowledge had ever seen an angel before? At least, not in my lifetime. It just didn't make sense.

Despite the baffling questions it raised, I couldn't ignore the fact that he was the only reason I was still here. He saved me not just by rescuing me that night, but by being there in the weeks to follow, giving me something to live for. If he hadn't been, there's no telling what would have happened. And maybe he didn't feel the same way about me as I did for him, and maybe he had fractured my heart beyond repair, but I would always love him for giving me a second chance at life.

And what was I doing with that life? Sitting in the dark in a condemned house screaming at my dead mother and crying over the loss of a fairy tale family that I'd never actually had. It made me laugh, a twisted, humorless laugh. How many hours had I spent hurting over the loss of my parents? How many tears had I shed throughout my childhood over my dad's abandonment, his weakness? How many sleepless nights had I spent in agony, haunted by memories of my mother's death that had me screaming in sheer terror? Too many, I realized. Far too many. I had let it consume me, let it define who I was. I was letting it dictate my future—I had come dangerously close to letting it take my future away altogether.

No more, I thought, with a stark realization. No more. I was not going to waste my life away—this life that had miraculously been handed back to me—wallowing in grief and self-pity. I had had my time to mourn. That time was over.

I was done teetering on the edge, threatening to go over at any time. I refused to end up like my mother. I would no longer give my father the power to make me feel unloved and unwanted.

I had been given a second chance, and I wasn't going to lose it.

Suddenly, I was ready to get out of there. This place held nothing for me anymore. I had memories of a mother who loved me so much that she made incredible sacrifices every day to keep me warm and fed and happy. And that was enough.

I stood up and brushed the dirt off my jeans. Taking one last look around the empty room, I turned to leave. As I reached the front door, I heard noises coming from behind me, from the back of the house. I froze, my heart and breath stopping simultaneously. It was footsteps, and they were growing louder. Coming closer.

I was just about to book it out the door when I heard a gruff male voice speak.

"Hello, Olivia."

CHAPTER TWENTY-ONE

I SPUN AROUND TO SEE a homeless man standing at the edge of the room, just inside the hallway. My skin pricked with fear, and I cursed myself silently for being so stupid. What was I thinking coming into a dark, abandoned house alone in the middle of the night?

"Who are you?" I demanded. "How do you know my name?"

I could barely see more than his silhouette in the dappled light, but I could tell that he was definitely a vagrant. Instinctively, I began to step slowly away from him, toward the front door, which stood open only a few feet from me.

The man laughed, only it sounded more like a dog's bark. "No need to be scared. I just want to talk to you."

No need to be scared. Right, I thought as I scanned the room for something to use as a weapon. *Isn't that what they always say right before they make you tomorrow's headlines?*

"Leave me alone!" I shouted. I had tried to disguise the terror I felt when I spoke, but failed miserably. Every part of me was shaking like a leaf, including my voice.

"Olivia, please. I'm not going to hurt you." The man was inching forward now, and I could see greasy black hair under an old, ratty baseball cap. He raised his dirty hands in a defensive gesture. "Really, I just want to talk."

I could feel all the blood drain from my face as he came closer; my heart threatened to pound right out of my chest. "Who are you?" I repeated.

"My name's Hal. I'm a friend of Jude's."

At the sound of Jude's name I froze, all fear suddenly vanishing. "What?"

"Please," Hal said, stepping into the weak beam of light, revealing his face. His skin was dark and had the look of someone who'd had prolonged exposure to the elements. The skin, the hair, the clothes, were all very off-putting, but there was something in his eyes that seemed kind, and they had a familiar depth to them that drew me in. "I'm here to help. There's some things about Jude that I think you should know."

I was so shaken by this sudden change of course that I couldn't think of a response. I glanced over my shoulder at the open door, thinking to escape, but I couldn't bring myself to leave. *He said he was a friend of Jude's.* How was that possible? Did he know about his . . . secret?

I turned back toward Hal. "Go ahead," I said in a tone that warned I was out of there at the first sign of foul play.

"This could take awhile. You want to sit?" He motioned toward the crate I'd just stood up from.

"No, I'll stand," I replied firmly.

He shrugged. "Suit yourself." He walked to the crate and sat down. "Where do I begin?" He said it more to himself than to me. "A month ago Jude came to me needing a favor. I hadn't seen him in . . . well, a while. He was real agitated, out of sorts. He said he needed to borrow my truck. I found it a little strange, but I've never been one to question things. Heaven knows I got my own skeletons. I let him take it, and he brought it back a few hours later. Still no explanation why."

I'm sure my bewilderment at a homeless man having a truck as nice as the one I'd ridden in so many times was apparent, but Hal continued like it was nothing out of the ordinary.

"Then he tells me he needs an apartment. Not just any apartment, but a specific one that may or may not be lived in already." He didn't have to say which one. I knew exactly which apartment he was talking about. "I pulled some strings, got him in there. Not too long after that, he tells me about a girl." Hal raised a finger and pointed in my direction. "You."

I found myself leaning slightly forward, barely breathing, not wanting to miss a single word of what he was saying.

"He tells me that the night before he came to me the first time, he did something. Something bad."

I stopped breathing altogether. Hal pursed his lips in thought, examining my face like he was trying to decide something about me.

"But before I tell you what he did, there's something you gotta know, or you'll never understand." He gave me a funny look then, narrowing his eyes and cocking his head to the side.

"You know, don't you?" It wasn't accusatory, the way he said it. It was more like he was in awe of the idea that maybe I did.

I was completely taken aback. How could he tell? I hesitated, not knowing if I should admit it or not. But then I was nodding. It was almost a relief to share the enormity of the secret with someone else.

Hal studied me for a second more before going on, maybe wondering how in the world I figured it out. Or maybe wondering if I wasn't right in the head to have guessed that about someone, to have ever even considered the possibility.

"Jude is an angel."

Hearing it said out loud, confirming what I'd only suspected, felt like smacking facedown against the surface of a lake from a long way up. "His job is to comfort people during their final hours. Like you."

I could only stare back numbly.

"He comforts them, then escorts them to heaven when it's time. You know how in the movies they always show people walking into the bright light when they die, and there's an angel there to guide them to heaven? That's what Jude's job is. But that's *all* his job is. To give comfort, give peace. But for whatever reason, that night when he was with you, and he saw you take those pills, something happened. He panicked, thinking he couldn't sit there and watch you die. It scared him to death, but it was such a powerful feeling, he acted before even thinking about it. He became visible, instantly severing his contact with heaven, and saved you."

I swayed where I stood, trying to remember how to breathe.

"Once he got you to the hospital and he was left alone, the gravity of what he'd done hit him hard. He was so overcome with guilt and remorse for failing his assignment, for breaking angel law, for going against God . . . that it almost did him in. But he couldn't bring himself to regret saving you."

I couldn't believe what he was saying. It was unbelievable. Did Jude really do that to save me? Could he really have given up a celestial existence because he did save me? It was too incomprehensible to even consider.

"He didn't know what was going to happen to him. No angel had ever done this before. He decided to stay here and try and take responsibility for his actions, made it his goal to watch over you and make sure you were okay. I think he thought that by doing so, he'd maybe somehow make up for what he'd done, that maybe they'd see his efforts and cut him some slack."

My heart sank, although I knew it was a silly reaction. Still, it hurt to think that that was why he'd tried so hard to convince me to let him be around. To redeem himself.

"So now he was here with no money, no job, nowhere to live. He didn't know what he was gonna do and that's when he decided to come find me. He tracked me down and the first thing he asked was to use my truck so he could go see you in the hospital, make sure you were all right. I gave him some money for clothes and stuff, and told him just to keep the truck. It was bound to blow my cover one of these days anyway."

I stood motionless, still in shock. I knew then that nothing would ever surprise me again.

"Then I got him the apartment, and that was that. He started keeping an eye on you, trying to be with you whenever he could, to make sure you really were okay."

Hal didn't start talking again, which was probably a good thing, since I wasn't sure I could handle any more. I was reeling, trying to unscramble this impossible information in my head and straighten it out into something I could understand. I had so many questions, so many things I wanted to say, but the only thing that came out was, "How do you know all this, about . . . angels?" It took considerable effort to get the word out.

"Because," Hal said, leaning back against the grimy wall. "I used to be one."

* * * * *

Jude felt the panic rising as he left Olivia's apartment. It was well past midnight, and she wasn't there. *Where could she be?*

He had just returned home from talking with Hal minutes before and gone straight over to see Olivia. What he planned to say he didn't know; he just needed to see her face. But she wasn't there. Her window was dark, her door was locked, and she wasn't answering.

He tried to think of every possible place she might go. He started with the coffee shop. It was locked up and empty at this hour, of course. Next he went to the pier. Empty. He tried the park, the house on the lake, even checked his own empty apartment, although he tried not to think about the disaster it would be if she was there. She wasn't. He felt no sense of relief though. In fact, the fear that grew each time she wasn't somewhere he looked was starting to suffocate him. He headed back to her building, thinking maybe she just hadn't answered the door. Maybe she was just furious with him for not picking her up from work, for having disappeared since they'd kissed, something he'd regretted severely. At the time, it seemed like the right thing to do—to stay away, not make things any harder for her or more complicated than they needed to be. But mostly, he didn't trust himself to be with her, at least not for a while. Not till he'd figured out what he was going to do. He couldn't be sure he wouldn't do something stupid again, like he'd done the last time he was with her.

But after more than twenty-four hours of not seeing

her, his resolve crumbled. He had to go see her, immediately, and told himself that no matter what he would be strong. He wouldn't even touch her.

Besides, he had some serious explaining to do.

Now, a wave of relief washed over him as he decided that had to be the problem. She was upset with him, that was all. He would go back to her place and if she still didn't answer the door, he would go inside anyway, the way that only he could. He had to know she was okay. He sprinted up the stairs to her apartment and started knocking on her door again, this time much louder.

* * * * *

No one had spoken in several moments. I was stunned into silence, thinking I couldn't possibly handle another shocking revelation. How was anyone supposed to deal with this kind of thing?

Finally, I asked, "What do you mean, *used* to be?"

Hal cleared his throat and I thought he seemed the tiniest bit uncomfortable when he answered, "I got myself kicked out."

I didn't know if I should ask, but I did anyway. "How?"

"Well . . . let's just say I wasn't really cut out for the seraphic life. Made a mistake. Got thrown out. I've been here, living among you mortals, ever since."

"So . . . does that mean you're mortal now?"

Hal shook his head, and I thought I detected a hint of sadness in his voice when he said, "Nah. That's part of my punishment. Not an angel, not a human. Stuck in limbo for eternity."

I didn't know what to say.

Hal laughed then, shaking it off. "Could be worse,

though. Could've wound up down there." He pointed at the floor, and I was horrified when I got his meaning. "You mean, like . . . a *fallen* angel?" Hal nodded. "What's the difference?"

Hal looked like he'd tasted something bitter. "Fallen angels are cast out, forsaken. Doomed to hell. I'm just someone that used to be an angel that's not anymore. I'm pretty much like you and everyone else on this planet except for I'm not mortal. That, and one other thing."

I had to ask. "What's that?"

Hal picked at the dirt under his fingernails. "I'm still compelled to serve, only now . . . I serve the angels." He glanced up at me looking penitent. "I have no contact with 'em when they're up there," he glanced skyward, "but when they're down here, I know it. I can see 'em, talk to 'em, and if they need anything at all . . . I gotta help 'em."

"Is that why you helped Jude?" I asked weakly. Hal nodded, a hint of something in his eyes I didn't understand.

"Is that why you're here telling me all of this? Because it will help Jude?"

"Yeah. That"—he shrugged — "and other reasons. Jude doesn't have it in him to tell you the truth, 'cause he knows what it would do to you, or did to you . . ." His words faded as something hit him. "You already knew. How did you know?"

I shrugged now, still trying to understand it myself. "I figured it out, as crazy as that seems. I just put some things together that didn't add up, and it seemed like the only logical explanation, as utterly illogical as it is."

"Huh." Hal was nodding slowly in amazement.

We were both lost in thought for a time until something came to me. "How did you know where to find me?"

"I didn't." He looked around, then back at me. "I live here."

My eyes narrowed. *Impossible.* "What?"

He raised his right hand and put his left hand over his heart. "I swear it. You came to me."

Suddenly I did need to sit down. I reached back, feeling for the wall for some support. Hal jumped up suddenly and disappeared toward the back of the house, returning moments later with a second crate. He planted it upside down not far from where I was standing.

"Thanks," I said, slumping down onto it. Then, still in disbelief, asked "You live here?" I eyed the less-than-stellar conditions of the room we were in.

Hal shrugged. "My name's not on the lease or anything, but I call it home. It's a nice place to get out of the cold and rain after a long day of begging." He smiled. "No one else comes in here. I think they sense a dark spirit lurking inside." He winked at me, and I expelled one short burst of a laugh, more out of incredulity than anything else.

"This used to be my house," I told him. "A long time ago. I lived here with my parents until I was five." I gazed at Hal in wonder. "What are the chances?"

"Slim to none," he replied. Then, "It's not as coincidental as you think. Everything happens for a reason."

I was beginning to see that.

We sat in silence until I remembered something Hal had said and an upsetting thought came to me. "What's going to happen to Jude?"

Hal's voice was bleak. "I don't rightly know."

I suddenly felt like I was going to be sick. How could I live with myself if Jude faced some horrible punishment for saving my life? Or worse, if he was stripped of his divine role and cast out of heaven forever? Hal's words echoed in my head, sending an icy cold chill down my spine: *doomed to hell.* I couldn't handle the thought, and I didn't know what was more unbearable; that, or the knowledge that the man I loved didn't belong in my world, and would have to leave me eventually.

I stood up quickly. "I have to find Jude. I have to talk to him." *And see him again, and touch him again.* "Do you know where he is?"

Hal shrugged his shoulders. "If I had to guess, I'd say home?" I didn't mention that I'd already been there and he wasn't there. Maybe he was now.

"Thank you, Hal, for telling me this. You were right. I needed to hear it, as unbelievable as it all is."

I turned to leave, but Hal jumped off his crate. "Where do you think you're going?"

"To find Jude," I said, confused. Hadn't I just said that?

"Not all alone at this hour in this neighborhood you aren't. I'll take you there."

"Thanks, Hal." I said, feeling an unlikely bit of affection for this haggard, ostracized being. We exited the house, Hal following behind me. When I got to the sidewalk, I started to turn around to take one last look at my childhood home. But just before I did, I made a last-second decision and kept going without looking back.

CHAPTER TWEN

HAL WALKED ME ALL the way to Jude's doo parting ways, I said, "Hal, thank you. Fo ing Jude, even if was out of obligation, and for tellin everything, even if it was a bit . . . jarring to hear."

"You're welcome. And, Olivia, just know that wheteve punishment Jude's in for, he'd suffer it twice for you."

My heart spasmed and I could do nothing but nod in response, instantly choked up. Hal gave me a little bow, then disappeared around a corner, no doubt taking the stairs instead of the elevator to avoid people staring and whispering, wondering what a filthy homeless man was doing in their building.

I steadied myself before entering Jude's apartment. Knocking seemed a little superfluous now, so I turned the handle and walked in. When I saw it was still pitch black, I was overcome with dread. *Where was he?* I was just starting to panic when I glanced at the window and noticed across the way that mine was lit up. There was a light on inside. Someone was there.

ttered in my stomach as I turned and ran out of down the hall, down the elevator, out the front up the stairs to my apartment. I didn't pause at just threw it open and rushed inside.

there he was. Sitting on my couch, looking like d-over death. It stopped me cold in my tracks. When ked up and saw me, I could see the worry and despair avaged his beautiful face, and it made me want to cry.

Hi," I said softly.

"Hi." His voice was rough, the word chopped up into o syllables.

We stared at each other for a long time, neither one aying a word.

Jude was the one to eventually break the silence.

"I've been all over the city trying to find you." I could read on his face and hear in his voice what he didn't say: that he'd been worried out of his mind.

My forehead creased with guilt. "I went to see my old house."

Jude looked bewildered. It wasn't until I said it out loud that I heard how crazy it sounded. It was a crazy thing to do. But I was crazy, at the time.

"And . . . I ran into a friend of yours." He raised his eyebrows. "Hal," I clarified, in case he had another friend running around that I didn't know about.

I watched as understanding crossed his face, and his eyes widened in horror.

"It's okay, it's okay," I assured him, before he could freak out too badly. "I already knew. I figured it out on my own."

Jude's expression would have been comical in any other situation, but I found no humor in it now. "*H-how?*" he stammered.

"I went to your apartment." Before the words were even

out of my mouth, Jude's eyes had closed and he was shaking his head, most likely picturing my reaction to seeing the empty place that he obviously didn't live in. I crossed the room and sat down beside him, grabbing his chin and forcing him to look at me. "Don't," I said firmly. "Please listen to me first."

He opened his eyes and looked at me, and I could feel the shame emitting from them.

"After that I started thinking about things, things that had never added up with you. I began putting them together, and when I did, the answer was right there, staring me in the face. I fought against it at first, obviously, but after hours and hours of thought I knew it was the only explanation. Obviously, it was a little disconcerting." *To put it mildly.* "I went into a bit of a shock, and started wandering the streets." Jude's face clouded over, and I quickly shook my head to remind him this wasn't the part to focus on. "I ended up on a bus that took me to my old house, the house I lived in when my dad left. It was empty—abandoned—so I went inside. And that was where I met Hal."

Jude's eyes widened in astonishment. Evidently it seemed just as unlikely to him that Hal would be living in my childhood home.

"He explained everything, including what happened that night. He told me about what you did in order to save me." I shook my head in wonder, thinking again at what he'd possibly given up for me. "I can't believe you did that."

"I had to." He reached out and laid his hand against my cheek. "I couldn't let you die."

All I wanted to do then was kiss him, feel his arms around me again, but I needed to know first. "Why, though? Why did you save me? Why me out of the countless people you watched die?"

He pulled his hand away, staring out at something unseen, in the general direction of my bed. "All the other ones . . . it wasn't hard for me. It wasn't my job to interfere. I was just supposed to be there with them through the end. I let it happen, because I was supposed to, that was my job. And I was okay with that. Until . . ." He turned back toward me, his eyes blazing green. ". . . you."

A tingle ran through my skin.

"I didn't know, at the time, what was different. I didn't understand it, tried not to think about it afterward. All I know is that when I saw you swallow those pills, something in me snapped, and the thought of sitting there watching you die was suddenly unthinkable. I had never felt such fear before, in all my time of doing this. And I just . . . acted. I didn't even think about it. It was like my body just moved on its own. I never thought about what it would mean, what I'd be giving up, or bringing upon myself. I didn't care about any of that at the time. All I cared about was keeping you alive. I didn't know why, and I wouldn't let myself think about it afterward because I knew if I did, I'd have to admit that the real reason I'd saved you was because I already felt something for you. It doesn't make sense, does it? One, I barely knew you. And two, saving you didn't mean I could be with you. But for some reason, I did it anyway."

I felt a little flushed listening to his account of what happened. To hear that even back then, when I didn't even know he existed yet, he felt something for me. My insides were burning, like someone had ignited a spark in my stomach and the heat from the growing flames was spreading throughout the rest of me.

"And that's why you kept coming around, even after?" I asked softly.

Jude nodded. "Again, I told myself it was only because

I had to make sure you were really okay, or that maybe by continuing to watch over you, I would somehow fulfill even a fraction of my assignment. But deep down I knew why." He grabbed my hand and began stroking the back of it with his thumb. "It wasn't long before denying it was useless. The draw to you got stronger and stronger, like I was being magnetically pulled in your direction. I fought it for a long time, wanting to do right, to be good, to not shame myself any further. But especially to avoid hurting you.

"It was the hardest thing I have ever done. Do you know how many times I had to force myself to walk away so that I wouldn't kiss you, or even touch you? Or how hard it was to have to lie to you constantly because I couldn't tell you the truth? It was agonizing, and it only got harder every day that we were together, the closer we became. And the worst part was knowing that just by being around you, just by forming even so much as a friendship with you, I was setting you up for unavoidable pain in the future. Once I realized that it went beyond that, that you felt something for me, too . . ." He didn't finish the sentence, as if he couldn't find the words. "I couldn't think of a way out, and I hated myself for my weakness, for not being strong enough to stay away in the beginning before you made any kind of attachment to me."

"Don't say that," I said, frowning. "Do you know where I'd be if you *had* stayed away?" He didn't answer, but I knew he knew. "You may as well have not even saved me, because I would have been right back there within days—I guarantee it. You are the only thing that kept me going. *You* gave me a reason to live."

Jude's face softened a bit, and it gave me hope that maybe he believed what I was saying, that he would realize what he'd done wasn't a mistake.

"And maybe we can never be together," I went on, my voice breaking. "But because of you, I'm strong enough to keep going on my own." I hated saying those last three words, hated it with every fiber of my being. I hated thinking of going on with my life alone, without Jude, but I was telling the truth when I said I could do it. I needed him to know that. That I wouldn't go back to the person he'd met. That I would be okay.

Tears spilled over onto my cheeks. It hurt so much to even think about. But more than that, the thought of the punishment that awaited him was excruciating.

Jude looked harrowed as he reached up and wiped the tears from each of my eyes. I realized he'd never seen me cry before. I fell forward into his chest, my tears soaking into his shirt, and he wrapped his arms tightly around me. Why couldn't I stay here in his arms forever? It was the only place I felt safe and calm and happy. In the perfect protective space it created, nothing could get to me, and nothing could hurt me. I laid my head in the little nook just above his collarbone that had to have been made for that purpose. I smelled the skin of his neck, drank it in deeply in huge, gulping breaths, trying to memorize it. It was unnecessary; I knew I couldn't forget that smell if I tried, not in a million years.

"Liv," he whispered, stroking my hair. "I love you."

I didn't move, didn't speak. I didn't want to disturb the echo of his words resounding in my head, over and over again. Never before had three words sounded so heartbreakingly beautiful. Jude's deep, humming voice made each word sound like notes in a melodic symphony.

I lifted my head and kissed his neck, then stretched up to whisper in his ear. "I love *you*."

Jude turned his head so our lips met, and he kissed me

in a way that made my bones turn liquid. His hands slid along my jaw to the back of my neck. I instantly went limp, relishing every second. He moved his lips to my cheeks, my nose, my eyelids, making his way back down to my lips, my chin, my neck just below my ear. A deep, shaky breath escaped from my mouth, much louder than I would have liked. Jude stopped moving. I could feel his lips spread into a smile, could hear a short, silent laugh that was more an exhale than anything. The burst of warm breath on my ear sent a shiver down my spine. He pulled away then, coming face-to-face with me, all traces of the smile gone. His eyes bore into mine with a feverish glow. I was pretty sure I'd never regain the use of my muscles again.

He dipped his head just enough to lightly brush his lips on mine one last time, never breaking eye contact. My heart felt like it was going to explode. He had to have heard it beating out of control.

He pulled me into his chest, wrapping his arms around me again, and for the first time I noticed the absence of a heartbeat in his chest. How had I never caught such a glaring omission before? The room was completely quiet except for my racing heart struggling to return to its normal rate.

"So . . ." I said quietly, after a bit. "You're an angel."

"I'm an angel," he repeated.

I didn't know if I would ever get used to the idea. "You're actually a celestial being from heaven."

Jude laughed. "Well, when you put it that way, it just sounds weird."

"Is there any way to put it that doesn't sound weird?"

He thought about it. "No, I guess not."

"I just can't believe that this whole time you've been . . . and I never had a clue. Well, I had lots of clues, but I just couldn't figure out what they meant."

Jude shifted, pulling me away from him so he could look at me. "What clues? How did you figure it out?"

"Remember the first time we went out? When I invited you to dinner so I could ask you a few things? One was how you got into my apartment when I was pretty sure it was locked, and the other was why you told the hospital staff that me overdosing was an accident. I knew you had to have lied to them, that you couldn't really have believed it was an accident." My eyes narrowed. "Why *did* you lie about it?"

Jude shook his head. "You have to finish answering my question first. What other clues?"

I frowned but kept going. "Anyway, that was when I knew something was off. Then when you were so maddeningly mysterious and wouldn't answer any of my questions, I grew more suspicious. But it wasn't until I went to your apartment and found it totally empty that I started thinking about everything and remembering things about . . . that night that I'd completely forgotten. Like that I positively *had* locked my door and that I heard you saying my name as I was blacking out, when we had never met before."

I could tell by Jude's reaction that he'd never thought of that—that by calling my name that night he was incriminating himself. Or maybe he had just thought I was more unconscious than I really was by the time he got to me.

"I saw you too," I said, watching his face grow increasingly incredulous. "You were the last thing I remembered before passing out completely. I thought at the time that you were an angel, come to take me to heaven." *Wow,* I thought. *I had actually been right.*

"So I was realizing all these things and then I saw the angel figurine you gave me, and that's when it clicked." I cocked my head to the side in thought. "Was that your way of trying to tell me?"

Jude looked a little sheepish. "I guess, in a *very* roundabout way. I never in a million years thought it would lead to you figuring it out, but I guess I felt like if I gave you even the tiniest heads up, that maybe hearing the truth wouldn't be a complete blow."

"Hmmm . . . that was thoughtful, but . . . no. It still was."

Jude laughed, raising his arms in a shrug. "I tried." Then, wanting me to go on, he asked, "So you figured out the angel thing, and that was that? You didn't think it could be anything else?"

"The evidence was too overwhelming. Somehow you knew my name before we'd ever met, and somehow you got into my apartment without going through the door, which was locked, and the window, which doesn't open. You were either an angel or a ghost, and I went with the one I could handle."

"And then you freaked out?" Jude asked softly.

"Yeah," I admitted. "I did. I went into shock. But it was that shock that led me to my old house, which led me to Hal, who explained things I needed to hear in order to be okay with it."

Jude shook his head in amazement. "I am really never going to be able to repay that guy."

"I don't think he's looking for any kind of compensation," I said, yawning.

Jude noticed and glanced at the clock. "It's three thirty! You need to go to bed."

He started to stand up and I grabbed his hand, instantly panicked. Knowing now that our time together was limited and having no idea how long we had, I couldn't bear to let him go.

"Stay," I pleaded. "Don't go."

Jude looked pained. "I would love to, but I don't know if . . ."

"Please," I begged, gripping tighter. "Just hold me while I sleep."

He contemplated it.

"Okay," he agreed. "I'll stay."

CHAPTER TWENTY-THREE

I WOKE UP TO A FULLY sunlit room late in the morning. The first thing I noticed was the arm draped heavily over me and the face nuzzled into the back of my neck. Sleeping with Jude there beside me had been the most peaceful, dreamless sleep I'd ever experienced without an IV stuck in my arm.

I could feel his breath now in my hair, tickling my neck. He was asleep. The realization was surprising; why would he be sleeping? His nonhuman body wouldn't require it. I remembered back to the first time he'd stayed with me all night. I'd seen him sleep then too. And eating. I'd seen him do it dozens of times. It didn't make sense. I sighed. I'd thought the mysteries were over.

I slowly tried to flip around so I could see him without disturbing him. But it didn't work; his eyes opened, and he reflexively lifted his arm, allowing me to roll over. When we were face-to-face and I saw that he looked exactly the same as he did hours earlier—like a painting—I quickly ducked my head and buried it under his chin before he could get a good look at me in all my human imperfection. I felt him kiss the top of my head. "Good morning," he murmured.

"Good morning," I said into his shirt.

"No nightmares," he pointed out.

"I know. It's because of you. I've never slept so well in my life."

My comment reminded me of the things I'd been wondering about moments earlier.

"Speaking of sleeping, why *do* you?"

"I *can* sleep. I don't need to."

"And eating? Same thing?"

"Yeah."

I thought for a minute about his answers, letting my mind adjust. My next question came out not much louder than a whisper. "You're immortal?"

He didn't answer at first. Then quietly, he said, "Yes."

My heart seemed to skip a beat, but I willed myself to relax. "Are you just . . . a spirit then?" He sure didn't feel like just a spirit now, with my head pressed up against his hard chest, his muscled arms holding me to him.

"No," Jude answered, pulling me away from him so he could look at me. I tried my hardest not to turn away, to look him square in the eyes and pretend I wasn't feeling horribly self-conscious. "I have a body. Just not a mortal one."

I scowled. "Angels have bodies?" That certainly went against everything I'd ever heard.

"Some of us do."

"Hmmm . . ." Suddenly I thought of something. "Where are your wings?"

Jude laughed, his dimples popping out of nowhere. "The thing most associated with angels is also the biggest myth. We don't have wings. No halos, either. Sorry to disappoint you," he said, seeing my face.

"No," I corrected quickly. "I'm not disappointed, just shocked. How did we get it so wrong?"

Jude shrugged. "I guess the world took the few things they did know, and it just evolved from there. The aura of light angels emit became a gold ring around their head. Their ability to travel between heaven and earth in the blink of an eye became flying, which led to wings. That's just my theory."

I raised my eyebrows in question. "You can't fly?"

Jude smiled and shook his head.

So much to absorb. My mind felt like it was spinning out of control. Suddenly I froze as another thought came to me. "You can't read my mind, can you?"

Jude laughed again, harder this time. "No! No superpowers. Well, except for the invisibility thing. And the traveling through space and time thing. Okay, a couple superpowers."

"The invisibility thing . . ." I echoed. I suddenly had a panicked thought. "Do you still do that? Around me, when I don't *know*?"

Jude's face fell. "No. I can't anymore. Not since . . . I showed myself to you."

"But before—"

Jude was already shaking his head. "Don't worry. It's not like that. I never saw anything I shouldn't have. I was completely honorable."

Still, the thought was . . . disconcerting. "So, you lost one of your . . . superpowers?"

Jude smiled. "I guess so. I don't know why. I just couldn't do it anymore after that night." I saw a sadness behind the smile that told me it bothered him.

"What about . . . traveling?"

"Yeah. For some reason, that I still have."

We stared at each other in silence.

"Wow," I said finally. "I just can't . . . it's just . . . crazy, you know?"

"I know," he said, squeezing my hand. "And you're handling it amazingly well, much better than I ever imagined."

"Hal told me you couldn't ever bring yourself to tell me, afraid of how I'd react.

"I tried to, several times, and chickened out every time. I thought for sure you would . . . not take it well." He glanced down at the bed when he said that, and I had the feeling he'd changed what he was going to say at the last minute.

"You thought I would go psycho again and do something stupid?"

Jude's face gave me my answer. He looked ashamed. "I should have given you more credit. I knew how far you'd come since then, but I guess I didn't really know just how far until now."

I couldn't help but feel a sense of pride to hear him say that.

"But why would you tell me?" I asked, miffed.

"Because, I knew I would eventually have to. We'd gotten so close, we were together all the time. I knew it couldn't last, that one day I would have to come clean. I couldn't just continue on, letting you get closer and closer to someone who would have to . . ." He trailed off, but I knew what he was going to say: *someone who would have to leave.* The reminder that this was only temporary, that at some point in the very near future we would have to say our final good-byes, brought me crashing back down to reality, and I couldn't keep my face from falling. It was a monumental feat that I kept from crying.

Jude looked as depressed as I felt. Neither of us said anything. What was there to say? We both knew what was coming, and that there was nothing either of us could do about it.

After a while I decided I didn't want to waste any of our time together in silence. "Keep talking," I said, propping myself up on one elbow. I was finally, *finally* getting the answers I'd wanted for so long now. "Tell me more."

"What do you want to know?" Jude asked, reaching out and stroking my cheek.

I tried to think of all the things I'd asked him that he never gave me a real answer to, but almost everything I could think of was suddenly irrelevant.

"What kind of angel are you? I mean, I know you're a comforting angel, Hal told me, but . . . have you already lived a life here and . . . *died*?" The word sounded weird coming out of my mouth. "Or . . . have you not even been born yet?" I tried to hide how unsettling I thought either possibility was.

"Neither," Jude said, to my surprise (and relief). "I was stillborn."

I knew my eyes were huge, but I couldn't help it. "When?" I breathed.

He hesitated, watching me closely. "Twenty-two years ago."

My brain was slow to catch on to his words. When I began to apprehend what they meant, I inhaled sharply. "That recently? That was only two years before I was born! You would actually be twenty-two?" This fact was so astonishing to believe, yet somehow it put me more at ease, to learn that Jude wasn't born three hundred years earlier or something. It made him seem almost . . . human.

He continued to study my face, I'm sure just waiting for

me to start freaking out at any minute. I swallowed, telling myself this wasn't any crazier than learning he was an angel. And yet . . . it was. To think of us having missed each other on earth by a mere two years was staggering.

"My parents were Erik and Lydia West," he continued slowly. "I was—would have been—their third child. They had two sons already, Paul and Luke. My mom was seven months pregnant with me when their car was hit by a drunk driver. They were all in the car, and they all died on impact except for Paul, who died in the hospital the next day. The medics tried to save me, but I never took a breath."

I listened, fully engrossed in the story of Jude's life that came and went in the blink of an eye. I pictured the tragic scene, playing out in my head like an episode from one of those medical drama shows. Except that it wasn't scripted, and it wasn't actors covered in red dye and corn syrup. It was Jude and his family. And it had really happened.

"My grandparents—my mom's parents—were left to name and bury me. I told you I was named after St. Jude. That was true. Jude was the patron saint of lost causes. They knew my mom had named her other sons after saints and had wanted to do the same with me, and they thought Jude was fitting because I'd never had a chance—I was a lost cause. Or so they thought. Because I had technically come to earth, but hadn't actually lived a life here, I was made an angel. A comforting angel, like Hal said, but more specifically, a comforting angel for lost causes." He looked apologetic as he said it, probably knowing I would make the connection to myself. That I had been a lost cause, and that's why he was sent to me. "I've never known if my grandparents were somehow inspired in choosing my name, or if my role in heaven came because of the name I'd been given on earth." He shrugged.

I was in complete awe. "Are you with them, your

family? When you're in . . . heaven?" It was still so unreal to think about, let alone say out loud.

He shook his head. "No. Spirits and angels are separated. We're all there, just . . . not together." He made a face that was half awkwardness, half frustration. "I can't really explain it." *So he wouldn't know if my mom was there or not,* I pondered. It was something I hadn't even thought of until now.

"Is that hard for you? To know that they're up there too, but you can't be with them?"

He thought about his answer. "No. I never knew them. Sometimes I wish I could meet them, see what they're like, but . . ." He shrugged again. I tried to picture it, Jude's family walking around up there. I wondered what they looked like, if any of them had his green eyes and dimples.

"What about your grandparents? Are they still . . . around?"

"No. They were old even back then. They've since passed on."

"And your other grandparents?"

"My dad's mom died when he was young, and he and his dad had some big falling out when he was seventeen. He left home and never spoke to him again."

"So you have no family left here at all?"

"I think I have some aunts and uncles on my dad's side, maybe some cousins. But I have no idea where." I could tell from his tone that he felt no ties to the relatives he'd left behind. I thought of something then, something that felt horribly morbid to even think about, but that I still felt compelled to ask.

"Where are you buried?"

Jude shifted on the bed. "Nevada."

We both fell silent, neither one sure what to follow that

with. Finally, I thought of another question that wasn't so grim.

"So, you said you were made a comforting angel. Are there other kinds, like guardian angels?"

Jude nodded, seemingly relieved at the shift toward a lighter conversation. "Yeah, and messengers. All with the purpose of serving the living on earth."

"What was Hal?" I asked, remembering what he'd told me at the house about serving the angels now.

Jude took a deep breath. "Hal was a guardian. Not a very good one."

"Why?" I asked. "What happened?"

"I don't know exactly," Jude answered. "Those kinds of things aren't . . . general knowledge. I only know that he failed an assignment."

"So he got . . . cast out?" I asked, completely absorbed in Jude's words.

"Sort of, but not really. More like . . . kicked out. He wasn't . . . damned or anything. Just stripped of his title and sent here. Kind of the difference between being executed for a crime and being fired for not doing your job."

I nodded, then frowned in thought. "How does he have such a nice truck?"

Jude laughed, and my chest ached thinking how much I would miss that sound. "Hal's made a small fortune conning people out of their money. He used to live like everyone else—had a house, a job, all of it. But when he realized he could make just as much money standing on a street corner holding a piece of cardboard, he quit his job and sold his house. He couldn't part with the truck, though." Jude smiled. "It was his baby."

"Till you came along."

"Right."

"So if it wasn't his house on the lake, who's was it?"

Jude looked mildly uncomfortable. "I don't know. Some rich friend's of his that's never there. Hal swore he'd be fine with us being there."

I felt a little weird knowing I had been in a complete stranger's house without them knowing it.

Silence fell between us again, and for a moment I savored just staring into the emeralds that were staring back at me, listening to him breathe. He was stroking each of my fingers, one at a time, and it was all lulling me into a relaxed stupor.

"Tell me about that night," I said, laying my head back on my pillow and closing my eyes.

Jude didn't answer right away, and I opened my eyes again. "Are you sure you want to hear it?" he asked quietly. I nodded. His expression was tortured, and it occurred to me for the first time that reliving that night would be just as painful for him as it would be for me.

He sighed and began speaking. "I had been with you for a while, going wherever you went, giving you whatever you needed in the way of comfort. Then, that night, it was especially bad for you, as you know. I tried my best to comfort you but I just didn't seem to be doing anything. And then . . ." he paused, and I knew he didn't want to say it, ". . . then you swallowed the pills and, I don't know, something just felt like it exploded inside of me. I suddenly couldn't bear it. I'd never felt so terrified, so panicked. Everything in me was screaming to save you. I wanted you to live. I *needed* you to live.

"So, I saved you. I became visible, picked you up, and took you to the hospital, where I had to tell them I'd seen you through my window. It was the only believable explanation I could think of."

The way he shifted when he said he took me to the hospital made something click in my head. "Did you . . . *teleport* with me?" I asked, using the only word I could think of to describe it.

"Yes, although we don't call it that." I tried to remember, strained to see if anything between blacking out and the hospital would come back to me. I was disappointed that nothing did. What would it have been like, leaving one place in Jude's arms only to appear the same instant in another, miles away? My brain couldn't even begin to fathom it.

"Once they took you from me and I was left alone, the realization of what I had done and the possible ramifications hit me hard. I had no idea what was going to happen to me, I couldn't even think about it. I was falling apart at the seams, but somehow, I was inexplicably more worried about you than me. All I could think about was if you were okay.

"When they came and told me you were going to be fine, I almost collapsed with relief. You were safe, and it hadn't all been in vain. I vowed to do whatever it took to continue my assignment, even though it would be incredibly difficult now that I couldn't be with you, unseen, at all times."

This reminded me of the question I'd asked the night before that he'd never answered. "Why did you lie and tell them it was an accident?" I cut in.

Jude shook his head. "I don't know why I did. I guess in some stupid way I thought I was protecting you, like if I told them the truth I was ratting you out. But in hindsight, I'm so glad I did. If they knew the truth, they would have forced you into therapy and I don't think it would have done you any good, with the mind-set you had at the time.

I think you needed to decide on your own to get help, like you did."

Finally, an answer to the question that had plagued me from the day we met. "And you called my work, didn't you?"

He looked sheepish again. "I said I was your brother, and that you'd had an accident and needed time off to recover. I knew that no one there knew anything about your family and they wouldn't question the brother thing. I tried to be as vague as possible. I didn't want them knowing what happened, but some of them might have guessed, based on your . . . emotional state leading up to it." He looked like he felt bad having to say the words. But I was well past feeling embarrassed about The Incident in front of Jude.

"So then what?" I urged.

"Then . . . I had no idea what I was going to do. I had no money, no car, nowhere to live, nothing. But then I thought of Hal." He paused. "Almost all demoted angels end up in big cities where it's easier to blend in. I know there are others here in Seattle, but Hal I actually knew, before he left. So I tracked him down, found him living in squalor. He was quick to tell me about his secret stash of money, though. I had forgotten that part of his being banished was that he had to serve us angels when we needed it, and, boy, am I ever grateful for it now. Besides his truck, he gave me money for clothes and whatever else I might need, and he got me the apartment so that I could still keep an eye on you, make sure you were okay."

"But you never lived there," I clarified.

"Right. Not if you consider living to be eating and sleeping there. But I did spend a fair amount of time hanging out there, looking out the window. So, anyway, that's what I did. I watched you when you were home and tried to be with you when you weren't, which wasn't easy to do without making it look like I was stalking you."

"So . . . the time you 'just happened' to show up to see if I wanted to go for a walk right when I was headed out . . ."

"I saw you through the window getting up to leave, so I came over. More so for the fact that it was late at night and there was no way I was going to let you roam the streets alone."

"How did you—I had a blanket over my window!"

Jude smiled, looking guilty. "It was a thin blanket, love."

And I was the idiot who thought it was such a coincidence.

"I thought I was doing a pretty good job of fulfilling my assignment," he continued. But then . . . things started to get complicated." He gazed at me, brushing his fingers against my bottom lip. "I started to fall for you. It scared me so bad. I'd never felt that before, and I didn't know what to do with it. I knew it was wrong, but I couldn't seem to fight it, and every time I was with you it just got harder and harder to stay strong.

"That night in the rain, and then again when I picked you up for dinner, and helped you with the necklace . . ." Jude shook his head, remembering. "Not kissing you was the hardest thing I have ever done. It took every ounce of willpower in me to walk away, both times. And then when you were so upset about seeing Ashley and trying to convince me that you hadn't got any better since your . . . since that night . . ." He paused, remembering. "You were looking at me, your face so innocent and pure and beautiful . . . my will finally crumbled. Or maybe I just didn't want to fight it anymore." He leaned forward and kissed me then, a soft, lingering kiss that sent electric currents down to my toes.

When he pulled away, a lump formed in my throat and

before I could stop them, the tears started flowing. "How am I ever going to be able to tell you good-bye?"

Jude didn't answer me, but his eyes, which had turned to a liquid jade, said it all. I reached out and pulled him closer. We lay there together, neither one saying what we knew we were both thinking.

Beneath my broken heart lurked something equally upsetting: the fear of the unknown—what lay in store for Jude. I tried my hardest not to think about it, but it kept creeping to the surface. I went back and forth between the two, like each impending misery was fighting for a front-row seat in my head. Somewhere in there a question formed, one I didn't want to ask but had to know the answer to.

"Jude."

"Hmm?"

"How long do we have?"

I felt his body tense beside me, heard him struggle to keep his voice even when he answered.

"I don't know."

CHAPTER TWENTY-FOUR

I HAD SEVERAL HOURS BEFORE I had to be at work, and we were perfectly content spending them right where we were, nestled together on my bed. Even though this new dynamic in our relationship had only developed less than forty-eight hours earlier, lying there with Jude and talking about his life as an angel and all that it entailed seemed completely natural, like we'd done it our whole lives.

The lies and secrets gone, along with the restrained feelings, finally allowed us to be what we'd both wanted to be for a while now: truly, honestly together. Being able to reach over and touch Jude's face like I'd wanted to so intensely before was wonderful. Having him lean in to kiss me whenever he felt like it was indescribable. Talking, kissing, holding each other, talking some more—this was the happiness I'd always dreamed existed but had never known. Lying there next to Jude made my once cold, lonely apartment feel like a home.

We talked about so many things. There wasn't much we didn't cover. I told him stories of my childhood, first the things I remembered of my family when it was still intact (which were few), and then life with just my mom. I told him of the happy times, pulling out the rosewood box and showing him each item inside and its correlating story—the ones I knew, at least. And I told him of the not-so-happy times: the cold, the hunger, the loneliness. I recounted my high school experience, flipping through my photo album that was a little worse for wear after it'd been chucked across the room weeks earlier. I told him stories of Ashley and some about other friends. Formal dances, sports events, my favorite teachers, my least favorite teachers . . . I told him in detail about moving out on my own, getting the waitressing job, and my downward spiral after my mom's death.

Jude listened intently, hanging onto my every word. It had seemed that in the whole time we'd known each other, all we'd ever talked about was me. But now, giving him a rundown of my life, I realized how much he still hadn't known.

After hours of talking I realized I was starving, so I got up to get something to eat. Jude followed me into the kitchen and watched in silence as I poured myself a bowl of cereal. When I sat down at the table, I hesitated. "Do you want some?" I asked, suddenly feeling awkward. I didn't know if I should offer or not, but I figured it was better to ask.

Jude pulled out the chair across from me and sat down. "No, that's okay," he said, smiling. "I'm good."

It was a little nerve-wracking sitting there eating with him watching me, so I quickly thought of something to ask him, to get him talking.

"Tell me about heaven. What's it like?"

It seemed to catch him off guard. "Uh . . . what's it *like*?" He shifted in his chair. "It's hard to say. There's so much that can't be described in words, or even if I could find the words, you wouldn't be able to understand."

"So tell me the things you think I would understand," I said between bites.

He let out a whoosh of breath before beginning. "It's . . . beautiful. Like nothing you've ever seen before, or can even imagine. And the perception people have of us walking around on clouds playing harps all day is incredibly false."

I laughed, almost choking on a mouthful of cereal.

"There are buildings, gorgeous buildings, and the streets are made of gold. It's very bright, always. It's nothing like it is here, which I'm sure you could guess. There's no sickness, no pain, no anger, sadness, jealousy. No fighting. Everything is peaceful and laid back and you feel content all the time. More than content. Joyous. It's just a general atmosphere of service, making someone's life better. When that's the common goal, everyone just works together to make that happen."

I stopped chewing, trying to imagine such a place. I thought of my world, where people were killing each other every day and war raged through devastated countries. Cancer and other horrible diseases plaguing our bodies and hardly a soul that could go a single day without saying something negative about—or to—another person. Our worlds were at complete opposite ends of the spectrum.

"And time . . . time is different there. Whole lifetimes can go by down here without a single second passing up there." I had set down my spoon at this point, my breakfast forgotten. "And when I say up, you know I don't really mean *up*, right? It's not up in the sky."

I had to think about that one. I guess maybe I had always thought it was. I was trying to think of some way of answering without revealing my ignorance when Jude continued. "It's just . . . somewhere else, like another dimension, I guess you could say."

I nodded slowly. I could sort of understand that, now that he put it that way.

"What else?" I asked, intrigued.

"Well," he thought. "It's huge. Infinite. Impossible to see it all. But no matter where you go, you always feel the presence of God." He said it with a hushed reverence I'd never seen him use before. It gave me chills.

"Have you . . . *seen* Him?" I asked dubiously.

Jude nodded. I got the sudden feeling he didn't want to say more on the subject, so I moved on.

"So, if all this is really true, if there are angels and God and heaven, does that mean there's really a devil? And . . . hell?" I was immediately unsure I wanted to hear the answer.

"Yes, there is," Jude responded, a shadow passing over his face. "He is very real, as are his angels."

I sucked in a sharp breath. "The devil has angels?"

"Unfortunately, yes. You've heard of fallen angels?"

I nodded, a cold tingling sensation spreading across the surface of my skin and raising the hairs on the back of my neck.

"They're the spirits that followed Satan out of heaven when he was cast out. They reside here on earth, permanently." Jude's voice had an edge to it now. "Every bad thing that happens here—every crime, sin, negative feeling, whatever—is them. You can't see them, but trust me. They're here, working their evil on everyone, trying to get as many as possible over to their side." Jude's eyes drifted away, as if he'd gone somewhere else mentally. "Sometimes I think they're winning," he said quietly, as if to himself.

Then he looked back at me, like he suddenly remembered he'd been answering my question.

I was motionless, staring back at him horrified. He saw my face and winced. "Maybe I said more than I needed to."

"No, it's . . . it's fine. I want to know the truth." The second part was true, but the first part was an outright lie. It wasn't fine. I wasn't fine. I was the opposite of fine, but I didn't want Jude to know that. I didn't want him to regret telling me or use it as a reason to not tell me things in the future because of it. *The future,* I thought with an anxious dread in my stomach. However long that might be.

"Can you see them?" I whispered.

"*I* can. You can't; no one else can."

"What do they look like?"

"Just like everyone else. That's the worst part. They're masters of deception. You'd never know by looking at them what evil lies inside."

Despite Jude's words, I felt a modicum of comfort knowing they didn't look like hideous creatures, like I'd read about in Dante's *Inferno* in my high school English class. I shuddered at the thought.

A heavy silence followed, which Jude broke by saying, "Ready to move on to a happier topic?"

"Yes," I agreed quickly. "Like what?"

"Like . . . how beautiful you are in the morning." He stood up from the table, walked around it to me, and grabbed my hands, pulling me up out of my chair. He wrapped his arms around my waist, resting his hands on the small of my back.

I smiled shyly, my cheeks burning self-consciously. "Yeah, I'm sure I look hot in my tank top and faded pajama bottoms."

"You do," he whispered, lifting my chin with his

fingertips. I looked up and met his eyes, which instantly locked into mine. For a long moment we stood staring at each other, our faces inches apart, and my heart was so heavy it felt like it would drop right through me. Knowing that sometime in the near future I would have to say good-bye to that face and never see it again. And worse, picturing it in pain as Jude endured some horrible punishment for what he did. For me. It was almost more than I could bear.

* * * * *

We parted ways when Jude dropped me off for work later, something that was incredibly difficult to do. As I watched him drive off, I couldn't help feeling a little bit petrified at the thought that maybe it was the last time I'd ever see him. *No way,* I told myself. He would never leave without saying good-bye.

I went inside and got right into the pattern of work. It wasn't easy, trying to resume normal life now knowing what I did. Everything had changed since the evening before, but I pushed through, determined not to let it affect me in front of all these people.

After our heavy conversation the day before, I was more than a little worried about what Jen must have thought of me now. I went out of my way to be casual around her, maybe a little too much. Either way, we had some good chats between tables. I learned she loved movies, and we decided to go see one together soon.

I was having a fairly good evening in spite of everything. At around eight o'clock, Bryan came out and said that things had slowed down quite a bit and he wanted to send a couple of us home. Jen volunteered, saying she was exhausted, and I jumped at the chance to be with Jude an hour earlier than planned. The only problem was that he wouldn't be coming to get me until nine. Jen offered to give me a ride, and I gratefully accepted.

We chatted on the way and learned we had several things in common. She was also an only child raised by a single mother, but she and her mom were really close. Instinctively I felt a twinge of jealousy when she told me this but quickly reminded myself that I was moving on from any negative feelings associated with my mom. We also discovered we both loved Asian food and decided to go try out the new sushi bar on Third. She told me about moving to Seattle her freshman year of high school after living her whole life in Oregon, and how hard it had been to make friends. She talked about her boyfriend that had dumped her when he went off to college, and I could tell that was a wound that had not fully healed. I listened, engrossed, and noted wistfully how much I'd missed girl conversation like this.

When she pulled up in front of my building, I thanked her for the ride and said good-bye. I started to head toward Jude's building in my excitement to see him, but decided instead to go home first and take a quick shower before heading over. I hurried in to my apartment, the whole time thinking about seeing Jude's face again soon.

I was surprised to see my answering machine light blinking, indicating that I had a message. It was so rare that I ever had one. I pushed the button as I grabbed a bottle of water out of the fridge. The recorded voice told me I had one new message, and then a familiar voice came on, almost causing me to spit out my water.

"Hey, Olivia. It's Ashley. I'm sure I'm the last person you're expecting to hear from, but I've been thinking about you since running into you the other night, and I thought I'd give you a call and . . . maybe we could talk. But, it looks like you're not home, so . . . call me back when you get this. If you want. Okay, bye."

I stared at the machine, wondering if my ears had really heard what my brain thought they'd heard. I hit the playback button and listened again. Sure enough, it was the same message. I debated whether or not I should call her back. Of course I should, but I was terrified to. I decided to wait until later, anxious to see Jude. Maybe he'd have some insight into what I should do. I headed toward the shower, but stopped halfway there and turned back around. Grabbing the phone, I dialed Ashley's number.

On the third ring, I found myself praying silently that she wouldn't pick up. But on the fourth ring, I heard a click and then Ashley's voice. "Hello?"

I took a deep breath. "Hi, Ashley." I hated how shaky my voice sounded. "It's Olivia."

"I know." The way she said it didn't sound unkind; more like it was silly of me to think she'd forgotten my voice.

There was silence. Was she waiting for me to say something? I was beginning to think what a mistake this was when she said, "I'm glad you called me back. We didn't have much of a chance to talk at the restaurant."

"Yeah," I said lamely. *Ugh.* I was going to have to pull it together if I didn't want to look like an idiot in front of her for the second time in a row. "It was . . . weird, seeing you after so long. I'm sorry if I seemed . . ." *Awkward? Embarrassed? Socially inept?*

"No, you were fine," she answered, jumping in and saving me from having to finish the sentence. "I can understand that it must have been . . . hard. After all, we didn't end on the best of terms."

A painful lull followed as we both remembered our parting moment.

"I want to apologize, for leaving you like that."

"Oh, it's okay," I replied automatically.

"No, it's not. I should have stayed, I should have given you the support you needed. I shouldn't have just abandoned you like that. If things had gone differently when you tried to . . . and you succeeded? I would never have been able to forgive myself. I just didn't know how to help you, and it freaked me out. It's no excuse, but it's all I've got. I am *so sorry*."

I couldn't believe I was hearing her say this. It meant more to me than she would ever know. "Thank you. It's okay, honestly. I was in a really, really bad place. I don't know if anyone could have helped me then."

Ashley's voice grew softer. "I'm just so grateful someone was there, that you've had someone there for you, during all of this. Jude seems like a really great guy."

"He is," I said, a dull ache settling in my stomach. He is, and soon he'll be gone. "Ashley, can I ask you something? How did you know? About . . . what happened?"

"My aunt's a nurse there at the hospital, remember? She wasn't going to say anything because of patient confidentiality and all that, but ultimately she decided that I should know. I'm so glad she did. I wanted to call you as soon as I heard, but figured it was probably way too soon, that you would need time to recover. Plus, I wasn't ignorant of the fact that I was probably the last person you'd want to hear from."

I didn't know how to respond to the last part, so I just ignored it. "Yeah, I was a hot mess there for a while after. It's been a rough road getting to where I am now, but I'm doing well. I see a therapist, and I'm taking medication. It seems to help." I wondered if I was sharing too much, seeing as this was our first real conversation after a six month hiatus, but it felt natural to confide in her. It was Ashley, after all.

"That's good. I'm so happy to hear it." I heard the sincerity in her voice. I could sense the conversation coming to an end, and I suddenly wasn't ready to hang up. "So, what about you? What have you been up to?" I asked.

"Me? Oh, same ol', same ol'. Still plugging away at school. I got fired from my job at Pete's. He accused me of stealing petty cash when everyone knew it was this girl, Julie. Whatever. Now I'm a receptionist at a car lot." She laughed. "So fun, let me tell you." I laughed too. "I have a boyfriend, too. Remember Josh, the guy in my study group who kept asking me out?"

"Oh, yeah," I responded. It hurt to hear how much of her life had changed since we'd gone our separate ways.

"Well, I finally caved and went out with him. Turns out he's a really sweet guy, and he loves to buy me things, which is always a bonus."

I laughed again. "That's awesome, Ashley. It sounds like you're doing really well too."

"Yeah, I guess so." Something in her voice sounded off, but I couldn't pinpoint it. "Well, I better go," she said. "I've got a ridiculously long paper to write that's due tomorrow." *At least one thing hadn't changed,* I thought. She was still a procrastinator.

"All right. Well, it was good catching up."

"Yeah, it was. We should talk again soon."

"I'd like that," I said, wondering if she meant it as much as I did.

"Okay, talk to you later."

"Bye."

I hung up the phone in a daze, unbelieving that that conversation had really just taken place. My spirits soared at the prospect that things between Ashley and me could possibly be repaired. I knew they would never be the same as they once were, but even the thought of being in her life again, of being able to call her a friend, made me feel like I could fly.

I all but skipped to the shower.

* * * * *

Something had been plaguing Jude ever since Olivia's question earlier.

How long do we have?

It was like a poison, seeping deep into the marrow of his bones. He knew she had to be feeling the same—consumed with the need to know, but terrified of learning the answer.

By the time he dropped her off at work, he had made a decision, formulated a plan. It was what he'd been dreading the most, the thing he'd been avoiding since the night he saved her. It scared him to his very core, but he knew it was what he had to do, that it was his only hope. He knew there was no guarantee that the outcome would be what he wanted, but he had nothing left to lose. If he did nothing, he would have to leave her forever. This way, he might at least have a chance.

He parked the truck and rode the elevator up to his apartment. Once inside, he stood in the middle of the vacant room, taking slow, calming breaths and trying to prepare himself for what he was about to do. He trembled, not believing that he was actually doing this. He closed his eyes and then, in a flash of white light, the room was empty.

CHAPTER TWENTY-FIVE

As I WALKED OVER to Jude's apartment, I had the thought that maybe he wouldn't even be there. The light was off, but that didn't necessarily mean he wasn't there. But what would he even do there now? He didn't need to "spy" on me anymore, and there was absolutely nothing else for him to do there. But I had no idea where else he would be, so I took the elevator up to his floor and knocked on his door.

No answer.

I sighed. Would there ever be a time I would knock on his door and he would actually answer?

Slightly dejected, I made my way back home, where I decided to make myself a quesadilla. I hadn't eaten since before work, and I was too hungry to wait around for Jude. Not that he'd necessarily be eating with me even if he were here.

I sat down and ate in silence, feeling better than I could ever remember. I hadn't felt this normal, this happy, since before my mom died. It just seemed like somehow, things were actually going good in my life, the thought of which scared me to no end. Like acknowledging it would burst the bubble. I felt like I had to hold on tight to the new relationships I had formed, with Jude, and Jen; as well as to the ones that were slowly being repaired. I smiled, thinking of my phone conversation with Ashley earlier and imagining things really, truly getting better between us.

And then, as if someone was reading my mind, the phone rang, making me jump in my seat. I snatched it off the base. "Hello?"

"Hey, Olivia, it's Jen."

"Hi!" I answered, surprised. She must have looked me up; I hadn't given her my number.

"So I came home from work fully intent on crashing, but I got my second wind and I was thinking of catching a late movie. Do you . . . want to come with me?"

I glanced at the clock, hesitating. Jude should have been here by now.

"If you have plans, or whatever, it's totally fine," she added quickly, picking up on my hesitation. "No pressure."

"No, not at all. I'm actually just sitting here eating. Alone." I heard the heaviness in my voice on the last word and hoped that Jen didn't. I started thinking quickly, trying to decide what to do. If Jude was still coming, I didn't want to miss him. Not knowing how much time we had together before he was gone forever gave me a panicky feeling that I couldn't miss a single minute that could otherwise be spent with him. I glanced at the clock. He should have been here forty-five minutes ago. I frowned. Maybe he was with Hal. Maybe I should go to Hal's and find him. No, I didn't want to be *that* girl. Besides, I didn't want to turn Jen down the first time she invited me somewhere. And Jude would want me to go, anyway. I could just go leave a note on his door saying where I'd gone, in case he decided to come over. Yeah, that's what I'd do. "I'd love to."

"Great! I'll pick you up in twenty minutes."

I finished eating and ran quickly over to Jude's, where I stuck a note to his door saying I'd gone to a movie with Jen (but not before knocking again to make sure he hadn't come home). Then I hurried back home just in time for Jen to show up. As I locked my apartment up behind me, I couldn't help but wonder anxiously what had happened to Jude. It was so maddeningly frustrating that I couldn't just pick up the phone and call him to find out. I decided that if he still hadn't made an appearance by the next morning, I would go see Hal. That wasn't being needy or clingy, right? That was what any genuinely concerned person would do if someone they cared about went missing. Yes, that was my plan.

Resolved to have a fun girls' night out, I shoved the thought from my mind and followed Jen outside.

* * * * *

Jude lay facedown on the hard, cold floor in the middle of his living room. His heart was beating wildly and he was breathing as heavily as if he'd just run a mile. His vision was blurred and his eyes stung. He blinked, feeling something dripping into them. He slowly raised his hand to his eye and instantly cried out. The small movement had sent a stab of something searing through his body. He brought his hand slowly away from his face and examined the offending liquid. Sweat. He was sweating, profusely. He marveled at this, and the curious sensation that had him moaning with each movement. Pain. He had never known it before. He had always tried to imagine it, to understand that horrible thing that mortals so often endured. But he'd never been able to.

Now he knew and wished he didn't. Now he understood why it caused them to scream, or cry, or even pass out unconscious. He understood why they avoided it at all costs.

He tried to pull himself up off the floor, but collapsed, gritting his teeth to keep from crying out again. Every bone in his body ached, every muscle, ligament, nerve was on fire. He took a deep breath, steeled himself, then flipped over onto his back, a mangled growl escaping through his teeth. He lay there, panting and sweating, disbelieving he had signed up for this.

There had never been a choice, really. After it was revealed to him that this was the only way he could stay with Olivia, he knew what he would do. It had been difficult, certainly. He couldn't let himself think about what he'd given up in return. But it was worth it. And he would do it again if he had to.

He only had to get past the initial adjustment to his new body (which he hoped was the explanation for all this pain), and he knew that he could. Somehow, he would. Besides the pain, he felt intense hunger and fatigue. And cold, despite the sweating. All things he'd never felt before, but knew what they meant, nonetheless. It was the most peculiar thing he'd ever experienced.

He waited a full ten minutes before trying to get up off the floor again. And he failed. Again.

He lay there staring at the ceiling, thinking about Olivia. What would she do when she found out? How would she react? How would he keep her from seeing him like this until it got better? *What if it never got better,* he thought, horrified.

Suddenly the exhaustion overpowered everything else and his eyelids felt like they weighed ten pounds each. He could feel himself drifting away, a sensation that wasn't altogether unpleasant. *Finally,* he thought. *Something that doesn't hurt.*

And he was out before another thought could assemble itself.

* * * * *

I was still laughing when I got home from the movie with Jen. We'd seen a comedy and had both laughed till our sides hurt. On the drive home, we kept quoting the best parts and laughing again. It had been so wonderful to laugh like that again with a friend. It was better therapy than I would ever get in a doctor's office.

By the time I walked into my apartment, it was past midnight and I was beat. I barely had the energy to wonder again what had happened to Jude, but knew there was a chance he had come by while I was gone. I quickly changed into pajamas and crawled into bed, fully prepared to sink instantly into a good, deep sleep. I should have known better.

I tossed and turned all night long, thinking of Jude.

* * * * *

Jude's eyes opened slowly, then blinked rapidly in the bright light. The tiny movement caused him pain, reminding him of the night before and the life-changing transformation he'd made. Slowly, carefully, he shifted on the wood floor that had been his bed for the last . . . how many hours? He cringed as pain tore through him like a fiery explosion, even worse than the night before, if that was possible.

He lay, panting, wondering how he was ever going to get off this floor. Just the thought of it made him hurt. But he knew he had to, and soon. There were things his body not only required now but were screaming for.

He gingerly pushed himself up into a sitting position, all attempts at staying quiet failing. He wondered what his neighbors must think of all the groaning and yelling. He sat there, catching his breath and gathering the willpower he needed to move again, before pushing his body up off the floor. By some miracle, he managed to get to a shaky standing position, but knew that if he didn't find some support soon he'd be back down in an instant. Breathless and aching from head to toe, and sweatier than he'd been even the night before, he made his way haltingly to the window seat, crying out with each step. Finally, he made it, collapsing in a heap on the hard, shiny surface.

What a mess I am, he thought, gasping for breath. How was he ever supposed to survive down here when he could barely make it halfway across the room?

He assessed his situation. He was trapped in an empty apartment, incapacitated and helpless, without a phone or any way at all to get help. No one knew he was here, except the one person he didn't want finding him, and a homeless man who would never come looking. He had no food, nowhere to sleep, no water even. He'd never bothered to have it turned on.

Things weren't looking good. He had to get some food and water in him and fast. His body had nothing to go on, nothing to give him energy to move, or heal, or keep breathing even. It was crazy, having to worry about dying. He didn't like it all that much.

His only hope was to leave, to go somewhere and get help. It would be a nightmare, traveling across the city in this crippled body, but he had to do it. And there was only one place he could think of to go.

CHAPTER TWENTY-SIX

As soon as the sun came up I threw on some clothes and hurriedly brushed my teeth. I didn't even glance in a mirror before running out the door. As I walked swiftly (jogged) over to Jude's building, I tried telling myself positive things, like Dr. Robinson was always encouraging me to do. I reminded myself that when Jude had disappeared two days earlier with no explanation, he'd done it for my benefit and didn't stay away for long. There had to be some explanation for this disappearance too. But even as I told myself this, a nagging, pesky thought continually tried to creep into my head, one that I fought to keep suppressed.

But when I got up to the fifth floor and saw the note still attached to Jude's door, the nagging thought began spreading its gnarled fingers throughout my brain, not even willing to stop there. Soon it had consumed my entire body, filling me with a dread I could hardly bear.

On the bus ride, I worked hard at filling my mind with happy images to counteract the bad ones. Like the way Jude's fingers had brushed against my exposed shoulder in my tank top. And the fire in his eyes that told me he was about to kiss me. The vibration of his chest against my cheek when he talked softly, holding me. Soon I was completely lost in a world of euphoria and almost missed my stop completely. Reluctantly, I tore my thoughts free from my own personal heaven and returned to the real world, the one where I had no idea where Jude was, where the persistent dread still coursed through me as the gnarled fingers stretched further and further. It felt like someone had dumped a bucket of ice water over my head.

I exited the bus and navigated quickly through my childhood stomping grounds. It was amazing to me how much my five-year-old brain had registered and hung on to. It wasn't long before I was standing, once again, in front of my old house. It wasn't until then that it occurred to me that Hal might have already left for work, or whatever he called it. But then, if he wasn't here, that most likely meant Jude wasn't either, and I couldn't handle that thought.

I pulled back the noisy screen door, careful not to rip it off its hinge and knocked on the door behind it. After a minute of no response, I started to question if Hal would even answer the door if someone came knocking. Probably not, I realized, and turned the handle, heaving my shoulder against the worn wood. It opened on the first try this time, I was happy to see. I stopped short when I stepped into the living room. The daylight that was absent two days earlier when I was here now streamed through the open door, revealing the true state of the house. Where before I was mildly disgusted by the state of the carpet and walls, now I was downright horrified. I felt contaminated just standing in the open air. The walls looked like someone had smeared every form of bodily excrement all over them, and the spot on the carpet that I had mistaken for oil in the dark was now clearly a blood stain. I shivered, my skin crawling under my clothes. It took everything in me to take a few more steps toward the back of the house and call out, "Hal?"

I heard distant sounds of movement and then Hal appeared in a doorway. He was dressed in layers of clothing, a duffel bag slung over his shoulder. I must have caught him on his way out for the day.

"Olivia!" His voice was laced with surprise, and my heart sank. If Jude were here, Hal would know exactly why I was here.

"Hey, Hal. I was just . . ." I sighed, feeling like I suddenly weighed twice as much. "I was wondering if you've seen Jude. He dropped me off at work yesterday and . . . I haven't seen him since." My face burned as I spoke, from embarrassment at sounding like a clueless girl who didn't know she'd just been ditched, and from fear and anger at not knowing what was going on.

The look on Hal's face told me everything I needed to know. I nodded, biting back tears, struggling to maintain composure in front of him.

"I haven't seen him." I didn't like the way he was looking at me. It was exactly the way people looked at me after my mom died. I refused to believe he was gone, like, *gone* gone.

"He has to be somewhere." The tears spilled over, hot and wet on my flushed cheeks. "He didn't leave. He couldn't have. He wouldn't have, not without saying good-bye." I shook my head furiously, unsure whether I was trying to convince Hal or myself.

Hal's shoulders slumped, and he looked like he was about to tell me he'd run over my puppy. I wanted to run out of the house before he said whatever it was he was about to say. But I didn't. I stood, frozen to the filthy carpet.

"Olivia," he said gently. "He did. He's gone."

I narrowed my eyes accusingly at him. "How do you know, if you haven't seen him?" Why would he rob me of the small strand of hope I had left that Jude might still be here, somewhere?

"Because," Hal answered. "I *know*. He's not here, not anymore."

And then I remembered. What Hal had told me two nights earlier about his remaining angelic powers. That he had to serve the angels that came to earth. That he knew when they were here, and when they were not. And that thin strand snapped in half, severing any last hope I had of ever seeing Jude again. I couldn't fight the little nagging thought any longer. It was the undeniable truth.

Jude was gone.

He had left me, without saying good-bye.

* * * * *

Jude sat in the driver's seat of his truck, attempting for the fourth time to get the key into the ignition. His hand was shaking so badly he couldn't get the key and the hole to align long enough to get it in. He was starting to get frustrated, convinced that he was doomed to die right there in the cab of his truck. If he'd had the energy to, he would have laughed at the irony of making a miraculous transformation into a human only to die less than twenty-four hours later from something as ridiculous as not being able to start his truck.

He still couldn't believe he'd made it to his truck at all. It had been sketchy, getting from his apartment to this point. He'd been lucky to find the hallway empty when he lurched out his door. He'd had to bite his lip to keep

from making any noise as he made his way to the tor, step by excruciating step. Once inside, he'd col to the floor, barely managing to reach up and hit the b for the ground floor. He'd had a few moments of pre rest before he'd steeled himself and pushed up off the f groaning in agony. As the numbers in the elevator rap descended, he'd taken deep breaths and focused every last of energy he'd had on standing still without shaking, kno ing there was a good chance someone would be standing the other side of the elevator doors when they opened. He been right. A middle-aged couple skirted past him onto th elevator, eyeing his jerky movements and the layer of sheer covering the surface of his skin. He'd tried to smile at them but it came off as a grimace. He'd gone outside, around to the back of the building as quickly as his feeble body would allow, clenching his teeth together the entire way. When he'd finally made it to his truck, he'd heaved himself up into the cab, collapsing onto the bench seat and immediately passing out. When he'd come to, he'd had no idea how much time had passed, but he could feel that he was even weaker than before. Sitting up had felt like it would most certainly kill him, and now he had spent the last fifteen minutes trying to get the stupid key into the ignition.

He was just about to open the door and chuck the keys as hard as he could (not that he could have if he'd tried) when fate seemed to smile on him and the key slid into the slot. He turned the key as hard as he could to get it to start, feeling warmer and sweatier with each passing moment. He somehow managed to shift into reverse, and then drive again, once he was turned the right direction, heading out of the parking lot. An overwhelming sense of fear came over him as he pulled out alongside the other cars, driving in his condition . . . in big city traffic, no less. If he didn't

die of natural causes en route, a nice fifteen car pile-up that he'd caused would surely do him in.

He said a silent prayer that he would make it to his destination in one piece, or at least not harm anyone else in his effort to do so. He knew it was going to be a long, terrifying drive.

The house was pitch black when Jude stumbled inside through the back door. It had been boarded up at some point, but the measly "X" created by two two-by-fours was a laughable attempt at keeping trespassers out. He didn't know how he did it, but somehow he worked his way through one of the four holes it created, falling through to the hard floor below. He knew he would never be able to get back up, but he also did not want to stay there by the open doorway. He crawled along what he guessed to be a hallway, feeling along with his hands, willing himself not to think about the disgusting layer of filth he felt under his fingertips. Besides touch, and the overpowering odor that now had his sense of smell alive and well, he had lost every other sense at some point on his journey. The last stretch of it was a complete blur. He had no recollection of how he had arrived at his destination, couldn't even fathom what miracle had gotten him there. He wasn't even sure where "there" was. He had lost the ability to think coherently, to see, to feel. The last one, at least, was a blessing. The pain was gone, replaced by a dull numbness. His thoughts blended together in one big blur, everything a haze of nothing.

But still he crawled, because if there was one thing he knew he sought, it was a comfortable place to lie down and die. It didn't take long to find it. His hands suddenly felt layers of soft cushiness, big enough for his whole body. He dropped onto them, his entire body giving one huge sigh of

relief. He had made it. Barely alive, but still, he was there. Maybe his plan had failed, maybe there was no one there to provide him with the things he needed to stay alive, but he had done all he could do. No one could say he didn't try. And with that last thought, he drifted out of consciousness, the only thing he seemed able to do effortlessly as a human.

* * * * *

When Jude opened his eyes again, it was because someone was shaking him, yelling in his face. But he couldn't see who, couldn't even be sure anyone was there. And then there was water everywhere, splashing all over his face, into his nose, down his neck. He choked and coughed, but the tiny amount of water that made it into his mouth seemed to wake something in him, some creature that had been sleeping, lying, ready to die, but had now found something worth fighting for. He turned his head frantically, searching for more. It came, and this time he opened his mouth and let it pour in. It was the most amazing, most delicious thing he had ever experienced, and he knew he could drink forever and never stop. He guzzled until the water stopped coming, and now he worked at focusing his eyes to see where it had been coming from in the first place. There was light in the room now, just enough that he could make out a figure in front of him, blurry at first, but then sharper, a degree at a time. Soon he recognized Hal, squatting down before him, holding an empty bottle. Jude's eyes zeroed in on it. He mumbled something indiscernible, but Hal seemed to know what he was asking. He moved out of Jude's line of sight, coming back a moment later with another bottle, this one full. He tipped the bottle to Jude's lips again, and Jude drank greedily until it was empty as well. Then he lay with his eyes closed, breathing heavily. After several moments he slowly reopened them and focused on Hal.

"Hey, kid," Hal said, eyeing the pitiful creature in front of him. "You don't look so hot."

"I don't . . . feel . . . so hot." Each word Jude tried to say came out in a short burst of breath.

"So, you want to tell me why you're here, lying on my bed, looking like Death himself?"

Jude looked at Hal and could see on the older man's face that he'd guessed what had happened. Most of it, anyway. But Jude didn't have the energy to talk yet, especially not to tell Hal the entire story.

"Food first," he croaked.

Hal scanned the room, his eyes falling on something somewhere behind Jude. He reached for it, producing a small bag of cookies. Tearing it open, he handed a cookie to Jude, who looked questioningly back at Hal before lifting a shaky hand and grabbing it from him.

Hal shrugged. "I just like to eat 'em every now and then. I know it's pointless, but they're really good." He watched as Jude bit into the cookie, saw his eyes grow huge as he chewed it.

"What?" Hal asked.

"I've . . . never had . . . food that . . . tasted . . . so good." He shoved the remainder of it into his mouth. Hal handed him the rest of the package, and Jude promptly devoured every last cookie.

Hal watched with a slight scowl. "How'd you get here, anyway?"

Jude swallowed, lying his head back on the rolled up blanket that must have acted as Hal's pillow. "I drove . . . the truck." His voice was still gravelly, but strengthening with each passing second. "Most of the way, anyway. It took me ten minutes to walk from my apartment to where it was parked behind it, and another five just to climb into it. I passed out from the effort. When I woke up and started driving over here, I could feel myself getting weaker and weaker, and about a mile away, right off the exit, I knew I had to pull over and stop before I passed out and drove into oncoming traffic. I don't know how I did it, but somehow I managed to get myself the rest of the way here."

Hal nodded and sat down in a rusty camping chair not far from where Jude lay.

He paused. "So, you gonna tell me what happened, or not?"

Jude sighed, wincing from the movement. The numbness was gone, the pain definitely back. He took it as a good sign. "I went . . . back. Home. To face what was coming to me once and for all. I was sick of worrying, sick of wondering, and I just wanted to get it over with. And also . . ." He glanced at Hal's face. ". . . to ask to stay with Olivia."

Hal raised his eyebrows. "That was the solution to this mess that you came up with?"

"It was the solution to me never having to leave her."

Hal didn't respond, but the look on his face told Jude what he thought of the whole thing. "So what happened?"

"They thought I'd come back because I was done, to report like normal. They had no idea what had happened, that anything had happened at all." He glanced at Hal. "So I had to tell them. Everything."

"And?"

"They were shocked, obviously. Some were appalled, even. They sent me out of the room so they could discuss the situation, decide what my punishment should be and whether or not they'd let me stay with her."

"And?"

"*And* . . ." Jude fell silent, not wanting to say the words. He could barely think them. He looked at Hal meaningfully, willing him to understand.

Hal stared back at first, and then his eyes began to grow wide as comprehension set in. He took in Jude's incapacitated body sprawled out on the shabby blankets that Hal used for a bed, and his mouth fell open. "You mean you . . . ?"

Jude nodded solemnly. "It was the only way, Hal. The only way I could be with her. Forever."

CHAPTER TWENTY-SEVEN

I CRIED AND CRIED THE rest of the day and most of the night, unwilling to believe that he was really gone, that I would really never see him again. That I would never kiss him again, or talk to him again, or touch him. That I didn't even get to say good-bye.

I wanted to be angry. Angry at him for leaving, angry at the universe for making him. Angry that once again, someone I loved more than anything in the world left me. But I couldn't be. I was too devastated to be angry. And besides, I knew that it was out of Jude's control. I knew that he would never have gone if there was any way possible he didn't have to. And I knew that he must have thought it would be easier on me, maybe easier on both of us, if he left without saying good-bye.

Sometime before dawn the tears stopped, and that was when I remembered the promise I had made to Jude, and more important, to myself: that I would be okay. I had meant it when I'd said it, and I had to mean it now, no matter how impossible it seemed. I didn't want to. I didn't want to be okay with Jude not in my life. I was furious that I had to be, that I had to accept it like I was fine with it. Because I was anything but fine with it. But I would do it, because I had to. I *had* to survive this. I refused to let this pull me back into the bottomless pit I'd crawled out of months earlier. I could not go back there.

After that, I was determined. I spent the rest of the night devising a plan to make it through the next few days, which would arguably be the worst. At times my resolve would waver, and I'd make up my mind to call in sick to work in the morning so I wouldn't have to get out of bed and face the day. But then I would remind myself what my life was like the last time I'd let depression swallow me whole, and all thoughts of wallowing in self-pity would vanish.

By the time sleep finally found me, I had vowed that no matter what it took, I would make it through this. It was going to be hell, for sure, but I'd been through that before. We were old friends by now.

The next day proved to be the longest of my life. Trying to keep your mind distracted every waking second is not an easy thing to do. It's akin to someone telling you, "Don't think of the color blue," so naturally, all you can think about is the color blue. If only it were the color blue I was trying not to think about.

I found things to stay occupied before work. I cleaned my apartment, something that had been sorely neglected in recent weeks. The first thing I did was throw out the wilted, dying flowers that stood propped where I'd put them the night Jude gave them to me. I could see them no matter where I was in my apartment, and I didn't need that constant reminder. Then I scrubbed every square inch from top to bottom. It was taxing on my raw emotions.

There weren't many places in my apartment that I couldn't picture Jude. Sitting at my table, sprawled on my couch, stretched out on my bed . . . Too many times I crumbled to the floor, sobbing uncontrollably and wondering how I was ever going to do this.

After that everything else on my list of things to do that day was neglected. Cleaning took every ounce of mental and physical strength I had in me, and I allowed myself to sit and stare into the oblivion for a while before work.

Work was difficult, to say the least, trying to act normal when inside I was slowly dying. But Jen was there, which made it marginally better. She even made me laugh a couple times by randomly quoting the movie we'd seen together, something I didn't think would be possible to do.

The true test of strength came when I was back filling up a tray of drinks, and Bridgett came back to get a pot of coffee. She glanced over at me, and I could tell I was headed into a conversation I didn't want to have.

"Hey, where's that guy of yours been? He hasn't been around in a few days."

Really, I hadn't noticed. I was trying to think of some way to answer that wouldn't turn me into a blubbering mess or end with my fist in Bridgett's face, when Jen came around the corner, saving the day.

"Bridgett, your fan club is at table four."

Bridgett grinned, her question instantly forgotten. "Male or female?"

Jen rolled her eyes. "What do you think?"

Bridgett quickly filled the coffee pot and breezed out of the room, leaving a cloud of overpowering perfume and cigarette smoke behind her. Jen made a face at her back, and I sighed in relief to have dodged that bullet.

After work I grabbed some takeout and a movie and curled up on my couch with my kung pao chicken and the latest romantic comedy. But I never took a bite, and I never pushed play. Instead, I cried myself to sleep.

And that was day one.

* * * * *

"How are you going to tell her?" Hal was sitting in his camping chair, watching Jude inhale a cheeseburger. After the shock of Jude's revelation had worn off and they'd talked about it in depth, Hal had gone to retrieve Jude's truck and made a stop at McDonald's on his way back. When Hal had come through the door of the room with the food and the smell hit Jude's nose, he couldn't get it into his hands fast enough. And since the water and cookies from earlier had given him some much-needed strength, he was actually able to prop himself up a little to eat.

Jude's face fell as he finished chewing. "I don't know. I haven't figured that out yet. That, or how I'm going to explain where I disappeared to this whole time."

"You know where she thinks you are, right?"

Jude sighed. "Yeah. I haven't let myself think about it. I know she's thinking I abandoned her, like everyone else in her life." The devastation on his face was apparent. "It'll ruin her."

Hal sat silent for a moment. "She came here, you know. Looking for you."

Jude's eyes flashed at Hal. "She did?"

Hal nodded. "Yeah. Yesterday morning, before I left."

"How was she? Was she okay?"

Hal didn't answer at first. "She'll be all right. She's stronger than you think she is."

This didn't seem to ease Jude's anxiety one bit. "What did she say?"

"She asked if I'd seen you and I told her I hadn't. And then . . ."

"Then what?" Jude demanded.

"Then I told her. That I knew you were gone." Hal rushed on before Jude could say anything. "I could feel it! I knew you weren't here anymore, not as an angel. Never for a minute did I ever imagine it was because you were human."

Jude's voice was soft, hesitant. "And how did she take it?"

"How do you think she took it?"

Jude squeezed his eyes shut and groaned. Hal continued. "What did you expect? You knew this would happen."

"This is exactly what I was trying to *prevent* from happening by going there in the first place!" Jude shouted angrily. "How could I have ever known this would be the result?" He motioned toward his weakened body.

No one said anything for several minutes.

When Hal spoke again it was in a much calmer tone. "Why didn't you go to her, after your decision, and your . . . change? Why drag yourself halfway across the city to me?"

"Are you kidding?" Jude laughed derisively. "And have her see me like this? Not only would she worry herself sick about me, but she would think I'd made the wrong decision."

Hal looked skeptical. "Even though it means being with her?"

Jude shifted his body, trying to get comfortable, and the movement took his breath away momentarily. "I don't . . . know. I don't know how she'll react. I know it's what she wants—to be with me—but not at this cost. She'll think it was wrong of me to do for her. Especially if she sees me like this. No way."

"So how will you tell her?" Hal asked again. "You're going to have to sooner than you think, especially with as much time as you spend with her. She's a smart girl. She's going to notice some very obvious differences about you."

"I know, I know," Jude answered, frustrated. "I *will* tell her. But on my own terms, at the right time. Not because she sees me and can tell that I'm human."

Hal looked like he wanted to say something but decided against it. Instead he stood up, grabbing a blanket from a pile of stuff in a corner of the room and throwing it down on the floor a few feet from Jude. "Well, I'm beat. You finish eating, I'm going to bed."

But Jude had completely lost his appetite. He stared at the half-finished burger in his hand and marveled at how something he had wanted more than air in his lungs minutes earlier could now have no appeal to him whatsoever. How could the way he was feeling emotionally affect his body physically? The human body was a mystery to him, albeit a fascinating one. He crumpled the remainder of his meal in its wrapper and curled up on the blankets beneath him. All he could think of now was Olivia and how she was going to react to this new . . . development. Would she even be happy? Or would she say he'd made a huge mistake? He felt sick—a different kind of sick than he'd been feeling all day—as he thought about where she was now, what she must be thinking, and feeling. He couldn't think about it, because he was sure he knew, and the thought that he was causing her that much pain was unbearable. Instead he closed his eyes and wondered how long it would take for his new body to fall asleep when it wasn't passing out unconscious. Not long, he discovered.

* * * * *

Jude woke up the next morning and had to take a minute to get his bearings. When he saw the familiar grizzled face a few feet away from him, he remembered where he was and why he was there. Hal was sitting in the camping chair, reading a book and eating cookies.

"How ya feelin'?"

Jude was almost scared to find out. If the food and water he'd consumed throughout the night hadn't helped him at all, then he didn't know what would. He braced himself before stretching slowly, carefully. A smile spread slowly across his face when the action didn't make him cry out in pain. He realized too that he was no longer sweating or shaking. His breaths came nice and even too.

"I feel pretty good," he answered, sitting upright on the blankets. A wave of dizziness washed over him, and he instantly had to lie back down. Hal chuckled. "Take it easy, kid. Baby steps."

Jude closed his eyes until the room stopped spinning, then stretched again, relishing the absence of pain. His joints felt stiff and sore, and that he could handle. For the first time since he'd had this mortal body, he had hope that one day soon he would feel normal . . . whatever a normal, mortal body felt like.

And then he noticed an uncomfortable, slightly painful sensation that he hadn't experienced yet, something that was demanding urgent attention. The look on his face must have given him away, because Hal said, "You better head outside. Nowhere to go in here." Now it was all Jude could think about or feel, and he tried to get up quickly without making himself feel like passing out again. Hal went to him and helped him up off the floor, and Jude was pleased to find that despite the dizziness, he could do it without wanting to scream. He limped alongside Hal, holding his arm for support, and made his way through the kitchen to the backyard, where Hal let him go on alone for privacy.

When he came back a minute later, he was shaking his head, looking a little bit stunned. "I can't believe all the stuff humans have to deal with. I don't know if I'll ever get used to this."

Hal laughed again. "Don't worry, you will. And you'll be surprised how fast." He led Jude back over to the bedroll and carefully helped him down to the floor. Jude fell back onto the blankets, spent from the physical exertion. He couldn't believe that walking a few yards and back could wear him out so much, but at least it was an obvious improvement from the day before. Hopefully it would only be another couple of days before he could move around with little to no effort.

Hal grabbed his duffel bag and turned to Jude. "Well, I'm out. Gotta work for a living."

Jude made a face. "What am I going to do here all day?"

"Do whatever you want. But if it were me, I'd probably lie there dreaming up a way to explain to my girl why I suddenly had the ability to bleed. But . . . whatever." Hal shrugged, and with that, he was gone, and Jude was left alone in the broken-down house.

* * * * *

I was hoping the next day would be easier, even by a minute fraction, but it wasn't. Not at all.

I tried so hard to stay occupied: reading, watching TV. . . . But no matter what I was doing, I would suddenly find myself staring out the window in a daze, unaware of how long I'd been doing so but knowing it had been a while.

After the fourth time or so of this happening, I began to wonder if I really was keeping my promise at all. It didn't seem like I was handling this any better than I was handling things before I met Jude. It all seemed too familiar. The numbness, the lack of desire to go anywhere or do anything, the fight to get out of bed and go to work . . . I was so fearful of the thought that I was back in that place. Petrified, actually. I considered calling Dr. Robinson, but remembered she was on vacation for a few weeks. So instead I called Jen and asked if she wanted to try that sushi place after work. Luckily, she did, which meant that from work on my day was scheduled, no time left open to have to try and fill.

The sushi turned out to be really good, but I struggled to appear like nothing was wrong. Luckily for me, Jen talked most of the time, and I was more than content to listen. She told me about her dad, who still lived in Oregon, and whom she missed dearly. She talked about the guy who broke her heart, and I fought to keep from crying out that I knew what she was going through. They'd dated her senior year and she'd been convinced he was the one, and that she was going to marry him. But he went to college out of state and apparently couldn't handle the long-distance thing. She looked pained talking about it, so I tried to subtly change the subject to *my* senior year, telling her about Ashley. I omitted the part where things went downhill, not a place I wanted to revisit just then. I also told her a little about my life before high school, and a little of after, stopping just short of my mother's death. The best part was that she never asked about Jude, not once. She had to have noticed that he'd gone AWOL recently, but she, unlike Bridgett, had tact enough to not ask.

It was a challenge, getting through that dinner without

breaking down, but I managed to not shed a single tear, which made the evening a smashing success.

I fell asleep in front of the TV again, since it had worked so well the night before.

Two days down, a lifetime still to go.

* * * * *

Day three: More of the same. I was completely out of ideas of things to fill my days, and had exhausted the last remaining ounces of willpower it would take to attempt them. So I didn't even try. Somehow I pushed through till work, something I was growing increasingly grateful for with each passing day. It was a wonderful five hours of being forced out of my apartment, forced to talk to people, and forced to do something other than stare out the window. I worked myself so hard in an effort to keep my mind occupied that by the time I was done I had no energy left to do anything but go home and flop on the couch, covering my eyes with my arm and wishing desperately I didn't have to do this anymore.

That was when I heard the knock at my door.

I sat up quickly, startled. *Who in the world would be knocking on my door at this time of night?* I wondered, slightly panicked. I considered ignoring it, pretending I wasn't home, but then, what if it was burglars who decided to come in and rob the place since it was empty? *You're being stupid,* I told myself. *Just answer the door.*

I went over and unlocked it apprehensively. I counted silently to three before pulling it open.

Standing there, staring back at me, was a face I knew as well as my own.

"Jude," I breathed.

CHAPTER TWENTY-EIGHT

I COULDN'T SPEAK, COULDN'T form a single sentence or even a thought. I didn't understand what I was seeing, or how he could be standing in front of me, looking like he never left. My mind rejected the idea that he was back, my emotions shutting down before they were allowed to feel something that was too dangerous to feel. I took a step back, wanting to separate myself from this moment. No matter how many times I'd dreamed of this happening in the last three days, no matter how badly I wanted him back, somehow I knew that this, whatever it was, was far worse. Because he couldn't be back. Not for good, anyway. It could never be for good. And I couldn't handle temporary. I couldn't handle him leaving again. I knew my limits, what I could and could not take, and seeing him again only to lose him again was something I was confident I would not survive.

"No," I whispered, shaking my head. "*No.*" I continued to step backward, away from the very thing I wanted to run to.

"Olivia," Jude said, taking a step toward me.

"NO!" I yelled, retreating further. Jude came into the room but stopped just inside the door. His expression was grieved, his hand slightly lifted as if to reach for me. I turned around and ran to my bed, crawling into it and burying myself under the covers. Maybe then he would just turn around and leave, and I could hide here forever, and never come out again. I started sobbing then. All the anger and hurt and betrayal that had plagued me since he'd left came spilling out of me, a torrent of tears and loud, wet sobs. Why was he here? Why would he come back when I had worked so hard at getting through the last three days? He had to know what torture it would be for me to see him again.

I heard the door close and stopped crying, listening. It had worked.

He had left.

But then I heard his footsteps on the wood floor coming closer and then felt him on the bed beside me.

"Olivia," he said quietly. "Please look at me, so I can talk to you."

His voice hummed soft in my ears, flowing into my head and coursing through my body.

"No. Just go away, *please*." My voice faltered on the last word, sounding as broken and wounded as I was right then. "Why are you doing this to me?" I whispered.

I felt the blankets lifted off my head, felt his hand on my hair. My heart constricted in my chest, threatening to squeeze all the life out of me. He moved the hair away that was covering my face, but I kept my eyes firmly shut. I refused to look at his face. One look in those eyes and I knew it'd be over for me.

He found my hand and pulled it toward him, resting it

on his chest. As soon as I felt the perfectly sculpted muscle underneath his shirt it caused a longing in me so powerful I thought I would shatter. But then . . . I felt something else. Movement, where there shouldn't have been. A rhythmic pulse.

A heartbeat.

I gasped, pulling my hand away. My eyes flew open, and I saw his face, his perfect, beautiful face that haunted me at night when I closed my eyes. He was staring back at me, his eyes wild and excited looking. They locked on mine, and that's when I noticed something was different about them. I looked closer, staring deeper. They were the same vibrant green as they'd always been, but something was definitely missing.

And then I realized what it was.

They stopped there. When I looked into his eyes, I could no longer see behind them, couldn't feel that fey, mystical feeling of eternity. They didn't go on forever, didn't give me any kind of glimpse into his soul.

My own eyes grew huge as the full extent of the realization set in. It couldn't be. It wasn't possible.

"Are you . . . you're telling me that you're . . . ?"

Jude nodded, looking like he was struggling to suppress some strong emotion.

"I don't . . . how . . . ?" I stammered in shock.

He hesitated, as if searching for the right words. "I'll tell you, but I need you to promise you'll listen to the whole story before you react."

"Okay," I said, taking deep, slow breaths. I pulled myself up into a sitting position, trying to get past the shock enough to listen to what Jude was going to say.

"After I dropped you off for work on Sunday, I went . . . back." I knew, without him saying, where "back" was. Although somewhere deep down I'd known this had to have been the case, it was still startling to hear him say it. "When you asked how much time we had, it did something to me, and I couldn't just sit there and accept our fate, waiting around for the time I had to go back. I *had* to do something, and the only thing I could think of was to go back and plead my case, even if it meant facing whatever punishment was coming my way for my actions here on earth."

I fought to keep my face expressionless as I listened, but inside I was reeling.

"I went before the Council of Angels. They thought I was coming back to report, like I do after every assignment. They didn't know anything about what had happened here, of what I'd . . . done. So I told them everything. And," he inhaled deeply, "I asked to stay with you."

I opened my mouth to respond, but Jude shook his head and put a finger to my lips. "You promised," he reminded me. I bit my lip and nodded.

"They were shocked," he continued, "as you can probably guess, and I think some of the Council members would have cast me out right then and there if it were up to them, but fortunately for me, they have to decide everything as a whole. They dismissed me so they could discuss what my punishment should be, if any, and to decide whether or not to grant my request. Ultimately, they decided to let me stay with you. And this was the only way, this body. I had to be human."

I gazed at him in shock. "You mean . . . you gave up being an angel? *Forever*?"

"It was the only way I could be with you," he said quietly.

I was speechless. Horrified. I couldn't believe what I was hearing. Jude watched me, his face blank.

"So what does that mean?" I finally got out.

"It means I'm just like you now. It means we can be together, for real. With no good-bye looming over our heads."

As beautiful as the picture was that he painted, I couldn't get past what it had taken to create it. My thoughts were a tangled mess of questions and emotions and things I wanted to say. It was too much. *Too much.* I couldn't dwell on any one thought for more than a few seconds. I couldn't straighten anything out, couldn't figure out the appropriate thing to say or feel.

Jude was watching me closely. I realized then that he hadn't got the reaction he'd hoped for.

I grabbed his hands. "I'm sorry, this is just . . ." I shook my head. "I just can't believe you gave that up for me. I feel so . . . I don't know what I feel. You have to understand that this is a lot to take in."

He nodded. "I do."

"So you're really . . . *human* now?" I studied his face, not knowing what I expected to see. Of course he didn't look any different, with the exception of his eyes, and that was almost imperceptible. He nodded.

I stared at him, my brow furrowed. "And you're sure you made the right decision?" Immediately I knew it was the wrong thing to ask. The hurt was evident in Jude's voice as he answered.

"There was never a question. I always knew I would do whatever it took, give up whatever I had to, to be with you."

"Yeah, but *heaven*?" *For me?* It just didn't seem right. Didn't seem worth it.

"Heaven will still be there when I'm done here." His voice sounded strange, but then again, so did mine.

The thought made me feel ill. Thinking of Jude . . . dying. "But it won't be the same, right? You won't be an angel."

"No. I won't be an angel." I could see he was fighting to keep his voice normal. He was staring at our hands, clasped together between us. His next words felt like a knife right to my heart. "Are you even a little bit happy that I did this?"

I suddenly felt awful, completely overcome by guilt. I had not yet shown any kind of gratitude or excitement about the fact that we could now be together, too in shock over everything to celebrate why it had all happened in the first place.

I thought for the first time what this must be like for him. I'd been so stupidly focused on myself. I couldn't even begin to guess what he was feeling, or thinking. How would it be, knowing you'd left paradise, even temporarily? Walked away from a consecrated existence, with no pain, no sickness, nothing bad or sad or negative in any way, to come to a place full of it? I couldn't even imagine, and I began to appreciate more fully what he must have been going through right then.

"I'm so sorry!" I exclaimed. "I'm deliriously happy that we can be together now, I promise! It's just so hard not to feel incredibly guilty that I'm the reason you gave that up. And hard to believe that it's really true, that we really can be together indefinitely now. I think it'll be a while before I stop expecting you to disappear."

"I understand," Jude said apologetically. "But you have to understand something as well. This was all me. This was *my* choice, *my* sacrifice. You have absolutely nothing to feel guilty about. I did this because it was what *I* wanted. What *I* needed. I *needed* to be with you."

My heart seemed to skip a beat, his words melting over

me like warm honey. He pulled me to him then, wrapping his arms around me. I could hear his heartbeat beneath where my head rested, and I listened with fascination. I touched the skin of his arm, knowing it was no longer invincible. He could get sick, bleed, feel pain. He would grow older, and eventually die. He could have children . . .

I pulled away from him so I could see his face.

"Are you . . . okay?" he asked, concerned. I could see how much my unfavorable reaction had affected him.

"I'm fine, I promise. Just really overwhelmed. I just can't believe that you're . . . *human* now. What did it feel like? Do you feel completely different?"

He sucked in a breath through his teeth. "At first it was rough. Really rough. I could barely move, everything hurt. Truthfully, I wasn't sure I was going to survive those first couple of days. It just kept getting worse before it finally—slowly—began to get better. But each day was an improvement, until finally I could move normally, without pain."

"So that's why you disappeared again? Where were you?"

"I went to Hal's—your old house. I hid out there while I tried to get used to this new body, waited for the pain to go away. Thank goodness for Hal. I don't know what I would have done if he hadn't been there to help."

"But I was there! I went there looking for you! Hal said he hadn't seen you, that you were gone for good. Did he *lie* to me?" The thought had my blood raging through my veins.

"No, no," Jude said quickly, shaking his head. "I wasn't there yet. It took me most of the day to get there, in my condition."

"Oh." I relaxed, feeling mildly guilty about being so quick to accuse Hal. "Why didn't you come to me?"

Jude frowned. "Can you imagine how that would have played out? I come crawling to your door, sweating and panting and crying out in pain, and that's how you learn that I'm human?" He shook his head again, looking appalled at the thought.

I grimaced at the image. "It was really that bad?"

Jude nodded. "But it's fine now. It only lasted a couple of days, and now I'm a healthy, normal human." He looked at his hand, clenching and unclenching his fist as if to prove everything worked perfectly.

"Human," I repeated, trying to get used to the idea. Just like that. It was inconceivable. "And you're here. For good. We don't have to constantly worry about when it's going to end, how much time we have left . . . we can actually be together." A smile was creeping across my face as I realized exactly what it meant. He really had fixed everything. I laughed then, giddily, and threw my arms around him.

Jude laughed too. "*There's* the reaction I was hoping for."

"So what now?" I asked, sitting back.

Jude took a deep breath. "Well, first of all, I need to furnish my apartment, since I actually have to live there now." He smiled. "Second, I need to find a job." He paused in thought. "Maybe that should come before anyth . . . What?" he asked when he saw the bewilderment on my face.

"I was just thinking how crazy it is to hear you talk about this stuff. I've only known about you being an angel for a week, but somehow, it's even more unbelievable to see you acting and talking like a human. As a human. Maybe it's because I know now that you've never actually been one."

Jude thought about it. "It is weird, but I've pretended to be human for so long now, it doesn't feel totally unnatural.

Although . . ." He trailed off as if his mind had wandered elsewhere. "I was wrong, there's something I need to do before anything else."

"What?"

My heart fluttered as he leaned forward, touching his lips to mine. I worked my way up onto my knees, so that we were eye to eye, wrapping my arms around his neck, wanting to make up for lost time. This seemed to encourage him, his arms wrapping around my waist and pulling me against him. His lips parted slightly, becoming increasingly more responsive to mine. He kissed me with a fervor I'd never felt from him before, a hunger in his movements that had been missing from every other kiss we'd had. I welcomed it, urged him on. It became nearly impossible for me to breathe, my heart was pounding so furiously. And just when I thought for sure I was going to go into cardiac arrest, Jude abruptly pulled away. "Whoa," he said between heavy breaths.

"What?" I asked, leaning back against the headboard, waiting for my heartbeat to return to a normal, safe rate.

He stared at me, his eyes ablaze. "That . . . was . . . different." He reached up and laid his hand on his chest, over his heart. I guessed it was beating as wildly as mine. "I had no idea. That's what you feel every time?"

I smiled, a little embarrassed. "Yeah."

"That's . . ." he stopped, at a loss for the words to describe it.

"I know."

"Whoa," he said again, and I struggled to keep from laughing. I couldn't deny feeling more than a little satisfied that he reacted this way to me now, the same way I had always reacted to him.

We were both quiet for a minute. I didn't know what else

to say. Jude reached up and brushed his fingertips over my lips, looking me square in the eyes. "I'm so sorry for making you think I'd left you, for doing that to you . . . again. It was the very last thing I ever wanted to happen."

"I know," I assured him. "You don't have to apologize anymore. I'm fine. Well, I am now. Not so much when I thought you were gone." My eyes fell in shame. "Evidently I haven't come as far as I'd thought I had."

Jude frowned. "Why do you say that?"

"Because," I told him, shame in my voice. "I went right back to the person I was when I met you. I was a complete wreck. I cried all the time, I didn't want to do anything, I'd even spend hours just sitting staring out the window."

Jude reached forward and gently lifted my chin so that I would look at him. "Liv, you need to give yourself more credit. Did you sleep all day long?

"No, but—"

"Did you wake up screaming at night?"

"No."

His eyes grew softer. "Did you swallow a bottle of Valium?"

I was about to answer defensively, hurt that he would even consider the possibility, when I realized he wasn't accusing me, or even genuinely asking. I could see in his eyes that he already knew the answer, and that he just wanted me to acknowledge it.

"No," I answered, resigned.

"And you don't consider that progress?"

I stared at him for a minute, struggling to accept that what he was saying was true but unable to argue it. He was right. Despite the thousands of tears shed and the despair that I thought would destroy me, I had survived it. The one person in the world that I loved—that loved me—had left,

I thought forever, and not once did I ever consider ending my life, not even close. And I hadn't curled up in a ball and let the darkness drown me. I had tried—hard—to push through it, to keep living my life with a shattered heart. I could see it now, looking back, the change in me.

Jude must have seen the resignation on my face, because he smiled and kissed me on the forehead. "You're amazing. You need to know that. You're the strongest person I've ever known."

And just like at the restaurant when he'd called me brave, I was overcome with emotion. I wasn't used to hearing these kinds of adjectives referring to me.

Jude squeezed my hand. "If you ever have to go through anything like that again, it won't be because of me. And I'll be here to help you through whatever it is, for as long as you want me," he said.

"I'll always want you," I replied.

"Then I'll always be here."

I leaned against his chest, listening again to his heart, willing its strong and steady beat to convince me that everything he was saying was true. That everything really was going to be okay from now on.

CHAPTER TWENTY-NINE

LIFE POST-JUDE'S TRANSFORMATION was an adjustment, to say the least. I just couldn't seem to get used to him needing to eat, needing to sleep, and needing to do all the other little things that he'd never had to do before.

The first priority was finding him a job. This proved to be a challenge, as he had no degree, no references, no résumé, no work experience whatsoever, no social security number, not even any kind of identification. It wasn't long before we realized that attaining some of these things needed to be our first priority.

Fortunately for Jude, the one person he knew on the planet besides me happened to have no shortage of friends who could get us what we needed. Just like with the apartment, Jude didn't ask about the details of how Hal came into possession of these items, and Hal didn't offer them. Within a few days, Jude had a social security card, a driver's license (which is when it occurred to me he'd been driving around this entire time without one), and a birth certificate, all with the name *Jude West* printed across them.

After that, he resumed the job hunt. Hal did his best to convince Jude to become his "partner," but Jude insisted he wanted an honest, legitimate job. Despite never having set foot in a school, he knew pretty much everything there was to know about everything, and could do anything he tried. The problem was convincing potential employers of this.

We finally had to accept that the only thing he was ever going to get was something blue collar, so we perused the want ads for anything available. An ad for construction workers led him to a building site, where he was hired on the spot and put to work the next day. Although manual labor was probably the one thing Jude knew nothing about, he proved to be just as good at it as everything else, putting his strong arms and chest to good use.

The first several days he came home sore, bruised, and exhausted, with blisters covering his hands. I hated to see it, but he always brushed it off like it was nothing. I got the distinct feeling he was trying to prove to me that he could do this whole human thing, so I wouldn't have one more reason to wonder if he'd made a mistake. What he didn't know was that he had nothing to prove to me. Of course I lay in bed some nights, overcome with guilt at what he'd given up for me. But the bottom line was that I wanted him here with me so badly, I stopped caring almost immediately about whether or not he'd made a mistake. If he had, it was one mistake I was happy he'd made.

Hal gave him another hefty loan, which Jude insisted he would pay back as soon as he started earning some money from his job, plus everything Hal had given him before. I had fun playing interior decorator, filling his apartment with a new couch, bed, dresser, table, everything—including a TV, which he insisted he didn't need. We also stocked his kitchen, supplemented his insufficient wardrobe, and had the water turned on finally. It seemed strange, readying this apartment for him that was so close to mine, living in buildings side by side but not together, when we'd already committed to each other for life. But even though it was something we'd never talked about, I knew it was something neither of us was ready for.

That's not to say I didn't convince him to stay with me sometimes. There were so many nights I just couldn't bring myself to say good-bye, and I would beg and plead with Jude to stay with me, to hold me while we slept. He never refused me, but I could always detect a hint of distance from him on those nights, a sense of caution.

One night as we lay in the dark together, I rolled over to face him. "What are you so afraid of?" I asked. His eyes were closed, but I could tell he wasn't asleep yet.

He opened them but didn't answer right away. I waited patiently, listening to him breathe.

"You know what I'm afraid of."

"But why?" I touched the small cut across his cheek that he'd gotten at work that day.

"I don't want to do something we'd regret."

"But why would we regret it?"

Jude sighed, taking my hand and weaving his fingers into mine.

"Is it because of . . . what you were? Where you came from?" I asked.

He nodded slowly. "That's part of it, yeah. I just . . . can't. Not yet."

"Then when?"

He lifted our hands up to his mouth and kissed the back of mine. "I don't know."

"What's the other part?"

Jude inhaled, then exhaled long and slow. "I just want

to be sure we're both ready, especially you." He paused, and then said "I've seen too many times what it can do to people who aren't ready, the consequences that so many don't even consider, or don't care enough about." He turned and looked at me. "It can cause a lot of heartache, and it's not usually the guy that's hurting."

I gazed at him in awe. It was crazy to hear a guy talk like that about it. They were usually on the other side of the argument, trying to convince the girl that it was okay. But then, Jude was definitely not a typical guy. He was being who he'd always been, whether human or not, doing what he'd always done—making sure I was okay, never pushing me further than I was ready to go. And he was right. I didn't know for sure that I was ready. Just like Jude, I was fearful of rushing into something and regretting it. I would never risk destroying what would otherwise be perfect between us.

And so I let it go, and we didn't talk about it again. And once we'd made the decision and both knew we were on the same page, we were able to relax completely around each other and just enjoy what we had, exactly as it was, knowing that it was a miracle we had anything at all.

We fell into a routine, and life became completely ordinary. Each morning Jude would go to work, taking his truck because the job site was way beyond walking distance. I would hang out, doing whatever, until it was time for work, which I was back to walking to. At nine, when my shift ended, Jude would come pick me up, and we'd eat dinner together (usually a second dinner for him). Then we'd try to make the most of our few hours together, sometimes going out to do something, other times staying in and just being together.

With each passing day, I thought for sure I couldn't

possibly love Jude any more. But then another day would come, and I would find I was wrong. I cherished every second I had with him, and I was without question happier than I'd ever been before in my life.

Sometimes I thought back to that night in March when things had been so bad that I'd seen no other way out than to end my life. I'd relive the whole thing, see that shell of a person sprawled on the bed, hanging onto the last seconds of life by a mere thread. It doesn't seem like that person could have been me. It felt like a million lifetimes ago. I would look at my life now and marvel at the night and day difference. I couldn't deny that I was lucky to have been here at all. Or maybe luck had nothing to do with it.

I continued to see Dr. Robinson, not fooling myself into thinking I was one hundred percent recovered. Two weeks after Jude came back for good, I sat in her office for one of our sessions. I hadn't seen her the last couple of weeks while she was on vacation, and a lot had happened in that time, almost none of which I could talk about.

"So, how are things going with the guy . . . Jude?" she asked in her throaty voice.

"Great," I answered, smiling. It was probably closer to beaming, as I didn't have a lot to complain about these days. "Things have gotten pretty serious with him, actually."

"Really? How serious?"

"Well, I mean, we're not engaged or anything, but . . ." I shrugged. What else could I say? So serious that he became human for me?

Dr. Robinson's eyebrows lifted. "Well, that's great. I'm happy you've allowed yourself to get close to someone."

"Me too. He made it easy to do."

"I'm glad to hear it." I couldn't read Dr. Robinson's voice. She had mastered the ability to speak with no inflection, giving nothing away of what she was really thinking. It made me constantly second-guess her words.

"And how is work?"

"Fine," I shrugged. "As good as work can be. Actually, I made a friend there. The closest girlfriend I've had in a long time. Her name is Jen. We've got a lot in common and she's fun to hang out with. She's one of those people that's really easy to be friends with. Not complicated at all—no drama."

"It sounds like just the sort of friendship you need."

"Yeah, it's been good for me."

"And what about your other friend, the one you ran into that night at dinner? Have you seen or talked to her since?"

"Actually, yeah, she called me. It was really unexpected. She said she'd been thinking about me since that night and wanted a chance to actually talk to me. She even apologized for abandoning me after my mom died. I still can't believe it." I shook my head, remembering.

"Wow," Dr. Robinson commented. "How did you feel about that?"

"I felt great." Obviously. "It's what I'd been waiting over six months to hear."

"Well," Dr. Robinson said, leaning back in her chair. "It sounds like everything is coming together for you really well. It's wonderful to hear. And are you still taking the medication?"

"Yes. I'm sure it's at least partially responsible for how good I've been feeling. I don't want to rock the boat."

She smiled. "That's what I like to hear. No stopping the meds until I say so."

"I know," I answered dutifully. "I won't."

There was a lull then, and I took the opportunity to say something I'd been itching to say. "Dr. Robinson, I wanted to tell you that . . . I know it's not just me grasping at the nearest thing that I think will make me happy. I'm not using Jude as a security blanket. You said to make sure I knew that it was real, and I do. A few weeks ago I thought that he'd left me. It turns out that he hadn't, that there was an explanation, but the important part was that I was fine. I mean, I was devastated, of course, but I was fine. I got through it. I did whatever it took to push past the pain and move on with life. Not once did I even think about raiding the medicine cabinet."

Dr. Robinson studied my face thoughtfully. "I have to say, Olivia, you surprise me. When I first met you in the hospital, I would have bet my medical license I'd never see you again. I pegged you as one of the ones that would be back having their stomach pumped within a week. Never did I imagine you would take your recovery so seriously. I want you to realize what an incredible feat that is, and in such a short time. There are too many who are not so successful."

I was embarrassed to feel tears welling up in my eyes, and I blinked furiously, trying to drive them back. She would never know what those words meant to me, especially coming from her, someone I always thought never believed I was actually getting better.

"Thank you," I managed to get out. "That means a lot."

"You're welcome." She smiled at me. "Now . . . I think that you are ready to graduate to twice-a-month visits."

"Really?"

"Yes, really. I don't believe you require weekly counseling any longer."

It was the best thing I could imagine hearing from her, second only to the compliment she'd just given me.

"Okay. Great! Then I'll see you in two weeks?"

She nodded. "Two weeks, same time."

I said good-bye and walked outside to Jude's truck. It was my day off, so I'd dropped him off at work and taken his truck so that I didn't have to take the bus to Dr. Robinson's office. It was nearly time to pick him up, so I headed straight to the construction site.

On the drive there, I replayed Dr. Robinson's words in my head. *There are too many who are not so successful.* And yet somehow, I had been one of the few who was. I wasn't going to lie to myself and say that Jude hadn't been a major part of that. But I had to give myself credit too. I had resolved to get better, and I'd done it. And that was huge.

CHAPTER THIRTY

I PULLED INTO THE CONSTRUCTION site and scanned the mass of working bodies for Jude. Finally I spotted him, standing up on the roof of the building, drinking a bottled water, with no shirt on. I watched the sweat gleam on his skin in the bright sun, unable to look away. I traced every line of his chest, arms and stomach with my eyes. I'd always guessed he was in good shape, based on the way he filled out his shirts, but I'd had no idea. He finished drinking, wiping the sweat from his forehead, before turning and seeing his truck with me in it. He grinned and held up his hand, fingers spread. Five minutes left, I knew he meant. That was totally fine by me. I could easily sit here and watch him work for five minutes.

I kept the engine running for the air conditioning, feeling sorry for all the guys out there baking in the sun. I watched as two guys working near Jude looked my way, then said something to him. He glanced at me, said something back to the guys, then started hammering something. One of the guys said something else, and Jude suddenly dropped his hammer and shoved the guy—hard. The guy stumbled backward, yelled something to Jude, and stormed off, the second guy right behind him. Jude picked up his hammer and resumed working, and even from a distance I could see that he didn't look happy.

A minute later a loud whistle blew, and all the workers climbed down to ground level, like ants spilling out of their hill. Jude appeared from behind the house, grabbed his stuff, and headed over to me, pulling his shirt on as he walked. He got in the truck, closing the door behind him.

"Hello, beautiful," he said, leaning over to kiss me. If it had been anyone else, I would have been grossed out by all the dirt and sweat, but somehow, Jude made even that look good. He didn't even stink, just had this sort of outdoorsy, musky smell that I found completely enticing.

"Hey, you," I said, pulling out of the lot. "What was that about?"

A shadow passed over his face. "Nothing."

"What?" I pressed. "Tell me."

He scowled. "Just some idiot guys."

"What'd they do?"

He puffed up his cheeks, then blew out the air slowly. "One of them made a comment about you being hot, and the other one agreed. I ignored them, 'cause I knew where it was headed. Sure enough, one guy took it a step further and said something he didn't need to, and it made me mad. So I shoved him. He didn't like that very much; he had a few choice words for me."

I listened, astonished. I had never had guys do anything like that over me. It had been a daily occurrence for Ashley in high school, but never me. It was kind of flattering, but mostly disturbing. I didn't ask what the guy said about me. I was sure I didn't want to know, and even more sure that Jude didn't want to tell me.

"I'm sorry," I said sympathetically.

He laughed. "Why are you sorry? You didn't do anything. It's not your fault those losers have no respect for women."

"Well, I'm still sorry it happened. But . . . thank you. For sticking up for me."

"It's not the first time," he mumbled. "And it won't be the last." Now I was shocked. It had happened before? Somehow guys had gone from calling me a freak to calling me hot? I couldn't believe it.

"Well," I said, changing the subject. Jude was clearly upset by it. "Where do you want to go tonight? We have all evening to do whatever we want."

"I don't care. I'm good for whatever."

"Ummm . . ." I thought about it. "There's this Japanese place Jen's been telling me about that I've been wanting to try."

"Sounds perfect," Jude replied, looking out the window. He seemed distracted. He must still be pretty upset about that guy, I guessed.

We went to Jude's place first so he could shower and get changed. I sat on the couch and watched TV while he got ready. It was strange being in here now, knowing he actually lived here. I still hadn't gotten completely used to him doing all the human things, like showering. I didn't know if it would ever not feel weird to me.

Fifteen minutes later Jude walked out, taking my breath away. He had on a vintage T-shirt, jeans, and flip-flops, and his hair, as always, was in perfect waves that bordered on curls.

"Ready?" he asked, holding his hand out to me. I grabbed it, pulling him down next to me and kissing him.

He kissed me back, and I noted how amazing he smelled. It made it extra hard to stop. But I did. "Okay. I'm ready."

We decided to walk, since the restaurant was fairly close and the night air was perfect. As we walked I told him about my visit with Dr. Robinson. He was happy for me when I told him about only having to go twice a week now, and he smiled when I told him what she'd said about me. But there was still something missing there, something that kept his full attention away from the conversation. Finally, I couldn't take it anymore.

"Jude, what's wrong? You're acting different. Are you still upset about what that guy said today?"

He looked at me in surprise, as if he'd had no idea he'd been acting any different. "No, it's . . . it's not that," he said, frowning. "I don't know what it is exactly. All day I've just had this . . . feeling. This bad feeling that won't go away."

"Bad feeling?" I repeated slowly.

"Yeah. I can't explain it. It's just this feeling that something's wrong. It's made me edgy and short-tempered all day. That guy ticked me off, but normally I would never have gotten physical with him." He turned to me, looking agitated. "Does that sound crazy?"

"No," I answered him. "Just . . . a little troubling. What do you think it could be?"

Jude shrugged. Something in that shrug made me nervous.

The Japanese restaurant was packed, and it took a half hour to get a table. We ordered our food, and as we waited for it to come, we chatted about our respective days. He told me about work, about the job they were doing and the electrical fiasco they'd had that had set them back days. I told him a little more about my visit with Dr. Robinson, and the errands I'd run before that.

Our food came then, and we started to eat. After a while I noticed that every few minutes, Jude would glance over his left shoulder. After the third time, I finally asked. "What're you looking at?"

"Nothing," he answered quickly.

But when he looked a fourth time, I demanded the truth. He was clearly looking at something.

"It's nothing, really. It's just that that guy over in the corner keeps looking at us, and it's making me uneasy."

I glanced over in the direction he'd been looking, trying not to be obvious. Sure enough, there was a man in a black hoodie and stocking cap staring right at us. It made me shiver in a bad way. "Creepy," I agreed.

"Let's get out of here." I nodded. Jude threw some cash on the table and put his arm around me protectively as we walked out of the restaurant. Once outside, we began our walk home in silence, neither of us in the mood now to talk.

We'd gone about a block before Jude glanced over his shoulder. I was just turning to see what he was looking at when I felt his body tense up beside me.

"What?" I asked, scared of the answer.

"That guy," he said. "He followed us out."

My breathing accelerated, but I tried to be rational. "Are you sure he followed us? Maybe he was just done eating too and was ready to leave." Even as I said it, I wasn't convinced. Not after the way he'd been watching us.

Jude shook his head, quickening our pace. "He hadn't even ordered yet."

My blood froze in my veins, and I had to concentrate on putting one foot in front of the other. "Why? What does he want with us?"

"I don't know," Jude answered, but something about the way he said it made me think that wasn't completely true.

We made our way quickly down the street, Jude glancing back every few minutes to see if the man was still following. Every time he faced forward again and pulled us along even faster, I knew that he was.

Fear spread its way through me the faster we walked, and the further we went with the man still on our heels. When we came up to an intersection, Jude shifted directions at the last second and led me across the main street instead of the side street we needed to cross to get home. "I'm not leading that guy to our apartments," he explained.

He started taking random turns at every intersection, hoping to lose the guy. But no matter where we went, every time we looked back, he was behind us. In fact, he seemed to be gaining on us.

"Jude, I'm scared," I said in a trembling voice. He squeezed my hand but had nothing to offer me in the way of reassurance. I could tell he was trying to hide his own panic from me.

On one of our last-second turns, we wound up in some kind of wide back alley, walled in on three sides. We stopped dead in our path, and I was convinced I was going to pass out with fear. We spun around quickly, hoping to get back out and onto the street before the man caught up to us, but it was too late. He was right there, twenty feet away. We were trapped. There was no way out.

"Who are you?" Jude demanded. "What do you want?"

The man didn't answer, just slowly walked forward toward us. I was shaking so badly I was almost convulsing. *This is it,* I thought. *We're going to die.* Jude's been human for less than three weeks and he's going to die.

When the man was about ten feet from us he stopped. We waited, frozen in place, waiting for him to talk.

He stood silent for several moments, purely to toy with us, I'm sure. It worked. The longer he stood there without speaking, the more paralyzed with fear I became.

Just when I thought he was never going to make a move or speak, that his whole purpose was to scare us literally to death, he reached up and pulled off the stocking cap, revealing a shockingly bald head underneath. Covering the entire left side of his bare scalp was a tattoo, some kind of tribal design. It made him look even more dangerous than he already seemed.

"Hello, Jude," he suddenly spoke, and I felt Jude tense beside me. The man's voice was eerily calm and had a high, almost feminine quality to it.

"How do you know my name?" Jude demanded.

"I know everything about you," he answered, pulling his lips apart in a sinister smile.

"How? Who are you?" Jude repeated. He was shifting backward, pulling me with him so subtly that I could barely feel it, and I knew the man wouldn't be able to tell.

"My real name is not something you would begin to understand. The body I reside in is named Caleb."

I felt Jude falter. In reaction to what, I didn't know. The guy was clearly a psycho, but I had no idea what he'd said that had upset Jude even more.

"What do you want with us?" Jude shouted, taking another infinitesimal step backward.

"You know exactly what we want. My associates and I are here to collect you."

"What associates?" Jude wanted to know, but I was more concerned with the "collect you" part. What was this guy *on*, and what was he planning on doing with us? I had never been so scared in my entire life.

Caleb didn't answer, but I noticed a tiny flick of his fingers on his right hand. Out of nowhere, people began jumping down from the brick wall beside us, off the roof of the building across from it, out from behind the dumpster in the alley behind us. There were at least a dozen men and women, all looking as vicious as Caleb. My knees weakened, causing me to lean on Jude for support. He already had his arm around me, but he tightened his grip, holding me like an iron vice against his side.

Now surrounded on all sides, Jude stopped trying to move away. It was futile, with just as many people behind us as were in front of us. Jude's eyes shifted around, gauging the situation. "Where exactly, do you plan on taking us?"

Caleb smiled again. "Not her. Just you."

Jude clenched his teeth. "And why would I go with you?" I could hear that he was trying to keep his voice casual.

Caleb laughed; it was an unnatural sound, like an animal being tortured. His cohorts joined in. "Because," he answered Jude. "You belong with us." He flexed his hands and made them into fists, in an obviously threatening gesture. The newcomers began to move in slowly, forming a sloppy circle around Jude and me.

I looked at Jude, and he looked down at me helplessly. I could see it then in his eyes, the same conclusion that I'd come to myself: we weren't going to make it out of here alive. He gazed at me sadly and mouthed the words, "I love you." I did the same back. At least we would die knowing that.

Jude turned back to Caleb and, lifting his chin in defiance, said, "With you is the last place I belong. You can tell your little puppet master to dream on." I looked at Jude in total confusion. What was he *talking* about?

Caleb snarled, incensed. "You're going to regret that." He cocked his head to the right and the circle of people around us rushed forward, closing in fast. I squeezed my eyes shut and prayed it would be over quick, burying my head under Jude's arm. I could hear the bodies moving closer and closer, their hisses and war cries as they ran in for the attack. Right at the moment that I braced myself for impact and, with it, an onslaught of unimaginable pain, I heard a yell, then several yells, and the next thing I knew Jude was pulling me, dragging me at a run. I tried to keep up with him, but all around us was complete chaos. I looked up to see that the number of people in the alley had more than doubled in size, but I didn't have time to wonder what had happened or what had saved us.

Jude pulled me into a doorway further down the alley behind some rusty metal canisters. He shoved me in first, then ducked down next to me, blocking my body with his.

Shaking violently, I tried to find my voice. "*Who are those people?*" I managed to choke out.

Not taking his eyes off the brawl playing out before us, he answered in a dire voice. "They're fallen angels." He glanced at me quickly. "The devil's followers."

Now my knees did give out, and I fell backward against the metal door behind me. Jude swiftly grabbed me and pulled me back up into a crouching position, then quickly resumed a close watch on the goings-on. I was pretty sure I was going to be sick. I took deep breaths, trying to calm down, but it was impossible. "How . . . can I . . . see them?" I managed between gasps.

Jude was shaking, but it seemed more like rage than fear. His voice was bleak when he answered. "There's only one way you could." All the color had drained from his face.

"They're not alone. They've joined up with their human counterparts."

"What do you mean?" I asked, regaining my breath.

Jude let out a deep sigh. "I mean that humans allowed themselves to be taken over. By the evil spirits."

My mouth fell open in horror. "You mean those people are . . . *possessed*?" I felt evil just saying the word.

Jude nodded. "Willingly."

I swayed again, but Jude held onto my arm to keep me from falling. I put my head down between my knees and breathed through my mouth to keep from passing out. I concentrated on the noises coming from the alley beyond and tried to make out what I was hearing. There were shouts and cries of pain, loud clangs and crashes. There was definitely a battle going on.

I peered up through the crack between the two canisters in front of me. "Who's . . . fighting them?"

Jude pointed out toward the huge dumpster. I followed the direction with my eyes, landing on a man with slick black hair who was fighting a guy almost twice his size.

Hal.

CHAPTER THIRTY-ONE

I STARED IN AMAZEMENT, thinking how much I owed that man. A wave of emotion washed over me as I watched him fight with everything he had in him. "Who are all the other people?"

"Other former angels like Hal. He must have rounded them up to come help us. Who knows how he knew we needed help."

I looked around at the others fighting. It wasn't easy with the lack of light, but I managed to tell which were the good guys and which were the bad. It was like watching a gothic cult duel with a bunch of homeless people.

I noticed then that the fighting didn't seem at all even.

There were more of Hal's group than Caleb's, but Caleb and his people seemed to have some kind of . . . *power* or something they were using against the others. Where Hal and the other former angels had to rely on their fists and feet and anything else they could use as weapons, the fallen angels were picking objects up without touching them and sending them through the air at their targets. I watched as one woman held out her hand toward the man she was fighting and lifted him up in the air from five feet away. Then she whipped her arm out and he went flying through the air, crashing into a chain-link fence.

I was aghast watching it happen, dismayed that such a thing was possible and filled with dread as I realized what it meant for our chances of winning. I turned to Jude. "Shouldn't we help?"

He looked at me in disbelief. "Are you kidding? And risk you getting killed? No, we're staying right here, hidden, where I can keep you safe.

I had to admit, I didn't want him to leave me, even if it meant helping Hal and the others.

We watched from behind our makeshift shelter, each minute that passed adding to our despair and feelings of hopelessness. I wondered how long our guys would be able to hang in there, up against such powerful opponents. I was mildly comforted by the fact that Hal and the other ex-angels weren't mortal and therefore couldn't die. But Hal had said they weren't immortal either, and I didn't know what that meant. By the looks of it, it wasn't good.

Suddenly a body landed just in front of the barrels, collapsing in a lifeless heap. Before I even had a chance to see whose side they were on, a pair of huge hands grabbed Jude by his shirt and pulled him out into the alley. "Jude!" I screamed as the large, beefy man dragged him into the middle of the action. Before I could make a move, a second pair of hands grabbed me and lifted me up out of the doorway. It was Caleb, baring his teeth at me like a wild animal salivating over its next meal.

I screamed again, and saw Jude's eyes focus on me in terror. "Olivia!" he yelled, kicking out at the man who stood over him. I watched as he tried to clamor to his feet, only to be shoved back down by the brute.

"Jude!" I screamed again, thrashing around, trying to escape from Caleb's grasp.

"Now, now," Caleb sneered. "Play nice little girl, or things might get ugly." He threw me over his shoulder and made his way through the clashing bodies toward the only exit from the alley. I screamed my throat raw, reaching for Jude as the distance between us grew with each step Caleb took. I saw Jude calling out for me, watched as the monster kicked him in the stomach. Jude doubled in half, and I felt his pain, screaming harder than ever.

Caleb turned a corner down another smaller alley, barely wider than a sidewalk. He threw me down in a pile of loose garbage, and I hit hard, something cutting into my side. My head felt like it landed on a rock, and I rolled over moaning.

"Now you listen to me, girl. You're gonna do what I say or you're gonna wind up a lot worse than that, you hear?"

I opened my mouth to scream, but no sound came out. It felt like every one of my ribs had snapped in two.

"I was sent here for one thing and one thing alone, and that was to get your little boyfriend back there. And I'm not leaving till I do."

He stood over me, rubbing his tattooed head as if deciding what to do with me. I tried to take advantage of his momentary indecision, to do something like the heroines in books and movies always do. Just when you think they're too weak to fight back, they always do something to surprise you, like kick out suddenly and knock the attacker on his back. But I couldn't move. I couldn't seem to work a single part of my body.

Caleb turned and paced down the alley a ways, then turned around and came back. *What is he doing,* I thought.

It's like he's waiting for something.

And then it hit me. He was waiting for Jude. He was using me as bait, knowing Jude would come after me. *Not a very good plan when his biggest guy out there is knocking Jude senseless at this very moment,* I thought, wincing at the image in my head.

"It . . . won't . . . work," I said, pushing my voice out with the little bit of air left in me.

"You . . . should . . . just . . . give . . . up. . ." The effort it took to expel that much breath left me winded and aching even more, as my ribs shifted around deflating lungs.

Caleb laughed cruelly, and I wished I had the strength to cover my ears. "I don't give up, sweetie. I get the job done." With that, he stepped forward and kicked me in the ribs, right where I was already wounded and bleeding. I cried out, the pain blinding. Caleb glanced over his shoulder toward the direction we'd come from, looking to see if Jude had come yet. If he'd heard my tortured cry.

When Jude didn't appear, Caleb let out a frustrated growl, kicking the brick wall. I was relieved that Jude wasn't coming, wasn't going to fall into Caleb's trap, but then, I knew the only reason he wouldn't come was if he was physically incapacitated. The thought made me see red, fury filling every ounce of me. I wanted to hurt Caleb like he was hurting me, and even more, hurting Jude. I wanted to scream and kick at him, inflict some kind of pain, but all I could do was lie there and cry.

Right at the point when it looked like Caleb was starting to doubt his plan, Jude came running around the corner, yelling my name.

I cried out when I saw him, both from relief at seeing him alive and from agony when I took in his broken, bruised state.

He was walking hunched over, looking exactly the way I felt. His left eye had a huge gash over it, blood flowing down the side of his face and neck. His shirt was torn, and he was cradling his left arm as if it was broken. But he was alive, and that was all that mattered.

"Jude!" I warned him, putting all my energy into getting the words out. "Don't . . . come! It's a . . . trap!"

Caleb, looking satisfied that his plan had worked, came over and grabbed me, hauling me up off the ground. A piercing pain shot through my ribs, and I was gasping for air.

"Put her down!" Jude yelled, rushing forward. "Leave her alone!"

Caleb whipped out a knife, seemingly out of nowhere, and held it up to my throat. Jude stopped dead in his tracks, unmoving except for his head, which was shaking back and forth. "No. No, don't. Please, I beg you. Don't hurt her."

Caleb laughed maniacally. "It's a little late for that, don't you think?" He gave my body a jerk, and I was screaming, on the verge of blacking out from the pain.

Jude cried out in agony. "STOP!" he screamed. "Just . . . put her down. You can have me, just *stop hurting her.*" His eyes looked insane.

Caleb paused at the same time that I screamed a hoarse "No!" He eyed Jude suspiciously. "What do you mean, I can have you?"

Jude looked ready to collapse. "I mean I'll go with you. Join you. Whatever you want, just leave her alone."

I opened my mouth to tell Jude to stop being stupid when Caleb suddenly threw me back to the ground. This time no sound came out as the wind was knocked out of me completely, all air pushed from my lungs. Jude screamed again, full of rage. But he knew he'd got what he wanted, so he stayed firmly in place, clearly fighting the urge to rush Caleb and do some serious damage to the demon. Our eyes met then, and Jude looked at me for a long time, total despair written all over his face. I reached out to him, pleading silently for him not to do it, unable to speak the words. I felt like I was dying as I watched Caleb approach Jude greedily, the hunter moving in on his prey. I wanted to close my eyes; I couldn't bear to see what was happening, but I kept them open, fixed on Jude.

Caleb lifted a hand as he neared the spot where Jude stood, to use his power to hurt or control him, I didn't know which. Either way, I was sure that seeing it would haunt me for the rest of my life.

Caleb opened his hand, and I knew it was only a matter of seconds before Jude would be gone, and I would never see him again. I couldn't bring myself to think about the life he would be forced to live then.

In the seconds that followed, I became disconnected from the scene. My eyes were on Jude, but my mind was thinking of the bitter irony that had been my lifelong companion. Three months earlier I'd tried to end my life, and now I was fighting desperately to stay alive. Jude had given up being an angel to become human, only to die; he had given up heaven for hell. I knew it had all been too good to be true. I'd known it all along.

Suddenly an explosion of light filled the narrow alley, blinding me and forcing my eyes closed. I heard Caleb scream an ungodly scream, and I pried my eyes open, shielding them with my hand. The white light burned into my retinas, and all I could see were shadows of figures: Jude's, standing hunched over; Caleb's, which seemed to be shrinking away; and a third, which was where the light seemed to be emanating from. I watched while Caleb's shrieking silhouette disappeared into nothingness, and instantly the light vanished, leaving behind only Jude and me in the dark alley.

Still blinded by the unnatural brightness, I blinked repeatedly to make sure it was Jude I was seeing, and that we were really alone. He was limping toward me, holding his wounded arm across his stomach. I tried to smile, to say his name and reach out to him, but everything was suddenly blurry and I was so very, very tired. My eyes fell closed again, and the last thing I felt was Jude collapsing onto his knees beside me, laying his head on mine.

CHAPTER THIRTY-TWO

"OLIVIA." SOMEWHERE, FROM a distance, someone was calling my name. I tried to open my eyes but it was too bright, like the sun was hanging directly over my head.

"Olivia," the voice repeated, and I tried again, this time managing to get them open just a slit, squinting against the light. I couldn't see anyone or anything; the light was too blinding. All I could hear was the voice calling my name. It wasn't a voice I recognized.

Slowly, as I adjusted to the glare, I was able to open my eyes completely, and, although everything remained ultra-bright, it no longer blinded me. I looked around, blinking, seeing nothing but white in every direction. The last time I'd opened my eyes and saw nothing but white I'd been in the hospital. *I must be there again*, I thought, which made sense since the last thing I remembered was getting the tar kicked out of me by a crazy demon.

But as I looked around, I knew that was wrong. This wasn't a hospital. There were no shiny silver instruments, no beeping equipment, no one in teal scrubs holding a chart. There was nothing at all. Just white, white, and more white, and I was standing in the middle of it. I felt like I should be alarmed, but I wasn't. In fact, a strange, inexplicable calm filled me, warming me from the inside out.

I saw someone then, in the distance. Or, at least, something that vaguely resembled a human form. In the glare of the light (where was all the light coming from, anyway?) it was impossible to make out any details. After a minute I could tell that the figure was coming toward me. As it grew nearer, I could see it was a woman, a beautiful woman with long chestnut hair and hazel eyes. She was wearing a flowing white gown that I found both bizarre and logical at the same time. I'd never seen her before, but something about her seemed vaguely familiar. Somehow I knew that she was the one who'd been calling my name.

When she reached me, she smiled the most beautiful smile that made me think of sunshine and fuzzy blankets and warm pie with ice cream melting over the top. It was impossible not to smile back.

"Hello, Olivia," she said in a soft, soothing voice.

"Hello," I responded, because it was the natural response.

"Do you know where you are?"

I looked around again at the glowing surroundings, then back at the beautiful woman in the ivory gown, and I suddenly knew.

"This is heaven, isn't it?" My voice was full of reverence and awe.

She nodded, still smiling.

"So are you an . . . angel?" I asked softly.

She shook her head gently. "No. I'm a spirit. A spirit who has completed a life on earth and returned home. As are you," she added. I thought of everything Jude had told me about heaven, about how spirits and angels lived separately.

And then her last three words registered, and my breath caught in my throat.

"Are you saying I . . . *died*?" It came out as barely more than a whisper. For the first time since waking up, I felt the first flutters of fear.

"Almost," she corrected, gently. "Not quite yet. There's still time."

"What do you mean?" I asked warily.

"You are very, very near dying. Hovering on the edge, actually. So close that you are here, but not quite home yet."

"I don't understand. Where's 'here'?"

The woman pursed her lips in thought. "It's sort of . . . an in-between. Not earth, not quite heaven, although technically, it is a part of it. Most people don't come here. When they leave their bodies behind on earth, they go straight home, to the heaven everyone pictures. But sometimes . . . sometimes a person is undecided. They hang back, fight harder, not ready to leave their life behind, for one reason or another."

I pictured myself lying on a gurney somewhere, doctors and nurses hovering over me, calling out orders and passing around tools, and charging the shock paddles and yelling "CLEAR!" It sent a shiver down my spine.

The woman's eyes seemed to bore into mine, like tiny spotlights that made me feel somehow exposed in the middle of this vacant place. "I know your reason for fighting to stay."

Jude. I closed my eyes, thinking of him back there, on earth, and me here. It was almost laughable, after everything we'd been through, everything that had happened in order for us to be together—him saving my life, becoming human to be with me—for it to end like this: separated again, by an infinite distance and an impenetrable barrier.

Laughable, if it wasn't so devastatingly heart breaking. Maybe someone, somewhere, *was* laughing. That's what I felt like. That fate was getting a big kick out of a really sick joke at my expense. It wouldn't be the first time.

I was so angry, so scared, so full of despair that I wanted to yell, scream, cry. But no tears came, a feeling I was all too familiar with. "This can't be right," I choked out. I was suffocating. There wasn't enough oxygen in this place. "This *cannot* be the way it's supposed to end."

"I know," the woman said, a mix of pain and sympathy washing over her picturesque features. Again I had the strangest feeling of recognition. "You need him. He needs you too. What he did, to be with you, it can't be in vain. You understand that, right? If you leave him now, and come here, everything he sacrificed *will be* in vain."

My forehead creased as I considered what she said. "So, what are you saying? I have the choice? I can just say I want to go back—to live—and I will?"

"I know it's hard to believe, but in this case, yes. You can. Because of the circumstances surrounding the situation, because you are here in this in-between, you can choose whether to stay here or go back. There is a way."

She had barely finished speaking when I blurted out, "Well then, I choose to go back! Now!" Something fluttered in my chest, something that I was terrified to give in to. Something like hope.

"I figured you would." Something in the way her voice wavered slightly made me think that she was hiding something, some emotion she was feeling and didn't want me to know about. "I'm happy to know he didn't choose that fate for nothing."

This stopped me cold. "Choose what fate? What are you talking about?"

The woman's eyebrows raised in surprise. "He didn't tell you?"

"He told me he gave up being an angel for me, became human to be with me."

The woman's face seemed to falter for a sliver of a second before returning to its composed, demure state, as if she too were trying not to cry tears that would never come. I wondered why she would feel affected by any of this. Maybe that's what happens when you're a spirit, once you've left the selfishness of the world behind. Maybe you're sympathetic to a fault, feeling others' pain and happiness as real as if it were your own.

"What fate?" I asked again, softer this time, not sure now that I really wanted to know.

The woman's voice trembled as she answered. "Jude gave up being an angel and became human, yes. But I'm not sure you understand what that means. He didn't become a regular human, like you, who will die one day and return here as a spirit." She paused, taking a deep, shaky breath. "He can never return."

"I don't understand," I whispered.

"He was given the choice: return to heaven, as an angel, or stay with you on earth, as a human, leaving all of this behind forever."

"*What?*"

"He chose you, Olivia. He was cast out of heaven. He . . . fell."

My throat tightened, threatening to cut off my air, and my chest seemed to be squeezing whatever life I had left out of me. "I don't believe it." My lips formed the words, but I didn't hear any sound come out.

"Jude is a fallen angel." The woman's tone left no room for argument.

I clenched my fist over my heart, which seemed to be on the brink of beating its last beat. I refused to believe it. That he had really made that kind of a sacrifice for me. It had been bad enough when I'd learned he'd given up being an angel, but now . . . this I absolutely could not accept.

"What are you saying, that . . . he'll go to . . . ?" I couldn't bring myself to finish the sentence. Like saying the word would make it true.

The woman looked as pained as I felt when she nodded.

I thought about my last memories on earth, of the alley and Caleb, and the reason he'd given Jude for coming after us. *My associates and I are here to collect you,* he'd said.

"NO!" I argued. "It's not true! Jude is *not* one of them! He *fought* them! He refused to go with them! He would never, *ever* join them!" I was hysterical.

"I know," the woman said softly. "It was incredible. Unheard of. No one who has ever been condemned to their side has ever refused to join them. Which is why you were sent protection."

"Hal?"

She nodded. "And the guardian angels."

I frowned, thinking back. "The blinding light." I hadn't realized it until just now, but I knew I was right.

She nodded. I was stunned into silence. I still could not believe it was true. That Jude really had fallen, to be with me. That he had given up everything he cherished, that defined his very being. He'd given up a life of divinity, immortality, salvation, everything he'd ever known and been for a life of eternal . . . I stopped there. I couldn't even think it. And for what? To spend, sixty, maybe seventy earthly years with me? That was hardly a blip on the radar compared to eternity.

Inside I was at war with myself, whether to feel

overwhelmingly grateful that Jude loved me enough to make that kind of a sacrifice, or devastated that I was the reason he'd condemned himself to endless misery. Even thinking the words made me feel sick, like I was some sort of temptress who'd lured him away to the dark side. And sicker yet was picturing Jude—my sweet, wonderful, angelic Jude, *there*. I couldn't do it. My brain wouldn't allow me to even begin to envision it.

The worst part about it was, it was all said and done. If what the woman said was true, and I had every reason to believe that it was, for she had no motive (or maybe even ability) to lie to me, then this had all taken place weeks earlier. There was nothing I could do to change it, nothing at all. I felt so helpless, so desperate, wishing more than anything that I'd known at the time what Jude had been planning to do when he'd dropped me off at work that day. I could have stopped him. I would have. Even if it meant we'd never be together again, I would have done it. Anything to prevent him from making such a choice.

"Is there no hope at all for him?" I finally got out.

The woman looked sad as she answered, "Jude made his choice. He must pay the price."

I felt as if the weight of the world was resting on my shoulders but knew there was nothing I could do. I only hoped that one day I would be able to pay him back for what he'd done for me. So that it wasn't in vain, just as the woman had said. She was right, I realized now. I absolutely could not let Jude's sacrifice be in vain. If I died now and left him alone on earth, it would be. I had to go back.

I was just opening my mouth to say as much, when she suddenly glanced over her shoulder—at what, I don't know—then looked back at me and said, "It's time. If you're going back, you need to go now."

For some reason I froze, unsure of what to do. I didn't remember getting here; I had no idea how to get back. "How?" I asked, feeling somewhat stupid.

"You'll know," she said, turning to leave. "I must leave you now." She began walking away, her long hair swinging behind her as she went.

"Wait!" I called out, right as a warm, tingling sensation began to prick at every pore in my skin. "Who are you? How do you know so much about me and Jude?" The glowing air around me seemed to be moving now, spinning in all directions, like a hurricane of golden light. At first it didn't seem like the woman had heard me, but just as I began to feel myself leaving, knew that in seconds I would be gone, she turned around. Her mouth was moving urgently; she was calling something to me but I couldn't make out what it was over the sound of the rapidly accelerating whirlpool of light and air whipping around my head. Then, just before everything faded away, before the last wisp of light surrendered to pure darkness, I somehow made something out, a fragment of a sentence, but couldn't be sure of exactly what it was. Something about . . . *sacrifice.* I called back, *"What?"* but she stopped talking. She just stared, and through the last swarms of light I saw a sudden flash of green in her eyes, a green that was as familiar to me as the back of my hand, and understanding filled me just as everything faded to black and was silent.

* * * * *

"Olivia."

A soft, deep voice hummed in my ear, ripping me from unconsciousness. *This* voice I knew. This voice I would recognize from the grave. I moved my face in the direction it was coming from, working at opening my eyes. The muscles in my eyelids weren't cooperating, but finally I was able to pry them apart and when I did, I saw the only thing in the world I would have wanted to see right then.

"Jude," I cried, or at least tried to. It came out as not much more than a wisp of air that took a surprising amount of effort to get out, and sounded like I'd said it in slow motion.

Jude was gazing back at me, a large bandage on his forehead over his left eye. He looked sad, and relieved, and worried, all at the same time, if that were possible. But I only felt relief at seeing his face again. I drank in every bit of it. I felt the need to re-memorize it, as if I would ever forget even one tiny detail. It was hard to focus, and everything had a hazy outline like I was looking underwater, but I didn't care. I studied the dimple in his chin, the two in his cheeks, his soft, full lips, his perfectly straight nose. His eyes that sparkled like gemstones. I had the irresistible urge to reach out and touch his face, and that movement too seemed sluggish and awkward. And it hurt.

"Ow."

"Yeah, you're not going to want to move much just yet," he said softly, stroking my cheek.

My eyes moved slowly to the IV in my hand, then followed the tube up to the bag full of clear liquid hanging above my head. Jude watched me. "Morphine," he said. "Lots of it."

So that explained the fogginess and delayed movements. "What's . . . why?" I frowned. That didn't come out the way I'd meant it to, but Jude seemed to know what I was asking.

"You broke some ribs, which punctured a lung. It was pretty touch and go there for a while. I thought . . ." he cut off abruptly, and I could tell by his face what he didn't want to say. That he'd thought I was going to die. I tried not to dwell on it but couldn't help thinking how it'd been twice now in less than three months that I'd come so close to dying and somehow survived. I really hoped this was the last time I looked death in the eye for a long time. "There were some other cuts and scrapes," he continued, "but those were all minor in comparison. The doctor will fill you in on everything when he sees you."

"What about you?" I asked, eyeing his bandage.

"Broken arm, head wound, some bruised ribs." I saw the sling around his neck, supporting his left arm, which I'd somehow missed before. "I'll be fine."

Everything was so fuzzy, it took so much energy to try and formulate thoughts and especially words. I tried to remember how we got these injuries, but all I could conjure were fleeting, blurry images of a dark alley, an intricate tattoo, a flash of light, and lots and lots of pain.

"What happened? I can't . . . remember." I hated how my voice sounded exactly like my dad's did when he used to get drunk, all slurred and sleepy sounding. Only his was usually laced with a meanness that had me hiding out in my room till he sobered up.

Jude leaned forward and rested his free elbow on the side rail of the bed, putting his hand over mine. "Not now. There's too much risk of being overheard, and, besides, you're too doped up. If I told you everything now, you'd never remember it later."

I sighed, which was a mistake. I gasped as pain seared through my rib cage. Jude winced as he watched me, looking like he wanted to help but didn't know how. The pain quickly subsided, though, and I made a mental note to try and remember not to move. Instead I just stared at Jude through half-lidded eyes, thinking that if I had to be confined to a bed, unable to move or do anything, I couldn't pick a better view. As I gazed into the bright green of his eyes, something tugged at the edge of my memory, just out of reach of fully remembering. Just like my memories of what had happened in the alley, it came in fragments, flashes of color and sound and feeling.

It must have shown on my face, because Jude reached out and stroked my cheek. "What?" he asked.

I scowled as I fought to remember. It was so hard trying to concentrate. "I think it was a dream I had, maybe, while I was unconscious."

"What about?"

"I—I'm not sure. I just remember bits and pieces. Lots of light, some woman with long hair. I think . . . I think we were talking about *you*." I started to laugh, knowing how ridiculous I must have sounded but cut off as soon as my ribs reminded me that laughing wasn't such a good idea.

Jude smiled back, amused. "What were you saying about me?"

I focused harder, straining to remember. It seemed as if every time I was just within reach of another detail, it would evaporate into thin air. I groaned in frustration.

Jude squeezed my hand. "Don't kill yourself trying to remember. It was probably just the morphine."

"Yeah," I conceded, but for some reason, I felt like it was more than that.

"You should get some rest, you can barely keep your eyes open."

I realized then that my eyes were barely slits, struggling to stay open, not wanting to lose the sight of Jude's face beside me. "Don . . . lee me . . ." I mumbled as my eyes fell shut, no fight left in them.

I felt Jude's hand on my hair. "Don't worry. I'll be here." I savored the echo of his voice that hung in the air after he'd stopped talking, the last thing I heard before drifting out of consciousness again.

CHAPTER THIRTY-THREE

We entered my apartment, Jude helping me make my way over to the bed. His right arm was around me, supporting most of my weight, acting as my crutch. Every step I took sent waves of pain through my torso, and other parts of me as well. There weren't many parts of me that didn't hurt, but I was so thrilled to be off of the morphine drip that I tried not to complain. I couldn't stand the constant cloudiness in my head, not being able to think clearly or stay awake for very long. It terrified me, that lack of control. I would take pain over that every day of the week.

It seemed to take a full minute to ease myself onto the bed, even with Jude right there, helping me down. Finally, I was laying, stretched out, the only position I'd found that was anywhere near the vicinity of comfortable.

"Do you want a pain pill?" Jude asked, and I was already shaking my head before he finished. He knew I didn't, and he knew why, but he was also worried that I hurt more than I was letting on because of it.

"I'm fine," I said, trying my hardest to speak evenly and normally, without the quick gasps of air that often surrounded my speech now. "I promise."

And I meant it. I was fine. I was more than fine. Sure, I was a little worse for wear, a little battered and beaten, but that pain was nothing. Temporary. Healable. That kind of pain I could handle, no problem. I was alive, Jude was alive, and we were together, with no threat of imminent separation hanging over us. How could I be anything but happy, truly, one hundred percent happy?

I lay, staring at the crack in the ceiling, as Jude moved around my apartment, putting things away and rummaging in the fridge. I thought about the crack, how through everything it had remained unchanged, while below it, everything else—*me*—had done a complete one-eighty. It seemed odd that the same crack I saw now, as I contemplated my perfect happiness, could be the same crack that stared down at me as I woke up screaming in the middle of the night, the same one I gazed blindly at as I waited for death to overtake me. Those memories didn't even feel like they could belong to me, like it was a different person completely who had been living that nightmare. It's amazing how drastically one life can change, in such a short amount of time. It's even more amazing how love can save a person.

Jude walked over holding two bottles of water, interrupting my reverie. He set them down on the small table next to my bed, then gingerly crawled onto the mattress beside me, carefully wrapping his good arm around me. My whole body seemed to sigh in relief. I hadn't felt Jude's arms around me—not like this—since before we'd both been hurt. And even though it was only one of his arms, it was good enough for me.

I turned my head toward him (about the only thing I

could move) so that we were face-to-face. He closed the inch of distance between us, kissing me lightly on the lips.

"I missed being able to do that," he said, when he pulled away. "I hated that stupid bar that separated us while you were in that hospital bed."

I smiled. "No more bars. No more separating us, ever."

"Ever." Jude echoed.

We lay in silence for a bit before my curiosity could no longer be contained.

"So, now that I'm no longer high on narcotics, will you tell me what happened that night?" Some more details had come back to me in the hospital, as I needed the morphine less and less. But there were still a lot of holes.

Jude chuckled, and then his face fell serious. "When I went back, to ask to stay with you, I was warned that coming back here human would put a huge target on my back. That I'd be pursued relentlessly by the devil and his demons, even more so than most humans because they would want me for their collection, so to speak. It would be an epic victory for them to bag an angel fresh from heaven, especially one who chose to leave. I would be their crown jewel." His eyes shifted as he spoke, and that subtle movement, in connection with the words he was saying, brought that same feeling that I'd had in the hospital of something tugging at the edge of my memory. But I couldn't put my finger on what, or what I should do about it, so I shoved it aside.

"I guess that's what I'd felt all that day. Remember, something just didn't feel right to me? It must have been that spirit—Caleb—tracking me. He must have rounded up his crew and recruited humans to house themselves in to take me down. Demons don't have bodies, not a single one. It's part of their curse—their punishment for going against

God. No one can ever see them, and their efforts to coerce someone over to their side are usually unseen to the human eye, only felt. They must have known it would take more than a temptation to recruit me, so they enlisted humans to gain a physical advantage in addition to their powers."

"So they cornered us in the alley and circled in to attack, and that's when Hal showed up with reinforcements."

Jude nodded, his face full of emotion. I knew he felt the same sort of overwhelming gratitude for Hal that I did.

My eyebrows knitted together as I tried to figure something out. "But how did Hal know we needed help?" I asked.

"He said an angel came to him and told him we were in danger." Jude paused, looking lost in thought, and I wished I could tell what he was thinking. He saw me watching him and explained, "Sorry. It's just that I wasn't expecting . . . I was told I'd lost that kind of protection when I left, that I was just as vulnerable now as the rest of you."

Again, I felt that nagging feeling that there was something I wasn't remembering, like an itch I couldn't scratch. It was starting to make me a little crazy.

I thought of something else then. "How did you escape and come to me? When Caleb carried me off, things weren't looking too good . . ."

Jude closed his eyes for a moment, remembering. His face looked pained. "I know. I never expected to get up off that ground again. And right when I was certain that one more blow would do me in, Hal jumped in behind the guy and bludgeoned him in the head with something. I never did see what."

I winced, picturing it.

"Once I realized I had a small window of escape, that there was hope for me getting to you, I somehow found the strength to drag myself up and make my way through the fighting without getting sucked back in. I followed the sounds of your screams, and when I saw you lying there, bloodied and broken, I thought I was going to lose my mind, I felt so crazed. Knowing that *I* was who Caleb wanted, that you were expendable to him, I did the only thing I could think of to save you."

"Again," I whispered.

Jude smiled affectionately. "Again."

I frowned. "Which I'll never forgive you for."

"What, saving you?"

"No, what you were about to do in order to save me. How could you willingly go there . . . with them?"

"I had no other choice," he said soberly. "I had to do whatever it took to save you."

How could I argue with that? "But it didn't matter, anyway." I remembered the brilliant white light, the way Caleb had vanished almost instantly. "We were saved. Was that what I thought it was?"

Jude nodded. "A guardian angel. And not just one. Another appeared back at the fight, driving away every demon within a mile." He smiled, obviously full of pride. It made me smile with him.

We fell silent, each of us replaying the scene in our heads.

A nervous thought came to me then. "Will they be back?"

Jude looked like he didn't want to answer. "More than likely, yes," he admitted. "If not them, then others. It never ends with them."

I felt like the temperature in the room dropped dramatically, but I couldn't deny that I'd already suspected the answer.

Jude touched my cheek, full of concern. "Don't worry.

We've got each other, and we've got Hal and the other ex-angels. And evidently we've got people up there watching our backs. One thing you have to remember is that good always conquers evil. It's not just a cliché. It's true. And I'll die making sure it happens."

I leaned into his touch, feeling the warmth of his hand on my face. Right then, with Jude inches away, hearing his voice and feeling his touch and knowing it wasn't just temporary, I could actually believe what he was telling me.

"Oh, and uh, one more thing I haven't told you yet," Jude said, his eyes full of mirth.

"What?"

"The powers that be witnessed Hal's courageous display of protection and took into account the other acts of service he's done for us, above and beyond the call of duty. They saw it fit to reinstate his status as guardian, giving him every privilege and power that comes with it. He's been assigned to us, indefinitely."

"You're kidding," I gasped.

"I'm happy to say that I'm not. It's true. He's right outside the door as we speak, although no one can see him."

I glanced over my shoulder toward the door reflexively. Then I looked back at Jude, shaking my head in utter disbelief. Nothing would surprise me again, ever.

"I'm so happy for him," I said, smiling. "And I have to say, I do feel much safer now knowing that."

Jude smiled a teasing smile. "You don't feel safe with me?"

"Of course I do. I would just feel a little safer if you still had your superpowers."

He laughed. "Sorry, love, it's just plain old me now. And you're stuck with me, forever." He leaned forward and kissed me again, lingering longer this time.

"I'll take it," I said, our lips still touching. I felt his lips stretch into a grin, and then we were kissing again, making up for lost time.

And then we just lay there, gazing into each other's eyes, which I always thought sounded like a really cheesy, embarrassing thing to do, but now saw the appeal. So much is said in those moments that words never could.

And it was then, as I lay there getting lost in the depths of Jude's emerald green eyes, that a flash of memory came tearing through my mind, hitting me with the force of a tsunami. Those same green eyes, flashing black at me through blinding, swirling light. Green eyes that belonged to a woman with long, chestnut hair and a porcelain doll face, who was wearing a white, flowing gown. And with that image, it all came flooding back, every single detail. It was almost as if I was back there, standing in the middle of all that white light, having a discussion about my impending death and the decision I had to make. Listening as she told me what Jude had given up in order to be with me.

Could it all have been real? Or was it nothing but a dream, a product of the drugs that filled my system at the time? It had seemed so real, had *felt* so real. But if it was real, then that would mean it was true. That Jude had given up everything, *everything*, to be with me. That he had made an unbelievable sacrifice and condemned himself to a life of tormented hell. That Jude was a fallen angel.

I hadn't been able to accept it in the dream, and I couldn't now. No way could it be true.

I stared at Jude, at the pair of green eyes staring back at me, and I knew then who the woman in white had been, dream or not.

Jude was watching me with the strangest expression on his face, and I realized I must have had some pretty strange ones myself as all of this went through my head in a matter of seconds.

"What?" I played dumb.

"You tell me," he said, one eyebrow raised in question.

"Nothing." I laughed, immediately regretting it as my ribs protested in pain. "I was just lost in thought for a minute. So much crazy stuff has happened in the last few months. It's a lot to think about." I watched his face, waiting to see if he'd buy it.

He seemed dubious at first, but then his face relaxed and he nodded. "I know. I don't know how you've handled it all." Inside I breathed a sigh of relief. "Actually," he corrected himself. "I do. You're incredible. Incredibly strong, and brave, and wonderful." He paused. "Do you know that's what made me start to fall for you? Your unfailing strength. I'd never seen anything like it, in anyone I'd ever been assigned to." He stared at me in amazement, something I was sure I would never get used to. "Everything that you've been through, with your parents and friends and personal struggles . . . when I met you, you were about as low as a person can get. And yet, you still got out of bed every morning. You still went to work every day. You pushed through, kept going. It was partly because of that that I felt so compelled to save you. And then, in the weeks to follow, you only astounded me more. The way you fought to get better, the courage it must have taken to let me in when you had every reason not to." He reached up and brushed away a tear that was silently making its way down my cheek. "It's what made me fall in love with you. What made me want to become human to be with you." He took my hand. "And this . . ." he said, placing it over his heart. "This beats for you."

His words gave me chills, my stomach doing little flips

inside of me. I wiped away the few tears that had followed the first and smiled. "You know what made me fall for you?"

"What?" he murmured softly.

"Your eyes. And your dimples." He fought against a smile and lost, his dimples appearing out of nowhere as they always did. "There they are," I said, smiling, and Jude looked embarrassed, which I thought was just about the most endearing thing I'd ever seen. I couldn't help myself; I reached out my finger and touched one, and then the other. "But that was just in the beginning, before I knew you. It wasn't long before your attentiveness and compassion, your respect and determination to protect me beat out all things physical." I paused, fighting back another round of tears. "No one has ever treated me like you do. Ever."

"I'm so sorry for that," Jude said, sadly.

"You don't need to be sorry! You're the one who showed me how a person should be treated, what it feels like to really, truly be loved. If you hadn't come along . . ." I drifted off, unable to finish the sentence, unwilling to think about how it would even end.

"But I did," Jude interjected. "And so we never have to wonder." I kissed him then, wondering what I'd ever done to deserve him. How had I been so lucky (blessed?) to have this guy fall in love with me, so much so that he gave up heaven to be with me? I suddenly remembered the words he'd said to me after becoming human, when I'd asked him if he'd made the right choice. *I always knew I would do whatever it took, give up whatever I had to, to be with you.*

And then I knew. Without a doubt, I knew that he had. He had given up more than just seventy earth years of heaven. He'd given up immortality, a sacred calling as an angel, a home in the presence of God. An eternity of peace and happiness, a pain- and sorrow-free existence . . . for everything the opposite. An eternity serving God's only enemy, in a place that I couldn't begin to imagine. An endless existence of pain, suffering, and misery. Although I couldn't bear to think about it, I still knew that it was true. That it hadn't been a dream. I had been there, in the in-between, as my body lay in the hospital back here on earth, hanging on to life by a thread. I had spoken to who I was now certain was Jude's mother. She had been the one sent to talk to me, to convince me to come back to him, so his sacrifice wasn't in vain. That's why she was so invested, so emotionally affected by the things we talked about. It was her son. The son she'd never known. The son who's features resembled her just enough that she looked familiar to me, when I'd never seen so much as a picture of her.

I was so touched then, so full of an overpowering feeling of unconditional love and commitment and sacrifice that I had to fight to keep the tears from falling again. I buried my face in Jude's neck, hiding my face—my eyes—from him, knowing they had to be showing at least some of what I was feeling. He squeezed me tighter, thinking I wanted to cuddle closer, and that was fine with me. I didn't want him to know that I knew. Not just yet, anyway. Maybe one day there would come a time when I would confront him with the truth, but today was not the day. He'd obviously had a reason for not wanting me to know, one that wasn't hard to guess, and I'd let him keep his secret for a while longer.

When I felt composed enough to come out of hiding, I pulled away and looked him square in the face. There was something I had to know.

"Do you ever regret it? Leaving heaven?"

Jude's eyes burned brilliantly as he gazed fiercely back at me. "Never. Not once." He leaned forward then and pressed his lips lightly to my ear, his breath warm against it.

"My heaven is wherever you are."

ABOUT THE AUTHOR

ALICIA K. LEPPERT always knew she wanted to be a writer, ever since Career Day in first grade when she walked around carrying a notebook and pencil. Twenty-some odd years later, after a short stint in high school where she dreamed of being an actress, a whirlwind Internet romance including a blind proposal that led to a fairytale wedding and two pretty-near perfect kids, her lifelong dream came to fruition with her first novel, *Emerald City.* She lives with her small brood in her beloved hometown of Pasco, which is located in the only part of Washington state that isn't green. When she's not writing, she can be found decorating novelty cakes and taking naps—her other two passions. Check her out at WWW.ALICIAKLEPPERT.COM.

0 26575 58646 6